Vinland

Viking Resurrection

R.G. Johnston

R.G. Johnston, **info@rgjohnston.com**
www.rgjohnston.com

Vinland Viking Resurrection / R.G. Johnston
ISBN: 978-0-9782978-6-2

1. Heroic Fantasy. 2.Vikings. 3.Vinland

Front cover image; copyright © 2018, R.G. Johnston

For,

Mom

R.G. Johnston

"Will this long winter ever end? I fear Fimbulwinter is upon us," my father growled, throwing a half-log on the fire; it exploded into sparks that raced up the chimney.

Already on edge, poised to flee as I spied on my father, I jumped and muffled an exclamation. I crouched outside his chamber in Borghild's Hall—named for my mother by my grandfather on the day of her birth—with my eye to the crack between the two doors.

Hamund was not distracted. "Your Majesty, changing our laws to accommodate twin heirs or even a child of questionable lineage on his mother's side cannot be condoned. If you will excuse my choice of words, a half-prince—as it's being whispered in every doorway within the castle walls and every village—is given a portion of your kingdom when you *have* two male heirs with lineage, on both parents' sides, going back a thousand years. Your jarls will not tolerate this; it will fracture them and the stable unification of your lands. We are finally experiencing a period of peaceful prosperity that you, Sire, have tirelessly given so much for and taken so little from in order to make it work—to the benefit of all."

"His mother is Wyfling. Of all people . . . Hamund, *you* are related to her! In Helgi, our union binds the wolf clan to the hound clan. Wyflings and Volsungs, united to live and prosper—together. And Borghild comes from noble ancestral bloodlines. Am I the only one not blinded by prejudice, who can see the historic significance of our union to the wolf clan?" Volsungsson demanded, frustrated. "In ancient times, we occupied the same land. It is time to put away our warring past," he snapped. "My jarls *must* accept him; I gave him a leek, to represent the land I've given him. Under clan law, it cannot be undone."

"Yes, Sire, but I am also a distant cousin of Sinfjötli and Sigird's mother, too. As your jarl, I cannot ignore the ripple this will send through the clan, and so I must warn you about the acceptance of your proposal—their minds and bodies will follow your words, my liege, but their hearts may resist. Those who talk of committing insurrection will use this point of contention to fortify their position."

The king rested his hands on his hips. "Hamund, I don't see how this complicates matters. After my passing, we will have a kingdom based on Cleisthenes's teachings: a democracy. When it moves through the althing, each son will have one vote for his third of the kingdom, to accept or reject the althing's decision for the realm. *Three* votes for the good of all, not a *stalemated* two-vote kingdom. We must leave our clan beginnings . . . behind *us.*"

"But Your Majesty, although I believe the logic of your decision—"

"Hamund, the discussion is over. I decree that my kingdom will be divided into three regions; each heir must designate their portion. My firstborn Sinfjötli and my thirdborn Sigird will have first choice; my second, Helgi, takes the remainder. We have more urgent problems—feeding ourselves, and quelling the clashes and skirmishes for food."

Hamund hesitated before saying, "Sire, there is a new problem . . . the clerics report that mothers are giving birth to stillborn babies throughout the land."

"What! Every baby stillborn? That defies truth." Volsungsson waved away the veracity of that with one hand. "Maybe it's linked to the food shortages."

"Yes. But it is happening with the livestock, too."

"Maybe it is the Great Winter?" King Volsungsson suggested. "Find out what the clerics want to do."

Sinfjötli pushed my head away from the door crack so he could peer through. "You will never live to rule, Helgi," he spat in my ear. "Sigird's and my mother comes from powerful regal bloodlines. Your mother is a Wyfling *whore*, ridden as easily as Óðinn rides Sleipnir across the sky."

"Your mother is Father's sister," I snapped back. "There are no words to describe the deformity that you are."

"We will populate the castle with so many heirs, by the time my father dies you will be the last heir behind a long line of younger ones; you will inherit nothing. I question my father's judgement."

"He isn't *only* your father; he's your king."

"Listen to yourself; you're squawking like Hamund—a bureaucrat."

My arms flailed at Sinfjötli. I grabbed his throat and watched his face turn red as I squeezed. He fell to the floor and I fell with him.

"You will not speak of my mother in that way!" I yelled, banging his head against the dirty wooden floor. "*She* comes from an ancient bloodline; she descends from Beowulf. At least Hamund's prejudices make sense."

Beside us, the crack of light between doors darkened. An iron latch clanked and rigid hinges stretched open. A fur-clad figure towered over us as Sinfjötli and I struggled to tear each other apart. A powerful arm pulled me off my half-brother, whose throat slid out of my hands.

"What is the meaning of this?" Father bellowed. "You are Volsungssons and Wyflings in brotherhood."

"You are the son of a *witch*," Sinfjötli spat.

"Your mother is *Auntie*," I hissed back.

"Borghild is of völva royalty; her ruling bloodline extends further back than the Volsungssons'—they were powerful beings, who ruled in union with others," I shouted.

"Silence, both of you—on your feet!" Father bellowed, shaking us as he pulled us to our feet.

"Leave us," he yelled to his nobleman and personal guard.

He pushed us into the room and the great door boomed shut. The bolts slipped into the floor, followed by the thud of a battle axe handle on the wood on the other side of the door.

"Both of you, sit."

"But Father, my wound," Sigird pleaded.

"Oh yes. Due to your injury, you may remain

standing." He glared at us. "When will this fighting stop?" He pointed his large finger at me. "Your mother, Borghild, was a Wyfling—a descendent of Beowulf, but she was also half völva, too. Sinfjötli, you and Sigird must cease these childhood arguments and consider yourselves all equals. You have different mothers, but you share the same father. This entitles each of you to a portion of my kingdom."

After my grandfather's passing and the marriage to my mother, my father moved his base of power within the stone walls fortifying Borghild's Hall. He loved my mother very much and wanted her to feel comfortable and safe in her ancestral home. Her family's völva temple was hidden in the lower catacombs that connected it with a keep and a sea cave harbouring his war fleet; when my father was away with my half brothers on campaigns, my mother and I played in the catacombs.

She showed me the secret passages in between the walls that connected the rooms and swore me to secrecy, threatening to put a charm on me if I told my father or my half brothers. I agreed, partly because they provided me with hiding places when I wanted to escape from Sinfjötli's wrath and Sigird's authoritative eye. My mother showed me the quickest entrances to some of the passages and the ones concealed by weight and lever doors, concealed in a room's shadows and protected by optical trickery—some with a völva charm. I'd enter and move through the walls, gathering information about my brothers' plans, my father's intentions, and rumours from the house staff. I'd watch and learn how my brothers moved when they practised with their trainers, and devise ways to undermine their axe, sword, and shield techniques.

"I've ordered my jarls to proceed with changing the laws. You are old enough to know the power of democratic rule to stabilize and strengthen. I have taught it to you from the day you could talk."

My father stared down at us—he still towered above us like Thør to dwarves. "King Granmar and King Högne arrive shortly; they will be guests at tonight's feast. You will not embarrass me in front of them. Now go to your chambers and never speak of this again." He walked to the door, his slight limp more noticeable from behind. "I think my jarls will be far easier on me than the three of you have been," he quipped. Father tried to make a joke after each "meeting of the realm," as he referred to his scoldings. It had stopped lifting our mood a long time ago.

The posts slid out of the floor and the door swung open. I turned in silence, feeling his absolute word weigh on my will. I stared down the corridor of wavering torchlights.

"Helgi, don't leave. I want to speak to you."

Sinfjötli shot me a glare.

"Put out the torches and keep the hearth burning," my father yelled to his servants. "It will be a cold night—I feel it in my bones." He closed the doors and dropped their posts into the floor again. We walked to the fire; the ash log burned now, throwing glowing heat at us.

"Did you hear my decision to Hamund? I am giving you a third of my kingdom. It's the only way for my wishes to be honoured. Our stability will come from our democratic constitution—each prince with one vote. And your strength to protect and govern will come from learning to work together."

"Father, I agree with your decision. You are a wise

king." I hesitated. "Father, will all three be king?"

"No . . . I will be the last singular king. You will rule as three monarchs when I am gone. The althing will retain its authority."

I nodded. "Your rule will be used as a map for future generations. But Sinfjötli and Sigird will vote against me in malice. And Hamund is right—your tax-paying landowners will feel the uncertainty that comes with power passing from ruler to son, multiplied by three."

Father dropped his voice. "If I could give you the entire kingdom, I would. You are wise beyond your years. I want you by my side forever. But, for your own safety, I must send you away. And regretfully, it must be to battle." He paused to hold my gaze. "Helgi, I am giving you your first command': my First Fleet. With my knarr leading, you will protect the Norðr waters. I've received reports that Hunding's heirs are getting bold—too bold for this king."

"What do you want me to do, Father? Do I demand tribute for trespassing, on threat of battle?"

"No, unless they show aggression, meet them with an open gesture as equals on the sea. They're in disputed territory, therefore it's not trespassing, per se. But be vigilant—they're sailing in the Norðr waters a little late in the season. I suspect it's in retaliation for our supply line blockade. We've been turning back the ships that supply their encampment in that part of the kingdom."

"Your blockade is necessary," I said. "With his actions, Hunding is inciting civil war."

Father grunted his agreement, then said, "You leave in the morning. Get your rest." He turned and looked into the blazing hearth, then grabbed a horn of mead that had been warming on the table and gulped it down.

I let myself out of the room. When my father turned his back, he didn't want to say goodbye. It was a stupid superstition, that if he said *those* words, his sons wouldn't return.

I passed Sigird and Sinfjötli, who stood talking near their apartments. They stopped their muted conversation when they saw me. I knew that they still spoke to others, putting fear into them about a Wyfling heir, smearing my name, suggesting I was tainted to those who would follow them in exchange for favour and power.

Sinfjötli silently left Sigird and walked back the way I'd come, slithering back to Father's chamber—no doubt to pass along what he and Sigird discussed. His posture as we passed said *one day brother . . . one day.*

My half-brother feared the völvur because he couldn't understand their power and couldn't control them. It was why he didn't accept my mother. Because I was part völva, I couldn't be controlled. In his eyes, an uncontrollable race must be eliminated.

℘ ℘

I was present when Father's cousins, King Granmar and King Högne, arrived at the great entrance to Borghild's Hall.

King Granmar was also of Wyfling royal lineage; he arrived with his four sons, Hothbrodd his heir, Gudmund, Starkad, and Dag. Their expressions seemed frozen in malevolence, probably from waiting for the day when an older sibling's death on the battlefield or a forest assassination would move them closer to the crown. This was familiar to me, of course; in each royal bloodline lurked the seeds for deceit, treachery, and murder. Parricide could easily move you up to be crowned king.

King Högne was accompanied by his son, also named

Dag, and his daughter, Sigrún, whom I had seen rarely. Her silver veil caught the wind, and I glimpsed the face of a luminescent goddess, her strands of long white hair shifting with the lucent fabric. Though I could tell she was slender, her full form remained hidden within the protective circle of her ladies-in-waiting.

Dag caught me staring at his sister and glared at me, long and hard enough to make me feel self-conscious. It wasn't threatening, but he started pacing nervously back and forth and darted glances around the room—always ending on me.

Despite his surveillance, my eyes strayed back to Sigrún. Her upper arms remained stationary, as if she were restrained by something. My look turned to a stare that waited . . . frozen in time.

I felt an elbow dig into my ribs—Sigird's.

"King Högne, it is always good to see Volsung kin," my father said.

"King Sigmund Volsungsson, I return the salutation," he replied, sounding more formal than sincere.

"This is my daughter, Sigrún. Give her no notice."

I ignored his instruction. *She is everything, but unnoticing.* A torc rested on her throat, its milky, polished amber stone gleaming through her veil.

My brothers fidgeted briefly, trying to see the mystery woman corralled by her ladies.

"Gentlemen, please follow us to my hall. A feast is prepared in your honour. My personal handmaiden Astrid will take Princess Sigrún to her apartment," Father said, sweeping his arm out. "This way, before the mead gets cold."

I stepped out of the way and allowed my father and brother to lead King Högne to the dining hall, acknowledging Högne with a bow.

Högne scowled as he passed me. "Keep your eyes off my daughter. Princess Sigrún has already been betrothed."

Högne's personal guards led the princess and her ladies to the other end of the Great Hall, where stairs rose to an upper walkway that connected to a tower via a parapet. The apartments in that part of the hall were rarely used. I walked along the shadow of the walkway and heard the collective footsteps of the ladies ascending the creaking stairs overhead, followed by the heavier treads of the guards. I glanced across the hall and saw my father's jarl Hamund leer at me before sneaking away to catch up with the king.

No one else was looking my way. I stepped to the wall and pulled aside the damask hanging and pushed a stone as hard as I could; a cupboard-sized part of the wall opened inward. I pushed on the slab and heard the rope running through a pulley. Reaching inside the four foot-high opening, I blindly fished for the rope. Got it!

I found a foot loop, stepped into it, and hung on as I ducked inside and dropped into the dark shaft. After a second of free fall, the rope went taut. A pulley squeaked and the heavy slab rumbled shut, again concealing the entrance. I searched for the floor with my other foot, then shifted my weight onto that foot . . . and stepped on something squishy and squealing—rats! I heard squeals and scurrying around me and felt their bodies brushing against my ankle as I slipped my other foot out of the loop. I smelled the stench of their urine trails.

Up ahead, the fiery setting sun streamed from the tower's putlog holes to spotlight the staircase. The golden light rode along the horizon. *The world is perpetually grey. The light of the sun no longer warms the land; the stale air is cold; the darkness is coming; the death of light; the fight for inner light; the final sleep.*

A shout pulled me from my trance. I climbed up the putlogs that were holding the tower's outside scaffolding in place and stood on the topmost log, using the wall to steady myself. A rope ladder hung from a wooden platform. I climbed it to the platform, then continued down a dark tunnel to stone steps connected to a passage in between the outside wall and the apartment walls of the tower rooms. Touching the wall for guidance, I walked along the passage.

Muffled voices slowly morphed into words.

"Take this belt *off* of me."

"I am sorry, Princess. You know that I can't—your father's decree . . . it's for your own safety."

I walked to a gap in the stone wall and removed a cloth plug.

Sigrún sat on a couch. Her veil had been removed. A woven gold belt confined her shoulders, covering her breasts. She sobbed, but her tears weren't those of self-pity, but the rage and humiliation of forced submission.

A fist pounded on her door, and it opened. "Leave us," a gruff voice yelled.

Her ladies-in-waiting stood, lowered their eyes, and hurried from the room. The latch clicked behind them.

"Father—"

"Sigrún, you will not shame me this weekend. Your duty is to secure the power of our family line. I only hope that you can understand. You are much more valuable to me as a troth than as a daughter. Hothbrodd will court you, and you will gain his favour. Don't make me look like a fool. Guard!" he yelled. The chamber door opened and he left.

She walked to a large upholstered chair by the fire and stood there, clearly weeping.

Knuckles lightly tapped on the door. . . then another tap. "My lady, may I come in?" a hoarse voice whispered through the door.

Sigrún sat down in the chair and wiped her tears away as best she could. "Come in."

The door creaked open and an old woman wearing a dark mourning gown slipped in. She approached the princess and placed a hand on her shoulder. "Let me wash you before you rest."

"I am not tired—"

"Please, I must care for you. Do not make it any harder for me, I beg of you."

I moved farther around the passage to get a better view at another grate. In the darkness I stepped on a sharp stone, lost my balance, and muffled a high-pitched squeak.

"What was that?" Sigrún said.

"Probably a rat."

Water dripped into a bowl.

"Lyana," the old woman called, "I need you."

I peered into the grate, pressing my forehead against the warm metal in an attempt to see Sigrún's front. Lyana walked in front of her and bent to unlace her dress, blocking my view. Then she walked over to a bowl and took out a wet cloth, which she wrung out and handed to the older woman. The old woman began to wash Sigrún. The two women stood with their backs to me, limiting my view. Lyana lifted Sigrún's leg and slowly wiped down her calf.

I turned away from the vent and muffled a cough in

my arm.

"I heard a cough," Sigrún said, her tone sharp.

"I think it's the crackling of the hearth you heard," the old woman said. "You're just nervous because you are away from home and everything is so new and unknown. After a bit of rest you'll feel fine. I'll put a few leaves in a cup and brew your tea."

"I can check the corridor if it will make the princess feel more at ease," Lyana said.

"Would you like your tea, dear?" The old woman asked.

Sigrún nodded.

Lyana went to the hearth and poured boiling water into a cup.

"Oh, you filled it too full," the old woman scolded as Lyana walked slowly back to them. "You're spilling it all over the floor."

Lyana lifted her pinafore and wiped off the outside of the cup before handing it to Sigrún. "I had the servants put a steaming pot on the hearth, ready for you," Lyana said. "Mind; it's hot. Inhale the vapours; they'll relax your head."

Sigrún inhaled the steam rising from the cup before bringing it to her lips. Her movements became clumsy, and Lyana took the cup away from her and set it on the table. Sigrún's body relaxed. Her head started to droop.

The nurse, still washing her, said, "Princess?"

"She's out; the drug was quick," Lyana said.

"And her body is tired." The old woman untied the golden belt and removed it from Sigrún's body, laying it flat on the table. She dipped and wrung out her cloth again; the water sparkled in the firelight as it dripped into the basin. Lifting Sigrún's arm, she gently stroked down the underside of it. Her skin there was covered in sores where the belt had bound her.

The cloth hugged her muscles, leaving a trail of glistening water on her taut skin. I smelled lavender. The sweat crawled down the creases on my skin and trickled into my ear and down my neck and back.

The door latch rattled and the door creaked open. I saw Greit, Mother's other attendant. "Excuse me," she said to Lyana. "Lynza would like to see both of you."

Lyana patted Sigrún's arm dry, then she and the old woman followed Lynza out the door.

Seeing my opportunity, I scrambled for a latch that locked the wardrobe in the princess's chambers, concealing a cubbyhole-sized hatch in the stone wall. It clicked, and I swung the wardrobe away from the wall and crept into the chamber.

Sigrún didn't move. Her arm drooped over the side of the armrest. I knelt down next to the washbowl and wrung out the cloth, feeling the warm water running softly through my fingers. Lifting her other arm, I cupped it in the cloth and caressed the underside of her arm down to her wrist. She squirmed. I stared at her fluttering eyelids, willing them not to open.

But her eyes opened and she stared at me, her expression disconcerted. She didn't move.

Frozen in the act, I held Sigrún's wrist, trying to take my next breath. Her eyes left my face to look down at her arm, breaking the spell. I plunged the cloth back into the washbowl and wrung it out again. She sank back onto the cushion and closed her eyes.

"I noticed you staring at me—earlier," she said.

I cupped the cloth around her breast, smearing and massaging the cloth over, under, and around it, brushing her pale nipple. Sigrún's breast moved and bobbed like a porcelain bubble rising to the surface of a pool, resting perfectly on her chest. I patted her dry with the towel. The lavender in the water made me think of summer fields.

"Hide. I hear them coming back," she whispered anxiously.

I jumped back through the hatch and pivoted the wardrobe closed just before they entered. The rattling door latch masked the click of the secret door. I slowly exhaled and leaned my head against the stone wall, feeling flushed and mildly dizzy, like I was about to pass out.

But my first whiff of the rat urine shocked away my daze. I tried masking a sneeze.

"Someone sneezed," Lyana yelped.

I muffled my mouth with my hands and rolled over, crushing my erection. I pushed carefully to my feet, grimacing in discomfort, and scurried back to the putlogs as behind me the nursemaid started yelling, "Guards, guards!"

My heart pumped wildly in my chest and the rush of adrenaline quashed my fear. I could still see the fire in her eyes in my mind as I returned to my bedchamber. She's interested, I thought, and smiled.

෨ ෬

Sigrún wasn't in the banquet hall for my father's feast. Father sat at the head of the table with Högne and Granmar on either side of him. Granmar's sons sat eating and mumbling to one another, seemingly uninterested in the conversations and the entertainment happening all around them. Dag sat next to his father, leaning into the conversation between Högne and Father.

I emptied my horn. The music played, swirling around my head as the dancers leapt and swirled around the floor. My servant filled my horn again and I felt a need to rise and make an announcement. I took a swig, stood, and raised my hands in the air. I felt the horn slip out of my hand and turned to see the servant taking it. I clapped my hands.

"Silence," I bellowed. "Your prince has something to say."

The hall quieted, leaving the room sounding hollow.

"Tomorrow I leave for the Norðr Sea to represent my father the king and you, his people. I do it not for *my* glory, but for the glory of all."

The chamber erupted with pounding fists, cheers, and shouting.

"Some say that I am young," I shouted. "That I am not ready for such an undertaking—to lead His Majesty's fleet into an uncertain situation. But I tell all of you—" I paused to take my horn from the servant and take a swig "—I *am* ready to represent my sovereign, my leader, and my father! I will not fail you—if I should, I will not return at all!"

The room erupted again. "Helgi! Helgi! Helgi!" they chanted. Their fists pounded on the banquet tables in time with their voices. Plates, bowls, and horns jumped, and the smiling servants scrambled to keep the food from leaping to the floor.

My father stood and raised his hands; the cheers quickly trailed off. "Guests we gather to feast and drink the mead of the gods to give us strength, as it did to Óðinn. We drink it as a reward for going into battle and know that if we die honourable deaths, we sit with Óðinn in Valhalla, where we will drink more."

"Hail!" the crowd cheered, lifting their horns high, splashing the mead on their heads.

Father turned toward me. "Helgi, you will come home a *hero*. Both of my sons will—Sinfjötli, too. I feel it in my bones."

Fists pounded on the tables again. Mother discreetly stood up and, still clapping, left the hall, followed by her guards and servants. She'd probably had enough and needed a break from the noise.

"Play," my father commanded the players and dancers. The room settled back into bobbing heads and voices raised in song as the musicians started playing again, and all eyes turned to the dancers.

I looked around the room, wearing a smile that I couldn't let go. I looked up the length of the table and met Father's eyes, and we raised our horns to each other and then drank, our eyes locked.

I turned back to the crowd. Sigird and Sinfjötli were leaving through the hall's main door. Sinfjötli looked angry, probably because father mentioned him as an afterthought. Father's mead consumption could be the reason for that blunder, but Sinfjötli's sour expression as he disappeared out the door was something that I would savour for quite a while.

I still couldn't stop smiling. I stopped a servant about to refill my horn and, like my mother and half-brothers, surreptitiously left the hall. High tide was only hours away, and my first day as leader would set the tone for the mission.

I dragged my tired body into my bedchamber, undid my scabbard and let it drop, and flopped onto my bed, hitting the horsehair mattress at the same time my sword clanked on the floor. Anticipation swam through my head

and I was still fired up from the feast and the adventure
of the voyage, so I doubted that I'd sleep much.

Indeed, I tossed and turned, feeling by turns proud,
frightened, and excited. The king's fleet didn't leave
the king behind without a good reason; in this case it
was because I commanded it, in the name of my father.
Sigmund Volsungsson was a man I would march with to
the end of Miðgarð. His faith in me was the basis of my
devotion. I'd march beside him to my death.

*Sigird and Sinfjötli must be burning up with envious
rage*, I gloated. Then I sobered. *I have to find out what
they're talking about.* I pushed myself off the bed and
drew my dagger; clenching it between my teeth to leave
my hands free, I pulled aside the tapestry on the wall
opposite my bed and pushed on a chiselled stone. It
pivoted and slowly returned to lie flush to the wall. A
section of wall moved inward and dropped to the floor.
Beyond, a knotted rope hung on either side of a vertical
shaft, dropping into darkness. On the wall between them,
chiselled rocks jutted out like steps. I stepped on one
and grabbed the rope, then slipped my knife into the
counterbalance so the doorway didn't close behind me.

I felt my way down the shaft in darkness, with my
feet moving from stone to stone and my hands slipping
down the knotted rope, as I had hundreds of times before.
I descended faster and faster, giggling at what I might be
missing: Sinfjötli banging his fists against walls and on
tables, stewing at being overlooked to lead a fleet, and
then Father mentioning him as an afterthought in front of
the clan and subjects.

I landed on the sandy floor of the tunnel connecting
the catacombs with the keep and the sea cave housing the
fleet. The torches in the tunnels remained lit, maintained

by the sentry patrol and the staff assigned to the cave port. The torchlight illuminated the ever-present vapour in the catacombs, making it look like writhing ghosts. I heard the grunt of an ox and the rattle of chains and the creak of leather, and a moment later the head of an ox and three men guiding the cart it pulled appeared in the tunnel, their movements dispersing the clouds of vapour.

One of the men immediately recognized me and grabbed and pulled on the ox's harness. The ox stopped. "Your Grace," he said as he grabbed his hat and dropped to his knees. Those with him followed suit, their voices echoing along the damp tunnel.

"Please stand," I said, approaching the man carrying a torch beside the cart.

"If you'll pardon me saying, I didn't expect to see you down here at this late hour, Your Highness."

I nodded. "The excitement of my mission kept me awake. I wanted to see how the loading is progressing."

"I can answer your questions, sir," the man holding the torch said. "If, if I may...I am Isung. I will be taking your orders on His Majesty's flagship."

"It is good to meet you," I said, extending my hand.

He looked at it, squeezing his hat with his hands, then looked at me with confused and fearful eyes.

I patted his shoulder. "Isung, please report."

"Ah—yes sir. We have two more carts like this one to load. We will be ready to sail at sunrise."

I nodded. "I will leave it in your hands. Please continue—and an excellent job, men." I walked past them, waving at the other two as the trio clambered up from their knees and urged the ox forward. They disappeared around a curve and I caught snatches of their conversation—merely words and incomplete sentences—

between the shaking of the harness and clanking of the cart, quickly receding as I too continued on.

I entered a large empty chamber designed by the royal völvur that acted as a drain when there was a storm surge, diverting sea water back into the ocean down a tunnel independent from the existing system of caves. It also kept the waterline within the harbour at a constant level. When the chamber was full of water it was impassable, and a longer route needed to be taken, but tonight the only indication of water was the salty smell in the air and the slippery stone underfoot. I stepped carefully over the slippery parts and entered the cavern holding the central pool, where I crouched forward and climbed into the descending central shaft.

I half crawled through a small chamber, hopping over drainage holes that carried any water back to the sea. A cold sea breeze blew up into my face. Opposite me, the tunnel continued, rising on an incline until it finally ended at the bottom of a steep staircase that rose between the stone walls of Sigird's apartment on the left, and Sinfjötli's apartment on the right. Tunnels, serving as conduits for air ventilation, branched off to the public and private rooms in each apartment.

I could already make out the iambic tones of people talking all around me, with shouting in one direction, as I travelled along the passage. Sections of the passageways were dark, but slits close to torch sconces provided enough light to see several steps ahead of me. I smiled; the shouts were unmistakeably Sinfjötli's, and part of his rant.

"I am the heir. I should command the royal fleet before—before him."

"Pounding your fists on my furniture will do nothing.

Talk to father—reason with him. Tell him the heirs of Sigmund must stand together in their rightful places—in front of Hunding's sons."

I moved to a metal grate with a cutout of a valknut. It provided me with a concealed vantage point to see and hear them.

"I will do that, Sigird. But what of your plan?"

"It has to be put on hold—although maybe this encounter might take care of the situation. Helgi will be at sea and Father will be without two of his three sons."

"Father wants me to meet with Högne and Granmar, to mediate a squabble they're having over fishing rights. He said it is part of my education as the third in line—I'll amount to nothing more than an administrator. I'd rather they go to war—mediation will drag on for months . . . or years."

"Högne is using his daughter, Sigrún, to forge an alliance with Granmar. Father is aware; that's why he's invited them to Borghild, to give his blessing and to not be left out."

Sinfjötli opened the door and left. Sigird turned and moved toward his bedchamber.

I stepped farther down the passage, passing Sigird's bedchamber. A woman—more like a girl—lay in his bed, drinking, waiting for her master. I recognized her; it was Mother's student, Lyana. Sigird's sexual exploits weren't a secret, but no one brought it up. "Tell Lynza that I approve," he said to her as I continued on.

I walked down the length of the castle wall and descended a flight of stairs. The passages that ascended to the king's apartments and down to the keep were a labyrinth of chiselled and wooden staircases. Mother's völvur ancestors had designed it all to be a trap for

invaders and an escape route for the royal couple. As
far as I knew, Mother was the only other who knew
how to traverse it. I quickly descended and ascended
staircases, leaping over steps and walking on one side or
the other, avoiding the traps my mother had made me
memorize. I leapt over landings and landed on keystones,
or avoided keystones on other landings. I avoided faux
rock trapdoors that opened over the rocky shoreline
and dropped the unaware to become battered corpses
decomposing on the rocks below.

Finally I left the maze of traps and ascended the
staircase to Father's spacious apartments. He used some
hidden hallways in his apartment to secretly move from
one room to another, but none of them connected with
the network throughout the castle.

There was movement in the darkness ahead of me. A
figure approached a crack filtering dim torchlight through
the wall. My heart pounded, then calmed as the figure
took shape.

"What are you doing here, Helgi?" Mother whispered
frantically.

"Mother . . ." I felt myself breathing again.

"Come with me," she commanded. She led me down
the passage to the other side of the apartment. We turned
a corner and she stopped at a wooden panel and lifted
it, pulling it out from the bottom. I immediately smelled
her lilac water. "Try not to get my clothes dirty," she said,
pushing me through her wardrobe.

I stepped in between a row of hanging clothes.

"Peek through the iris," she whispered, "Lyana might
be tending my bedchamber."

If Sigird is finished with her. I looked through the
decorative cutout. No one was in the chamber. I opened

the wardrobe's double doors and walked into a room filled with the smell of burning cherry wood.

I heard my mother slide the panel in place behind me just as Lynza entered with a full mug of steaming liquid on a tray.

"Ah!" she screamed, seeing me. She managed to recover in time to catch the teetering mug on her tray. "My apologies, sir; I didn't expect to see you, wif your trip tomorrow and all."

I raised my hand, attempting to calm her.

"Is Her Majesty, here?" she asked.

I jumped as I heard a loud bang inside the open wardrobe.

"By all that is holy—it got away," Mother yelled.

I turned in time to see her roll out of the wardrobe with a shoe in her hand.

"Did you see it? A rat the size of my arm."

I smiled.

"No, Mum; I waf talking to His Majesty and didn't see anything."

"Well . . . keep an eye out for it and warn the other servants," Mother ordered, getting to her feet. She nodded toward the mug sitting in its puddle on the tray. "Lyana, what do you bring me?"

"Yes, Mum. I waf wondering if you could sample my tea."

"Yes, of course," she said, taking advantage of the diversion from seeing the queen rolling out of a wardrobe. "Lyana is studying to be a völva," Mother told me, accepting the cup and swirling the contents under her nose. "It's an aphrodisiac," she said between sniffs ". . . for men."

Mother looked at her student. "Lyana, why do I know

what it is by smelling it?"

"Because, Mum, I fink it's the scent of the nettle, ginger, and damiana when they're combined."

"You are correct," Mother replied with a smile. "Now to taste, to make sure the amounts are in the correct proportion."

"I beg your pardon for interrupting, Mother," I said. "What effect will it have on a female?"

"Nothing, it is like a sip of warm tea," she replied, lifting the cup to her lips. "So recognize this smell if you are offered a cup of tea from a female völva." She set the cup on the tray. "It will do its job," she said to Lyana. "You make me proud. You may go."

"Yes, Your Grace; thank you, Mum." Lyana stepped back and curtsied, then left without turning her back on us. I could tell she was excited about Mother's praise.

"That was close," Mother said, breaking out in laughter as Lyana's excited steps receded out of earshot. Then she grew solemn. "Helgi, I showed you the passages to protect you, not to spy on your father in his apartments."

"Mother, what were you doing—"

"Do not question your queen and mother," she snapped. Then she calmed down. "Your question is a valid one. My völvur are telling me that the castle is filled with rumour and innuendo. I was trying to get to the bottom of it."

She cleared her throat. "Recently I've heard that Sinfjötli is planning something. Where Sinfjötli goes, Sigird knows. I was in the passage confirming a report that Sinfjötli was seeing his father. That is all: to verify and leave.

"Sinfjötli's mother and father are brother and sister,"

she continued. "Your half-brother is a victim of the risks of family copulation. The gods have cursed Sinfjötli, born from incest—he is a bloodthirsty killer and a rapist. It's said that he orders his men to watch."

"Why did Father engage in such a practice?"

"He didn't have a choice in the matter," she said. "So Sinfjötli's lineage is unquestioned and cannot be disputed."

"Mother, is your life in danger?" I asked.

"I know that I am a target. But no, not with my staff carrying bodyguards present. Sinfjötli and Sigird's accomplices would be mad to attack me, unless they were drugged. I'm trying to corroborate a rumour about a secret meeting between Hunding and Sinfjötli," she said. "And an assassination plot. I'm leaving tonight.

"Your father will be upset. But I'll tell him that I will meet with the Norðr völvur, to find out what Hunding is up to. While you are on the sea, I'll be spelunking through the cave systems to talk with my völva sisters, to see what I can find out about Hunding. They've infiltrated his clan."

"I suspect you'll learn something," I said.

A fist pounded at the door.

"Come in, Sigmund," she called. She looked at me. "I can recognize his pounding fist anywhere."

My Father pushed the door open and sauntered in. "My love," he said, bowing playfully to Mother and receiving a giggle in return. "A servant girl said that she saw you in here with another man."

My mother giggled again.

"I told her it can't be true, because she only has eyes for her Big Dog." He winked. "Ruff, ruff!" He turned to me. "Hello, son."

"Hello, Father," I replied, feeling a little embarrassed that I had to see that

"Sinfjötli is accompanying you because it will look better if we show unity in family and clan. *You* are commanding the mission and he knows it."

"Yes Father; I will work to make the mission a success."

He smiled awkwardly, stepped forward, gently wrapped his hand around the back of my neck, and shook it to acknowledge that he was pleased with me.

"I might see you later," he said, turning to Mother. From Mother's giggle; I think Father winked at her as he left.

"People think I have charmed the king," she said, staring at the closed door, "but they have it backwards; he charms me." She turned to regard me, her expression concerned. "Son, have you been hearing the whispers in your head?"

"Yes."

"Close your eyes," she commanded.

She took a deep breath and I heard her mumble the sounds of the runes. Her hands rubbed together and I smelled one of her many potions—peppermint overpowering lavender. I felt her hands waving around my face and forehead. Her armlets rattled in front of me. The smells lightened my head and my thoughts became muddled, giving me momentary peace.

"Mother, I should get some sleep. My fleet leaves in two hours."

"Yes, of course." She walked over to a cupboard and opened it, studying the shelves within before selecting a number of items. She walked over to me, her hands full. "Take these satchels of death's herb and henbane—in small doses they cause unconsciousness; too much will kill." I accepted them and she held up a vial. "Here's some opium-infused walnut oil. A few drops mixed with drink causes unconsciousness; dripped on the tip of a blade, it causes incapacitation." More vials followed. "Here is elixir of Baldur's brow and sea mayweed; a few drops will revitalize you. And a vial of hound's cover; it will help you pass among those of Hunding's clan with certain anonymity."

She waited while I secreted everything on my person. "Remain on your guard. Isung is husband to one of my völva. He will guard you." I recognized the name; I had met him down in the catacombs. She stepped forward and gently kissed me. "Trust no one and guard what you say; there are spies—*everywhere*," she whispered in my ear. "Come home safely."

₲ ℛ

I heard the rush of the cold ocean wind against my ear as it drove the cold rain to sting my face. A second wave hit our dragon boat and my fur collar weighed a little heavier. The rain was freezing on our clothing.

"How do we look, Isung?" I yelled to my navigator. "Do you see the rest of the navy?"

"If it weren't for my icicle-crusted nuts and the worry of not bearing sons at my young age, I'd say that we *look* pretty good."

I smiled. "Have you seen *Hel's Rival*?"

"Not unless she's on the other side of the swell. Helgi, don't worry; we have more than enough firepower to handle what's ahead of us. Your father's forces contain the top fighting men in the realm. We will not fail."

"Ægir's daughters, the sisters of Kolga, are unrelenting," I commented, looking at the rolling waves.

"Yes, the waves are testing our resolve," Isung replied.

Isung was my father's top navigator. Until now, he'd never left the king on land. It was a point that stuck in my head. If their voyage was to safeguard the king's interests, why the need for the First Fleet and his top navigator?

"Navigator, when do we reach the edge of the Norðr Sea?" Sinfjötli yelled, appearing through another drift of ocean spray.

Isung stole a glance at me, fearing the position that question put him in.

"The boat is navigating growlers; she must be prevented from capsizing. We don't know when we will get there," I said, taking the focus off of Isung. "Once we're through the swells, we'll regroup with the other ships in the fleet and head, as one force, to meet Hunding's sons."

I stared at Sinfjötli, waiting for a gesture or verbal reply to my matter-of-fact report. I didn't want my answer to sound like I was leaning too heavily on my authority as captain of the fleet and the expedition. After all, Sinfjötli was my future king and Isung, his subordinate.

The deck yawed. The rowers raced the rise of the ocean, struggling to turn the dragonhead into the wave. The ocean rolled into a wall and the oars snapped in two like dried sticks.

Sinfjötli turned.

"Brother, wait," I yelled as the wave punched the ship; it tipped us to steerboard and swallowed rowers into its churning black curtain.

A growler catapulted from the wave and shot down the swaying deck, heading for Sinfjötli. I grabbed the yardarm and thrust out my arm, grabbing him around his waist. We slipped on the streaming deck and landed hard.

"What the Hel—?" he screamed in indignation.

I spun around, sliding past him as the chunk of ice exploded on the main support of the mast. It creaked in the wind before the torrent ripped it completely from us, spinning it over our heads and sucking it out to sea.

Sinfjötli looked at me but said nothing. He slowly stood, using the side of the knarr for support, and clambered across the deck.

I returned to my duties.

"Your Majesty—"

"Helgi . . . call me Helgi," I commanded, pulling a windblown tuft of my blonde beard out of my mouth.

"Helgi . . ."

I looked up. The freezing rain was getting worse; it quickly coated our hair and beards. I pulled off my fur collar and shook the weight off into the wind.

"Helgi, look," Isung yelled, pointing into the air.

I squinted through the rain and ice. Chain lightning tore open the clouds. Silver lights dropped out of the arcs and fell to earth. The blasting wind caught them and they rode the currents as if they had ridden them forever. The unrelenting drop and thud of the knarr leaping over the world serpent Jörmungandr's back wavered—a little. Thør's hammer drifted to a distant rumble, but the lightning cracked the stony ocean and sky, beating down the world serpent, trying to release its grip on the voyage.

Sinfjötli stalked up the deck, wearing the raging storm on his face. His unsettled eyes stared into mine and I saw his frustrated and anxious mind as I'd experienced it my entire life.

The first time was when our father gave us each a

puppy, as his father and forefathers had given their sons puppies. The stewardship was a sacred duty: to show leadership and demonstrate the importance of training one's followers to protect the leader in the pack.

We were outdoors playing with our gifts when I heard whimpering and then a yelp. I turned. Sinfjötli was choking his dog with his bare hands. His eyes bored into mine.

"It wouldn't do what I told it," he almost gasped, so heavy was his breathing.

The memory dissipated as Sinfjötli leaned toward me and whispered, "I see Hunding's fleet."

I scanned the ocean, seeing only the churning water and sky. I glanced at Isung. He gave an imperceptible shrug and lifted an eyebrow to indicate Sinfjötli was seeing things.

"I see them—"

"We will keep a watch on them," I said in a low voice. "Father instructed me to not engage them unless they become a threat."

My words seemed to calm him. I'd seen Sigird's do the same, many times before. "Of course you must engage them—if they become a threat. It's father's royal fleet. If Hunding wants to start a civil war, he must be destroyed—" he turned and stared at the churning sea "— to show that the sons of Volsungsson intend to carry on the monarchy, with force, if necessary."

Lightning tore across the sky's blustering roof. In the distance, pewter clouds parted and the distant sunset stained the sky with the blood of Baldur.

I looked up, remembering the silver lights moving with the storm currents. They were nowhere, neither behind nor in front of us. Recalling them made me wonder about Sinfjötli's apparition. Suddenly a sighting seemed possible.

I see it! Seven points of light swooped through the wind and the rain, riding its sleeting currents and descending in formation. I resisted blinking in the icy wind, fearing they might disappear forever.

"Helgi—look," Isung yelled.

Longships, with twenty-foot flames flapping in the storm, glowed through the sheets of freezing rain. One tipped and the world serpent's waves consumed it, flames and all. Another longship followed, it's burning main snapping in two. The flames caught the wind, which fanned them at the rowers; they screamed, covering their faces in pain. The ship rolled over and disappeared in another wave with the first.

"We might be able to save the flagship," I said, noticing Hunding's flapping crest, untouched—the flames weren't consuming it as quickly as the others.

"Let them *burn!*" Sinfjötli barked with the ferocity of the ocean.

The sleet stopped and the grey storm clouds parted; shafts of light hit the burning ships and the lights were gone.

"There's a break in the storm," Isung yelled.

"Where's the rest of the fleet?" I asked, looking around me in horror.

"I see four ships, Helgi."

Half the fleet . . . gone. Three hundred and twenty men, swallowed by the dark, cold water: the sisters of Kolga captured them, and Hel feasted. I pushed that thought aside; there would be time later to mourn. "Take us to those ships!" I ordered.

"Weigh oars; steerboard rowers, lower oars . . .

heave—ho!"

The dragon boat turned, struggling with the dipping and swelling water. Sixty rowers were left; spread out and struggling with the weight of the oak hull and the crew, fighting the serpent's perpetually writhing back.

I looked back, periodically staring into the sky, searching for the lights.

The other ships saw our course change and turned with us. The waves pushed us faster and faster to Hunding's burning flotilla.

"Helgi—" Sinfjötli's stinging voice yelled from behind.

"Sinfjötli, I'm *thinking*," I yelled back.

"You are not thinking of rescuing the sons of Hunding?" he sneered. "Let them die. They spilt *our* blood first."

"Sinfjötli, I see this as an opportunity. Father wants to find other solutions besides killing. Especially when it's our kin. There are also reports of völvur in the area. I don't think Hunding has wand carriers." I turned and raised my voice. "Isung, take us alongside; archers at battle ready."

"Aye, Helgi." Isung raised a yelling horn and called over another boat. We headed to the burning ships.

"Sinfjötli," I said, turning to him and pointing up. "This is an opportunity to settle our families' dispute. The light of Baldur has laid this opportunity at our feet."

Sinfjötli's eyes seemed to lose their focus and his irises shone the colour of fire. "Helgi, kill our enemies; Father—"

"Hunding's ships being in our territory is not worth starting a war. We are kin. If we slaughter them, they will retaliate. Sinfjötli, their ships are in flames; they are not a threat. We have the upper hand."

Like so many times during our childhood, Sinfjötli's rage and hate blinded him. He temporarily lost contact with the real world, as if Loki forced his way into Sinfjötli and took him over. "All the more reason to destroy them," he replied, "when they can't fight back."

"We take this opportunity to leave the dark times behind and live in the light," I decided. I walked to the bow of the longship, hearing the clank of swords and the oars dragging through the water.

I saw four figures standing motionless on the deck of the ship we approached, their swords drawn. From this distance, they seemed ready to fight to the death. Men were leaping from the other burning ships and dragging themselves onto flotsam bobbing in the water, but this ship seemed intact. Altogether I saw about a dozen men standing behind the five foremost figures. Not enough to overwhelm us. But it didn't mean that they'd surrender, when fighting to the death guaranteed the front door of Valhalla would be wide open for them.

"That's close enough." I yelled to Isung as we turned, positioning ourselves near enough to talk but with enough icy sea between us to kill anyone stupid enough to attempt a hijacking. "Greetings from my father, King Sigmund Volsungsson," I called across to the other ship. "Can we help?"

They looked at one another, confused. Then the middle man called, "I am Hjorvath, first son of King Hunding of the Saxons. I stand with my brothers, Alf and Hervarth, and my sister, Ayolf."

"I am Helgi. This is my brother, Sinfjötli." I gestured toward him. "Where is the youngest heir—Hæming?"

"He is not with us," Ayolf replied.

"We don't need your help. The fire is out," Hjorvath—
the regent cox—said, indicating the charred and steaming
stump of the mast. "We're making the half day journey to
Sigarsholm, to repair our ship and then journey home,"
he added.

"With a full crew," I said pointedly, eyeing the twelve
men behind them, "it will take you longer than a half
dægur." I looked around at the few survivors clinging to
the charred timbers bobbing on the water between my
ship and theirs. They must have been attacked recently;
they'd not had time to spread the survivors among the
undermanned, floating relics before we arrived. "Those
on the other ships were not so lucky. There are few left to
fill out your crew. Will the sons of Hunding row?"

"And the daughter of Hunding," Ayolf interjected.

"Who attacked you?" I asked, ignoring her.

"And why are you here?" Sinfjötli added.

"We don't know who attacked us; when the storm
passed a bank of fog rolled in," Hjorvath said. "There
was a blinding flash of light, like hundreds of burning
longships attacking us. Indeed, we choked on the fumes
of burning tar and saw the flames of our other ships
through the dispersing fog. It was too late to help them;
with many of our rowers already lost in the storm, there
weren't enough left to turn back in time."

"Sinfjötli," Ayolf yelled, "we are here to verify a
report of strange lights in the sky and a sighting of a ship
appearing out of the sun."

*Or, are you here to assess our presence in these
waters?*

"Do you think that was the same ship that attacked
you?" I said.

"What kind of ship?" Sinfjötli interrupted.

"A ship of light," Ayolf answered.

"How many longships in your fleet?" I asked.

"There were eight," Hjorvath replied.

"You lost many crewmen." From the corner of my eye I saw Sinfjötli peer at me. I ignored him and noted the direction of Hjorvath's eyes as the rest of my fleet pulled up alongside us, the oars poking from under the shields swishing to keep them stationary.

"We will follow you," I said, feeling Sinfjötli's piercing glare on me. I turned aside and whispered to him, "Sigarsholm is disputed territory. They have the right to beach there to make repairs. And so do we. Besides, we should see if their story floats." I looked to my navigator. "Isung, we're going to Sigarsholm; notify the fleet."

Back to Hjorvath. "I offer you a loan of rowers," I said with a wry smile, suspecting they'd refuse armed men on board.

"We'll manage," Hjorvath grunted.

The daughter and sons of Hunding, along with what remained of their crew, disappeared behind their shields. I heard Hjorvath's muffled voice barking orders. Twelve midsection and portside oars lifted out of the water, circled backward, and splashed down. The oars pushed against the rolling ocean. The knarr hardly moved.

"It will take them forever to get to Sigarsholm," Sinfjötli said.

"Once they build momentum, they'll get there soon enough."

Our longships moved to the Hundings' starboard and port, waiting for them to complete their maneuver. We remained at a safe distance off their stern, keeping the dragonhead central in our view and our eyes on their deck.

As *Hel's Rival* flanked us, a bobbing keg drifted over her wake. "Get that barrel," I ordered two oarsmen. Then I headed toward midship to meet Isung.

"Isung, Hunding sends eight ships carrying six to eight hundred crew on a 'scouting voyage.' Does that seem like too many to you?"

"Aye, Helgi, it does. But Hunding does like to make a show of things."

"A show of things," I said, "is important when you're going to battle."

"I see your point."

I heard footsteps and the sound of a rolling barrel creaking down the deck. "Isung, get me a drinking horn." I stepped in front of the two crewmen and they stopped the barrel. I knelt and rolled the barrel to find the cork. It was sealed with resin. Isung pushed the horn in front of me as I loosened the cork out with my dagger. They slowly rolled the barrel and I gently wiggled the stopper out; a thin stream poured out, and I caught it in the horn, then pushed the stopper back in and hammered it with the handle of my blade.

I put my nose to the horn. "It's mead. But there's something else, a moldy smell. I think it's drugged— soaked fly mushrooms." I handed the horn to a rower. "Drink." He took it reluctantly.

I stood. "The sons of Hunding are lying to us. Drugged mead means berserker fighting. I think we know why they're voyaging out of season. They must be launching their attack from Sigarholm."

"It sounds like they've occupied Sigarsholm," Isung said, nodding.

"They probably annexed it and are using it as a base

for their attack," I said. "We're heading into Hunding's forces."

The man had finished the mead. I rinsed my horn over the side. "Isung, keep an eye on him. And keep Óðinn's good eye on the horizon," I added.

"Aye, sir."

ᛉ   ᛈ

Vígríðr's summit loomed in the distance. It was an ever-present reminder of Miðgarð's eventual ending: a final battle on its summit for peace. I scanned the skyline, looking for yellow dots on the crystalline surface of the sunstone.

"I have the sun's position; we're heading in a norðr¬-austr direction," I said, handing the stone back to Isung. "I see spots arranged on one side of the crystal; there's a land mass there." I pointed as Isung looked through the stone.

He nodded. "It has to be Sigarsholm."

I rubbed my eyes and looked out into the grey morning. The choppy water seemed to be swimming through my head. I leaned over the hull and scooped up handfuls of frigid salt water, splashing it over my face and rubbing several times until the sting jolted my body awake. My beard, full of salt, had hardened, the hairs bristly to the touch. I shook the remaining water off and stared into the dark water. I felt heavy, burdened with little sleep and saddled with the responsibilities of life.

Heavy footsteps approached. I looked up and saw Sinfjötli. Stroking back my hair, I straightened with a grunt, trying to conceal my sigh. "Good morrow, brother," I said.

He managed a nod and some lip movement, as if what was in his skull might spill out over my dripping

43

head. "Helgi, I was told that you're sharing our food with Hunding's pups."

"Sinfjötli," I said, lowering my trousers and hanging my ass over the hull, "if they don't eat, their arms will weaken and we will never make it to Sigarsholm."

Isung handed me a rag and I dried my cold face and head.

"Hey Isung, how is the oarsman?"

"You are right; the mead is drugged with fly mushroom. He rowed nonstop, well into the night. I told him to eat and rest, but he was soon back, complaining that he couldn't sleep. He rowed till dawn and asked to be relieved. He's sleeping the rest of it off."

I washed my ass with the cold seawater and dried myself with the rag. I dressed.

"Isung, prepare for battle."

₮ ℂ

Sigarsholm was a rock and shoal island with volcanic mountains, valleys and woodlands. It was in a strategic location, situated in the centre of a seaway separating King Hunding's and Sigmund's lands. Passing icebergs, floes, and growlers of all sizes protected the island from invaders while floating far enough away from it to not be a threat. Both the Hunding and Volsungsson clans claimed ancestral ownership. The absurdity was that they were both right, because both sides originated from the same clan.

The day had been long and made more tiresome and tedious by Sinfjötli's constant questioning of my every stratagem. I did have command of what was left of the fleet, but he was prince too. We were not just ranking officers; we represented the dynasty and the realm. My replies had to be tactful and my disagreement . . .

discreet.

For the moment, Sinfjötli was on another longship. I'd given him command of the fighters. He would lead them into battle. That was keeping him out of my hair and gave him something to do. Because of his violent nature, he was happiest being a hands on leader. We would be encountering unknown numbers and he'd do well on the battlefield. He thrived on the savagery of hand-to-hand combat. Splattering blood and the sensations of a sword striking flesh and bone appealed to his personality.

Isung and I had spent most of the night creating our battle strategy. Without a völva to consult, we didn't know how to counter the volatility of the berserker, or how to use the fear and paranoia side effect from the drugged mead, to our advantage. I knew that strength alone wouldn't win the battle against them.

"Isung, how close are we to Sigarsholm?"

"They will see us soon."

"Get us to the Hundings' longship."

I stood at the masthead as Isung signalled the archers aboard the adjoining ship to match our course and swordsmen lined up behind me.

We easily gained on the Hundings' ship; the ocean was glass and the light morning mist hung in the air, wrapping around us like translucent cheesecloth. We approached their stern and I raised my sword to notify the archers and the warriors, then grabbed the dragonhead and swung onto their boat.

"Don't!" I yelled as they dropped their oars and rose, scabbarded swords in hand. "Look to port."

The sound of arrows scraping across hemp and the creak of flexing bows broke the silence of the morning.

Arrowheads pierced a deck of sunlight as the sun, peeping over the horizon, formed a wall of morning light on the mist. The clanking of swords behind them followed.

"What do you want, son of Volsungsson?" Hjorvath growled, sounding betrayed.

"The future of the Saxon dynasty. Throw your swords in front of you and we'll *talk*."

They glanced at each other, then obeyed.

Warriors passed me in trios and escorted each prisoner aboard our longship. The others remained aboard to keep it stationary. When the last of them were on board, their captors cupped cloths over their faces and held their heads forward. Their violent struggling quickly faded into unconsciousness; their prone bodies littered the deck.

"Remove their clothes. Wait—oh no."

"What is it, Helgi?" Isung asked.

"Who will dress as Ayolf?"

We shot glances back and forth, our expressions frozen in half no's, as if the answer would land on one of us and stick.

The king's fighters were seasoned and experienced. Most of them had bushy beards down past their breastplate and rough, blotchy cheeks scarred by a lifetime of salt sea and mead. Even with Ayolf's statuesque height, they were still too big to fit into her clothing.

"Helgi?"

"Yes, Isung."

"If I may; you are a wise *young* leader. Recall the fair haired Thør, who infiltrated the land of the Jötunn dressed as the bridal goddess Frejya, with Loki as her matron, to steal back his hammer Mjöllnir and stop their invasion into Asgard. You have the opportunity to emulate the bravery of our god-protector and save us from a possible Saxon invasion. Besides, in stature you are closest to Ayolf."

The heads in the huddle nodded hopefully and waited, their eyes on me. Invoking the feats of gods was an argument I couldn't touch. It carried with it the deeds that leaders and heroes must be obliged to emulate to be seen as anointed. And most important of all, it was what the people expected and wanted.

"I . . . will honour the diversity of the gods and sacrifice my new beard to protect my people," I decided, smiling.

Time jump-started and they turned to unclothing the prisoners. Then, shivering, we removed our clothes and quickly passed around their garments. My crew were the best fighters and equal in experience and combat skills, but that was secondary to fitting into the tunics, trousers, armour, helms, and most important of all, their headdresses.

I drew my dagger. Isung took it and carefully scraped off the beard that marked me as a mature male, periodically rinsing the blade in the sea. The cold blade numbed my face and the nicks didn't hurt. I was surprised by his nimble hand, moving confidently as the longship bobbed and tipped.

"All done," he said, holding my chin and moving it from side to side.

I leaned into the water and shook my face, then dried off and sat down again.

"I'll tie your hair at the crown; the helm will hide it, along with your nose and cheeks," he said, looking at me. "We'll powder your face with flour. Her gauntlets will help to conceal your hands and her molded breastplate will add shape to your chest."

"Isung, I wish you were coming."

"Helgi, I can coordinate the fighters in the field if I remain here. Please, sir, don't forget to practice with your sword with the breastplate on. You're working with an extended chest with more weight on it. You have to get the feel of it, because your balance might be slightly off."

"I keep looking behind us, hoping that more of the fleet made it through the storm," I said. "We could use more fighters."

"Aye, we can always use more fighters," he replied. "We have the element of surprise. If the fog keeps up, we can use stealth to our advantage and avert a Saxon invasion. What should we do with Hunding's heirs?"

"From what I've seen, Hunding wants a war. I doubt that diplomacy is part of his vocabulary. Let's push back! Throw the heirs of Hunding overboard! I'll see you on the other side," I said, raising my hand and nodding.

Thirty warriors lined up on either side of the longship and took up oars. Isung signalled the longship full of archers to accompany us. As our ships moved forward, I and the other Hunding imposters found elkhound headdresses and fur collars to add to our disguises.

"This will add to our camouflage. . . sir," said one of us.

"Who are you?" I asked him.

"I am one of your lieutenants, Hrafn; your personal guard," he replied as he fit the headdress to his helm. The head, snout, and ears concealed his helm nicely.

"I'm happy that you're by my side," I said, tilting my head back to meet his eyes. There was something familiar about him. He possessed notably eastern features. For him to achieve the rank of lieutenant, his accomplishments were probably great. My father accepted only the best and unquestioningly trusted his men.

When we reached the shore, I handed around my mother's bottle of disguising serum and we splashed it on our faces and chests. It smelled like animal urine, poorly concealed with mint and rosemary. I grimaced. I didn't feel different, and the others didn't look different, as they ducked into the cover of the woodland. But I trusted Mother's abilities. Besides, with our headdresses tilted forward, our faces were heavily shadowed.

We lifted the knarr out of the water and hid it in underbrush; long pine boughs provided more cover.

Then, moving away from the main beach that led directly to their fortress, we approached the island's forested side. This end of the beach provided protection and concealment while we got a sense of our surroundings and planned the next steps. If Hunding's forces had overtaken the island, there'd be bloodshed.

A temple, its construction clearly indicating that it had been built by Irish monks, towered over the trees in the distance. Legend said that Saint Brendan of Clonfert constructed it and many others like it. It was made out of flat grey rocks. The weight of the slanted walls, leaning against each other, kept the stacked rocks tightly compacted and the structure standing. Its flattened pyramid shape made it stand out from its natural surroundings. It had been pillaged, though, and afterward it was converted to a hóf, a place of Norse worship. The Hundings would be stationed there; it was a natural fortress-type structure. They would also be in the area surrounding it, and sentries would be stationed in the wooden towers we'd seen on the shoreline.

"Why is this part of the beach not better defended?" I wondered, looking around.

"Maybe our longboats were seen and they were called away to defend the main camp," someone answered.

There was charred wood in a firepit just in from the beach where we'd landed. I touched the rocks. They still held a trace of warmth. "This fire isn't too cold. You could be right," I replied.

We walked across the beach, stepping into the footprints already there to conceal our approach. The footprints would eventually wash away, but until that happened, our arrival couldn't be tracked. We stepped through a line of cedars into an ash forest. The underbrush was low and most of our sight lines were clear.

"The plan is, approach the structure and scout. If we see a chance to infiltrate the temple, then we take it," I said.

"Atli, is that you?" I asked, reaching out to pull the headdress away from the face of the man on my right. "My father didn't tell me that he was sending his jarl's son."

"Yes, I was assigned to Sinfjötli. He's remaining with the rest of the fleet, so I'm here to protect you, too," he said. "My father is here as well; you met him. He's Hrafn."

"I keep remembering when we were kids—" I caught something moving from the corner of my eye. "Get down," I whispered. Everyone dropped or scuttled for cover. I hid behind a bush and carefully peeked out.

"Psst!" Hrafn hissed, drawing my attention. There

was fear in his face; his arm hugged his chest. He uncurled a finger from his fist and pointed behind me.

I slowly turned, then scuttled backward, stopping against a tree. A hound larger than a wolf sauntered toward me. It stopped inches from my face. I held my breath and turned away as his flat snout sniffed my face. His jowls smacked together, slobber dripping from the corners. He sniffed my chest, pressing his snout against it. I slowly reached for the dagger in my belt, caressing the hilt.

The hound sneezed and backed away, leaving a spray of slobber and snot on my leather armour. It paused, lifted its leg, and pissed on the tree next to me, then sauntered over to Hrafn.

Mother's potion is working to get us through their defences, I realized.

I signalled to Hrafn and Atli to join me. They scrambled over. "They have hounds guarding the forest; that's why we haven't seen Hunding's men," I said. "We shouldn't have a problem getting to the hóf."

"Let's hope we're not humped to death by a playful one," Atli quipped.

We continued, remaining on the lookout for Hunding's men, but the only thing we attracted were more sniffing hounds. We descended into a wooded valley. Ravens flew in circles overhead, squawking; I caught a whiff of hot metal. "Careful," I whispered. "I smell a smithy close by."

We crept along the underbrush, twigs crunching and snapping under our feet as we tried to blend into the foliage. Hounds brushed up against us, smelling and marking us with their scent. Hrafn and Atli were always in my sight, and I in theirs.

The temple towered over us and the frigid air carried the distant sounds of humans. I crawled to the edge of the long grass. A ghostly memory of wheat yellowing in the sun crawled through my head. I heard Saxon voices, barely audible.

"Once we kill Volsungsson's forces and murder his progeny, Hunding has promised his chiefs property and wealth."

"We're taking back what was stolen from us—what is *ours*." Another voice replied.

It's civil war. My blood boiled. *Betrayal*, I thought, finding myself agreeing with my brother. They were seizing the opportunity of an aging king to strike us down and cut up our ancestral lands. The old values of family and honour were dissolving before my eyes. To betray kin was madness; it weakened all of us and left us open to outside attack. Where clans outgrew themselves, kinship and family were no longer enough to bind us together.

I peeked through the tips of the grass as I heard the voices recede. The area in front of the temple entrance was clear, except for roaming dogs. We descended into a wooded ravine. Squawking ravens circled overhead. I caught a whiff of the smithy—again. "Stop."

Suddenly a horde of voices thundered through the air, announced with horns and the discordant racket of swords beating on shields. I crouched. Atli and Hrafn crouched next to me. Warriors were running to the beach. I looked out to sea. A lone ship was heading to Sigarsholm. I seethed. *Sinjotli, you idiot.*

Flaming arrows catapulted from the mist-enshrouded longships; carried by the wind, they reached the shore and were followed by another volley, and another. Armoured men ran from the structure, answering the call to battle. Their faces were flushed with the effects of drugged mead. Shouts and grunts mixed with the clatter of arrows hitting shields. With each wave, bodies fell with the clattering arrows.

"He's clearing the temple," I said, happily-surprised.

We stood and walked up the embankment to the entrance, unnoticed in our headdresses. I tried to emulate how my mother walked. Her gait was strong, powered with the movement of her hips. "Hey Hrafn, would you say that my walk is more strong female, or mannish?"

He stopped and looked at me. "I say strong woman. What do you say, Atli?"

"Yeah, it's a little . . . provocative, though with a strong gait."

"Okay, I'll have to tone it down a little bit; we could be walking into a building full of men."

"I thought there was a rule about touching a female of royal blood," Hrafn said.

"Would *that* stop you?" I chuckled.

I fixed my headdress and crept along the wall to the gated entrance. No one saw us enter the temple. Slivers of light penetrated crevices in the walls and ceiling to shine on three statues: Óðinn in the centre with Þør on his right side and Freyr standing to his left. I used the statues for cover and peered into the next chamber. It was empty; it would be a good place to make further plans. I glanced upward. A series of staircases, the steps slabs of chiselled rock, jutted from the sides of the temple. At the top of some were open doorways. I saw no signs of life.

Exploring farther in, we carefully crept to the dark opening of a tunnel. I looked down a torchlit staircase to a closed wooden door. "You two stay here; I'm going up to a room to get a better view of the battle," I said.

I climbed a staircase and entered a covered balcony. I found a large enough gap in the stone wall to see a good portion of the beach and water. The longships remained offshore, the rowers trying to stabilize the ships in the large swells while the archers launched arrows toward the shore. The swells made accuracy impossible, but their arrows often hit their targets.

I heard the squeak of goose-greased wheels and heaving grunts. Oxen and humans harnessed to a trebuchet and ballista were pulling them toward the rocky beach. Once there, they stopped in a semicircle, aiming at the open water.

"Hey," I yelled down. "I need you two to find Hunding's longships."

I turned back and heard the trebuchet's arm creaking back, then the vibrating backlash of the boulder being released. I didn't see where it landed and I heard nothing that indicated it had hit anything. A voice yelled out numbers, quickly followed by the creaking of levers being moved.

I had confidence in Isung's abilities, but I wasn't sure that Sinfjötli had enough sense to order the longships to retreat beyond the range of those weapons. I knew that Isung wouldn't put the fleet at risk even if that meant disobeying an order.

Hunding's men grunted as they adjusted the position of the trebuchet. Once in position, its rope sling flipped into the air and hurled a boulder directly at the longships. I heard the smashing of timber and an uproar of cheers from Hunding's soldiers.

Next, tar-soaked balls were loaded as payload. "Ready," a lieutenant yelled as warriors touched a torch to the ball. It burst into flames. "Fire!"

The arm flipped forward; the back wheels jumped off the beach, thrusting the burning boulder into the air. It rumbled, trailing black smoke. I pushed my face out as far as I could, hoping to see where it hit.

"Helgi," Hrafn yelled from the doorway.

"What!" I yelled behind me.

"I saw two longships navigating around the island. There might be a port on the other side of Sigarsholm."

"There are caves on the other side of the island," I said. "I wonder if they constructed a cave port."

"Atli is taking a closer look," Hrafn said.

As I passed into the next chamber and approached Óðinn's statue, I heard voices outside. "Seal the temple," one of them yelled.

I peeked around the corner in time to see a circular rock slab rolling over the tunnel entrance. The ground shook as the slab rumbled into place, the sound echoing inside the temple.

"They sealed us in," I said, running to find Hrafn. "They must be defending something."

"Maybe the cave port is somewhere beneath the structure."

I nodded.

We searched for Atli.

"Helgi," Atli said, rapidly descending the stairs. "Hunding's ships are leaving port."

"How many?"

"Six longships; three ships have one hundred shields"

"We'll be overwhelmed," Hrafn said.

"Let's get down to the cave."

We walked down a sloping corridor. The slate walls, floor, and ceiling were polished to a gloomy sheen; light flickered across the corridor from wall sconces holding burning torches. I slowly drew my sword, listening to my blade scrape along my scabbard's metal rim. As we descended, a cold dampness blew past my face. I smelled the sea.

Helgi . . .

"Who said that?" I said, startled.

Atli and Hrafn looked at one another. "Helgi, I heard nothing," Atli said, turning to Hrafn, who shrugged.

"It sounded like a woman calling my name."

"Maybe you're beginning to think like . . . a princess." Hrafn sniggered.

I chuckled and dismissed the phantom voice.

At the bottom of the corridor, we stepped into a tunnel. Torches flickered along the wall; some had blown out. I grabbed one and kept walking. We stopped at a T intersection and looked down another tunnel. More flickering torches lined it. Farther down, the torches had blown out, concealing the end in darkness.

Helgi . . . A soft breeze stroked my face.

"I heard the voice again," I said. "It's coming from this tunnel."

We descended and stepped into a port—nestled in an ocean cavern. A doubled-hulled dragon boat was moored on the other side of a dock.

"Helgi!"

I turned toward Hrafn's voice. He was a short distance away, standing over a cowering man, the tip of his sword pressed against the man's neck. Atli and I hurried over.

"What is your name?" I asked him.

"Thør," he replied, wide eyes on the length of the sword at his neck.

"Well, namesake of our protector, I am Helgi, son of King Volsungsson and Queen Borghild."

"Ah . . . a p-prince," he stammered.

"Let him stand," I ordered.

"Sir?"

"Thør, stand."

As he rose in front of me, his whitish-blond hair and beard seemed to grow. The wooden dock creaked as he straightened, though his muscular shoulders hunched forward. Hrafn tipped his head to look up at him.

"You have chains on your ankle," I commented.

"Yes; I am a prisoner of Hunding. When they invaded they spared my life and enslaved me, because of my skill and physical strength. When I am left alone, I am chained to the rocks until someone frees me." Thør's hawk-like nose pointed downward as he bowed his head.

"Hrafn, Atli, free him."

They lifted their axes and attacked the rivets holding Thør's chain to the rocks. The rivets eventually broke and his chains dropped to the ground.

"Thør, we'll get the anklets off eventually. There's no time right now. You appear to be a man I want fighting by my side. Do you swear your allegiance to me?"

"Sir, I . . . I don't know. I work alone and—"

"Suit, yourself. Hrafn, Atli—"

"Wait—what will I get in return?"

"You get allies, friends, safety, and kin, if you want it. You add to *us* and learn from *us*. And when the end comes, your name lives on with ours."

Thør stared into his blackened hands.

"What is it, Thør?" I asked.

"It's funny," he said with a rueful chuckle. "I didn't realize that the chains could be broken; I could've freed myself."

"You didn't know any better, because you thought that you were a captive," I said.

"You *are* a leader—I'll follow you," Thør declared. "I'll get my hammer and gloves." Thør thumped down the tunnel.

"Helgi, we are taking a stranger on his word," Atli said.

"Yes, but there are three of us and one of him. Atli, we have nothing to worry about, because we have you. I heard that you slayed the Jötunn Hrímgerðr."

"Helgi, there was no one there to witness it," Hrafn said.

"Yes, I did kill her, because she prophesied your death, Helgi. Your brother made a rash oath and it would have killed you."

"You know better than to listen to a frost Jötunn," Hrafn said. "Jötunn are chaotic liars that kill us on a whim. Jötunn in the sea pull us under; ice Jötunn freeze the life out of us; some Jötunn incinerate us into black soot . . . they're *all* lying drunks."

Thør returned wearing chain mail gloves. He carried his hammer on his shoulder.

"How heavy is your hammer?" Atli asked.

"Find out for yourself," Thør offered, putting it on the ground in front of him.

Atli dropped his axe and stood over it. Using his arms, back, and legs, he heaved upward with a long, strained grunt—then let go. "It's too heavy."

"Try lifting it with one hand. And here, put these on." Thør took off his gloves.

Atli donned them and grabbed the hammer and lifted it with his right hand. His arm muscle tensed against the weight as he lifted it waist-high before putting it down again. "That must hurt when it hits," he commented.

"When it was forged, it was left for too long. The handle is shorter. But its defect is actually its strength; it's harder to capture, because if it can't be lifted with two hands no one will bother trying to lift it with one. My gloves make it lighter, so I can strike with deadlier blows. The only thing missing is my gold belt; with that tied tightly around my waist, I can lift and throw Mjölnir farther. I whisper its name and it returns to me."

Atli backed away nervously. He looked up at Thør with an uncomfortable grin. "How does it return to you without a rope, or a chain?"

"I don't know; its shape? Its short handle?"

"Thør," I said, "your first task, as the newest member of the group, is to tow us out in Hunding's new toy, the double-hulled longship."

"How far?" he asked, walking down the dock.

"Till you're about knee deep."

"Watch out for eels," Atli shouted wryly.

"Are you sure we can trust him?" Hrafn asked, watching Thør move away.

"Yes," I said. "I'm trusting my instincts. You know, size can also shield a noble heart, as well as destroy."

Hrafn untethered the boat and we all climbed aboard; Thør held the tow rope over his shoulder and walked along a rocky path along the cave wall, beyond the end of the dock.

"Do you need a hand?"

His large hand waved me off. I turned my attention to the longship. Its two hulls were attached with a bridge near the port and one near the bow. The one we were on also had a mast pole rigged with a sail. This model looked like it could accommodate two hundred or more rowers, making it an excellent attack vessel, ship-to-ship and ship-to-shore. Atli and Hrafn began rigging the sail as I looked out to sea. The four of us would never get the boat moving without wind.

The boat didn't use a steerboard. The centre mast was rotated using a cogwheel. One handle lifted the cogwheel up and the other handle rotated the mast until it needed to be locked in place. The weave of the sail was tighter—heavy wool woven into hide. It appeared that it would be much more durable in higher winds.

"I'm taking royal privilege and steering first," I announced.

Thør gave the rope one last tug and jumped into the boat as it passed through the cave entrance. We remained around the mast. As the momentum pulled us into a crosswind, I grabbed the sail-rod, waiting for the others to lift and unlock it from its cog.

Hrafn nodded and lifted the cogwheel.

I braced myself and pulled, slowly turning our sail. My arms shuddered as the ship entered the wind current. Maneuvering it felt like the movements the seagulls made when riding the currents in the sky. The sail shook and *boomed*, shaking our footing on the deck as the wind dragged us out to open sea.

The twin hulls gave us more stability and we easily glided through the choppy water. The wind pushed us into a wide arch, taking us to the end of the island.

"Helgi, what will we do when we encounter Hunding's men? We don't have a crew and the only weapons we have . . . we're wearing."

"We'll set the ship on fire and jump ship. The wind

should fan the flames enough to set one or two of his ships in flames as it rams through his fleet. With enough luck, we'll be rescued and head for the beach to finish them off." *If not, we and Hel will feast together*, I thought. "Hunding might be on one of those ships. We can't let him get away, not after his betrayal of the clan. Especially not after he swore an oath in front of our king—my father. No, the wound grinds too far into my bones."

We turned the sail, taking the ship in a wide curve around the tip of the island. Heavy spray hit us, driven by the cold sea wind. Blowing snow concealed our approach, but it also blinded us to what was immediately ahead of us. The snow intensified, blowing from our backs as we snuck through the storm.

I pointed to a checkered spot riding the storm-tipped waves; we headed toward it.

The weight of my headdress was getting unbearable, despite the protection it offered from the wind and rain. The wet pelt froze in the wind and I kept bending it around my neck and shoulders.

"It's a dragon boat," Atli yelled, looking at me.

We caught an inshore wind and managed to turn the sail in time to ride the wave, gliding on an intercept course with the ship heading to Sigarsholm.

"Can you see the figurehead?" I asked.

Atli shielded his eyes and squinted into the storm, strands of his hair blowing wildly in the wind. "It's . . . a hound's head—*Hunding*!"

"Hard to port!" I howled, feeling the fire in my head boiling my thoughts and breath into a red-hot rage. I reached for the yardarm and looked up at the sail, ready to catch the next inshore wave. "Wait for my signal!"

Suddenly, ridges blew across the sail.

"Turn!" I pushed on the rod as hard as I could while Thør, standing on the other side of the mast, pulled. Hrafn locked the cogwheel. We leaned to port as the wind lifted our side out of the water, arching just behind a wave crest.

"I see them," Thør yelled as the boat thudded on the water.

The sail filled and we headed for them. I prepared to draw my sword, imagining Hunding's neck within reach of my blade.

"We're going to hit her port side!" I yelled, peering through the blowing storm.

A swell rose up behind Hunding's boat and pushed it sideways—toward us. We were caught behind them on the downslope of the trough. Our boat was heading for their midsection.

The water rolled out from underneath us and the stern hit the bottom of the trough hard. It thrust our bow up, and our keel shuddered across their gunwale. Oars snapped as our keel crushed bones and pushed bodies into the dark water. Their mast wedged in between our two hulls and we pushed them along with us. They remained afloat, but waves splashed into their ship.

I had my sword out, and swung it at any moving form, feeling the blade slicing into their flesh before swinging again, desperate to make the next kill that would take me closer to Hunding.

Hrafn and Atli had joined me, mindlessly attacking what was left of Hunding's crew. I looked overboard, hoping to see Hunding's face in the sea of heads swimming in the dark water. Instead I saw a tail sweep up, high above our mast, then drop to slap the water.

"Jötunn! It's mine," Thør yelled, slipping Mjölnir out of his belt and throwing it at the monster. It arced through the air, hit the plunging creature, and returned to Thør's outstretched hand.

On Hunding's ship, men were grabbing for our gunwale. I yelled a warning, but the crest crashed behind us, drowning out my shouts. Fighters were scrambling over the side behind Hrafn and Atli. They were almost aboard when Atli swung his axe, pushing them back into their longship. Another wave was scrambling behind them.

I turned. Hunding stood behind me with his sword drawn, fighting the wind and the waves. He looked ready to fight me. I swung my sword, hoping that I could see him die before the yawing deck or the force of the waves thrust him into the water.

The monster surfaced again, Thør struck the beast, sending it back into the open sea. "I hate monsters!" he yelled into the wind and rain.

Our sail caught the wind and our boat spun around, dragging Hunding's boat with it. Hunding ducked; I was knocked off balance and tumbled into the bottom of our ship.

Hunding stared down at me. His expression didn't need words; his thirst to kill the son of a Volsungsson was clear. I scrambled away and pushed to my knees, my sword in my hand.

"If you give me your sword and beg for your life, I might let you go," he gloated.

I stood. "Your heirs are dead," I told him. "*I* killed them. Hjorvath, Alf, Hervarth, and Ayolf lie beneath your feet. *Hel will feast!*"

He charged at me, his rage alone keeping him

stable on the bucking deck. I grabbed my sword in both hands, ready to absorb a hit. Sparks jumped when our blades connected, to be torn away into the wind. Snow had changed to blowing rain that blurred our vision. The deck jerked, sending us stumbling back away from each another. The wind shifted the rain and water into a whirling torrent, throwing us off balance, sending us toward the side of the boat.

Hunding's hand cracked on the edge of the gunwale, sending his sword overboard. My ass hit the gunwale and my balance tipped—toward the dark, rolling water. I blindly kicked, hoping my lashing boot hooked Hunding to pull him into Hel with me.

I grabbed. . . something—an arm?—and squeezed, using my enemy to pull myself back aboard. Blinded by the flying rain, I landed on the tilted deck. Hunding, on his back, struggled to heave me back into the water. I wasn't letting go; I locked my leg around his arm. If I went in again, he'd came with me. I tried to swing my sword downward, but Hunding's flailing arm kept wrestling me back.

I savoured the pain on his face as I scissored my legs, twisting and turning his arm into torture. The deck yawed and I wrenched the arm more . . . and more. I was panting as I flipped my sword to plunge it through his chest, feeling the rush of the kill, anticipating the feel of the sword slicing through his leather armour and into his skin.

The deck creaked and shuddered; Hunding's boat was being pulled into the water-whirl, thrusting our boat away from it. The keel was sliding backward across their gunwale. The bow plummeted and bounced up, flipping me over Hunding. His arm slipped out of my leg lock and

I thudded onto my back. I gasped, caught my breath, and rolled over.

A hand grabbed my hair and pulled my head back—one of Hunding's men was hanging over the side of the boat. I hit him with the hilt of my sword, and kept hitting him until he let go.

I gagged as I felt another hand grab a fistful of hair and pull my head backward over the gunwale. Flipping my sword, I thrust the blade past my neck. The tip pierced flesh; I pushed until he let go of my hair. My head flipped forward and the ocean rippled and sky twisted over me. I steadied myself on my arms. My hands stung as the frigid salt water cleaned my cuts.

Hunding was on his feet, stretching his arm out to the grey ocean. The falling rain made his form seem to shudder. A weighted rope slapped onto the deck, its other end tied to the mast of Hunding's boat. He knelt and coiled himself in the rope, favouring his shoulder injury, and yelled. He was immediately pulled into the air.

"You coward," I screamed as Hunding disappeared into the blowing rain. My only desire was that if I couldn't kill him, he and his boat would be ripped apart and his corpse would remain down there forever.

Thør's monster had disappeared and he turned to protect the ship. He grabbed the rods and moved the sail, using the storm wind to get us free from Hunding. I leapt across the deck.

Hrafn and Atli stood back-to-back, axe fighting with the last of Hunding's men. Another one tried climbing into our boat, until Atli managed to kick him back down—again.

Atli looked like a dwarf next to Thør. His smaller size and agility let him duck a few blows, but the yawing deck was another adversary. Atli swung his axe wide, blocking another strike. The deck tipped sideways and the blade missed Hunding's man. I scrambled up the deck and jumped at the invader, hitting him in his midsection and sending him over the gunwale into the frothy ocean.

I looked through the blowing rain. Hunding gripped the end of an oar and was being pulled into a dragon boat. The sky boomed; my chest quaked. "I'm coming after you, you *bastard-dog*! I will *tear your flesh apart* and *feast on it!*" I yelled into the storm.

I whirled away from the gunwale. "Hrafn, Atli—man the sail! I'm going after Hunding!"

"Helgi, our sail is splitting," Thør said, pointing up.

"Do it!" I stormed back to the mast. Thør was right; the stress from the storm and the raging ocean was splitting the sail. As I stood there, the mast snapped with an enormous crack. The storm was ripping the rigging apart and we'd soon lose our sail.

A gust caught us and I tumbled forward, landing in the other longship. We slid sideways, down an ocean swell, spinning out of control. All we could do was hang on, Thør, Hrafn, and Atli's watery forms riding the next crest alongside of me. I gripped the gunwale as another ship wavered into view up ahead.

Massive oars poked through the rolling wall or water. Their gunwale hooked on our masthead and they rolled on top of us—or we dipped under them. Oars and oarsmen tumbled on top of us. I jumped across the bridge as the longship crashed down, smashing it and disconnecting our two longships and the mast pole.

A wave consumed me and I tumbled through snapping oars and mangled bodies. The ocean's stinging slap knocked me into shock. The cold felt like it was pulling the breath from my body. There was a flash above me, and the wind and the crash of the waves ceased as I submerged into dark death. The muffled shouts disappeared in the humming inside my head and a silence fell over me. Hunding's dead and injured men floated around me in the grey light.

I twisted and kicked toward the surface, hitting bodies on the way up. I broke the surface, and driving rain stung my face. My headdress was gone, exposing me to the wind. My cloak tried to drag me down. I submerged and twisted out of it, feeling the weight lift as the cloak drifted away. I frantically flailed my arms and kicked myself back to the surface, fearing that the current was pulling me away from the boat. I had to get out of the water; my legs were going numb and I was floating bait for Jörmungandr.

A shape bobbed in the distance—*a hump?* I panicked as I watched it dragging down a swell and up the other side, moving toward me.

It's the flipped-over dragon boat, I realized.

I swam, gasping and wildly moving my arms to fight the swells, trying to push the calming numbness of the cold away from me.

The sky flashed and I saw the keel. I reached for it, gasping and kicking myself out of the water. I was tiring. *I feel like I'm turning to cold stone. The grey water is absorbing the light from me.* My body tried to fight, but my mind wanted to sleep.

Too numb to hold on, I closed my eyes and relaxed my body and let the waves take me. My mind fell from the light. I felt the sword in my hand, but the dark cold was slowly pulling it out of my grip. The shafts of light in the water were dimming. My body drifted in the eddies, like a feather in the breeze. I couldn't move. My will slowly released its hold on me.

Suddenly the surface concussed over me and water rushed toward my back. I was tugged upward and broke the surface in a rush, sound again roaring through my head.

Someone straddled me; legs wrapped around my waist and chest and pulled me up. I felt the break of the icy ocean surface and passed out.

℘   ℭ

Soft fingers stroked across my skin and a palm felt my forehead. I tried to open my eyes, but my lids felt like stones. Arms surrounded and cradled me, protecting me from the storm. I heard the beating of a warrior's heart, pounding against my head. I remembered split-open milkweed pressing against my face.

A cradle of light touched me. Sinewy arms held out the shattered pieces of a sword, beckoning me to take it.

Above us, flocks of ravens circled a glacial summit, an ice field atop a mountain. A ring of fire burned above Vígríðr in the dark night.

There's warmth . . . a light . . . a presence. . . It's pulling me, forcing me from stillness, dragging me across a stormy plain.

℘   ℭ

I opened my eyes.

A woman sat with a baby in her arms, looking at the hazy glow of the morning sun. She appeared to be frustrated.

As the longship dipped, her nipple dropped out of a baby's mouth and he started to fuss. She grabbed it and pushed it back in—till the boat bobbed it out again. "You look as frustrated as I feel, Snorri," she said to the baby, and chuckled.

As Snorri settled back into her arms again, she looked down, watching him suckling her breast. Her nipple dropped out of his mouth again as his head rolled away from her chest and flopped against her forearm. She wiped off her nipple and sighed in relief.

Snorri looked like he was a child of the ocean. The world serpent had rocked him to sleep.

There was a tarnished look to the morning, an aging light that my stiff, sore shoulders and back felt as they crept to life. I squirmed in pain, fighting the movement of the ship. I knew there was nothing broken, because every part of my body ached and burned.

The mother looked up. Behind her, a chained silhouette slumped over the masthead in the copper sunrise. It was a woman, displayed in public disgrace. The mother tipped her head back and closed her eyes, appearing to bask in the morning light; she clutched Snorri close to her and sighed.

A tall figure came and stood beside her. She blinked and squinted upward, smiling in recognition at the man. His strands of long, silvered hair and his beard blew in the wind and glistened in the light. "Thorfinn, my love, you are troubled. Is it the same thoughts?"

He nodded. "Gudrid, I'm haunted by the end. Vinland was a timeless place. I can't help but feel that our lives exist only in the richness of our past. Our saga is over; beyond it, there is nothing."

"Living with me all these years has certainly rubbed off on you," Gudrid said with a smile, trying to lighten Thorfinn's mood. "You're developing more insight. The end will come, as it always does."

"Freydis's husband, Thorvald, is not among the crew," Thorfinn said, changing the subject.

"Thorfinn, I can't forgive Freydis, but I do sympathize. Like all cowards, he ran away and Freydis must bear both of their crimes. She will have to face humiliation when we arrive at Brattahlíð. The tales of her shame will most likely reach home and they'll be told as part of our saga, as a cautionary tale."

"But, she may have been possessed by Loki."

"I don't believe her possession story."

"How's my strong boy today?" Thorfinn suddenly growled, snatching Snorri from Gudrid's arms.

"Thorfinn, he was sleeping," she scolded. "I just fed him, so I wouldn't—"

Snorri let out a screech, followed by throwing up, splattering in Thorfinn's hair, his beard, and down the front of his fur collar. He passed Snorri back to Gudrid with a grimace and closed his eyes, appearing to be trying to settle his stomach. Then he gently patted Snorri's back and rubbed his downy skull. Gudrid looked on in amusement. "My strong boy," Thorfinn mumbled.

"How is the *Hringhorni* handling with less crew to sail her?"

"It practically sails itself," Thorfinn answered. "It appears sunny all the time because *Hringhorni* is refracting the light at the circle on the boat's stem."

"It was Baldur's ship; he was the god of light before Loki killed him," Gudrid said.

Thorfinn dropped a rag over the side of the longship and wiped his son's breakfast out of his hair.

"You haven't talked much about losing . . . the alfather," Gudrid said.

"I thought we'd play a much larger role in helping to

save Miðgarð; what will we do now?" Thorfinn said, his voice trailing off.

"Thorfinn, you must find a way to pull yourself together for the three of us. Regardless of how we feel, the end of the world is *coming* and there is nothing you, I, or Óðinn can do about it." She sighed. "I know how you feel, my husband. It's hard to believe that the end is near when I hold my son. Remember the Ouroboros, biting its tail; the end is not only an ending; it's a beginning, too." Her calm voice held a stern edge.

"But that's the part, I *don't understand*," Thorfinn blurted, his hands waving and his voice cracking.

"I don't understand it either. We don't have to. The only way to face it is with our hearts, not with our heads. Thorfinn, the Ragnarök is something that we can't think our way out of."

Gudrid lay Snorri in a basket and placed a thin piece of linen over it. She walked to the centre of the longship and slowly approached the mast, walking around it with her eyes focused on the birds' behaviour. "Look, we picked up some ravens," she said thoughtfully.

"It's a good sign to have a pair of ravens. . . they could be Huginn and Muninn." Thorfinn laughed.

"Memory and thought," Gudrid mumbled. "Óðinn's ravens fly over Miðgarð and report back to him; they're his eyes."

I raised myself on one elbow and saw a flash of lightning on the distant horizon before I collapsed to the deck. The wind was still and I felt the warmth of the sun on my face.

A shadow moved across my closed eyelids and a soft hand warmed my cheek. "I think our stowaway is awake," Gudrid whispered.

My chest pushed out and I heaved in a deep breath. My eyes opened and the clear sky burned into them. I sat up and threw up all over myself.

"Thorfinn, get me something to wipe him off," Gudrid said, then turned back to me. "You're with friends," she said.

The smell of vomit nearly overwhelmed me, and I felt globs dripping down my chin. I stared at Gudrid through a head full of fog. I forced myself to remember everyday words that kept dissipating before I could form them into sentences. "Who. . . am I?"

Her eyes stared into mine. Her face was kind and soft; she had a mother's look. "I don't know who you are. We found you after we left Vinland. No one knows you."

"Please help," I said, trying to get to my feet. The deck bobbed. The ocean spun and my legs collapsed beneath me. Thorfinn caught me and I used him as support, pushing myself upright to stand trembling. Blurry figures glided across the deck, looking at me through the haze.

"The water is calm and the sky shines like gold," I said, feeling the memory of a storm passing through me. I looked toward Thorfinn. "Please put me back down."

He lowered me and I leaned against the curved bulkhead, cradling my head on my arm. "Where . . . where are you headed?"

"Back to Grœnlandia," Gudrid said.

"I've never heard of it."

"It is a land settled by Eirik the Red."

"Is he your clan leader?"

"He's more like a chieftain," Thorfinn replied. "We rule ourselves by an althing—a parliament of our community leaders. Eirik oversees the althing."

Gudrid wiped my face with a cloth; it felt cool and calming. Ravens squawked and I followed her eyes up the mast, squinting against the brightness. Ravens fluttered around one another, wings spread, levitating against the golden sky. A winged woman, shadowy in the hazy copper morning, suddenly appeared above them, her hair radiating like the sun. She held the top of the sail as if towing the ship along. I cowered into the curve of the bulkhead.

"What's wrong?" Gudrid asked, looking down at me.

"I saw a shadow—a woman with wings."

"A Valkyrie," she said.

"She's gone," I noted, seeing only the ravens ruffling their feathers in the breeze and the wavering sail.

"I feel like I know you," Gudrid said suddenly.

"Do you have the sight?" I asked, sinking into the fur of the pelt under me.

"Yes, I do."

I nodded, then looked around. "This place is strange."

"How so?"

"It's like the light when the moon is eclipsed. I see it bending and curving around everything—around you and me," I said, staring at my hand. The light flowed through my fingers as if I were trailing them in a clear pool.

"I sometimes feel my skin tingling in the light. It usually comes right before I have a vision," she said.

"I remember . . . a sword fight . . . a dark and stormy sea . . . and an island . . ." I said, struggling to make the scattered memories coming back to me coherent. I shook my head. "It sounds like a lush land."

"Pardon?"

"Grœnlandia: land of green. It sounds like green

fields go on for days."

"You must rest," Gudrid said, pouring an amber liquid into a horn and handing it to me.

"I recognize the scent of this elixir," I said, inhaling. "It's a plant extract—a medicine."

I smiled and tipped the horn to my lips, smelling it as I sipped. "It's skullcap; I know it well. I remember drinking it as a child." I lay back and closed my eyes, waiting for its effects to take over.

My head swam and I heard the ocean lapping against the boat. The sun warmed my face.

Footsteps scuffled next to my head. "Gudrid—"

"Shh! He's getting off to sleep," she whispered, stepping away.

"Gudrid, why doesn't he know about Grœnlandia? Did he hurt his head?"

ℰ   ℘

I woke abruptly and recoiled as a stench tore into my nostrils. Something brushed against my cheeks, startling me. I opened my eyes and stared into a sagging face that peered down at me, its folds conjuring a sea Jötunn in my mind. "Is that your breath?" I said, screwing up my nose.

"Silence!" She snapped. She looked up and the loose skin of her face settled over her skull, the excess hanging as jowls on either side of her mouth. She took a puff from a smoldering pipe and looked at Gudrid. "I see it," she said, coughing out smoke. "It looks like . . . Óðinn's handwriting."

"How do you know, Grimhild?" Gudrid asked.

"I saw his likeness when I stared into Óðinn's missing eye."

"I know him," Gudrid said, looking at me.

"From your past?" Grimhild asked.

"Yes . . . but there's something else," Gudrid said, rising and peering over me.

"Óðinn *is* the ultimate weaver," Grimhild commented. "If he had gained the wisdom of the runes, he could've influenced Urðr, Verðandi, and Skuld— the three Norns. That which happened, that which is happening, and . . . oh, what's the third? That which should happen."

"You're wearing a tattered pinafore." Grimhild shouted, measuring her words. "Are you a boy or a girl?"

"I'm a man," I said.

"Oh yes," she said, rubbing my beard. "It's hard to tell these days. It's your features; they still retain the softness of youth." She took a puff from her pipe then clenched it in between her teeth. She reached out and rested her hands on my head. Her hands massaged my skull and calmed my mind. I drifted into a light sleep.

"He has a large lump on his head. It might be the reason why he can't remember," she said, startling me back to consciousness.

"I remember . . . a battle in a storm—"

"No one's talking to you! But that's where you got that bump," Grimhild said, taking a congratulatory puff and appearing triumphant at her perceptiveness.

"I . . . I fell in the water and woke up here."

"You wouldn't have survived long in the water," she said.

"Did someone rescue you?" Gudrid asked.

"Or did someone stow you away on the boat before we left Vinland?" Grimhild demanded. Puffing on her pipe, she turned to Gudrid. "There's nothing more I can do here, Gudrid. If his head hurts, give him a horn or two full of mead. And for Óðinn's sake, don't give him drugged mead," she added, walking away.

෨ ൙

Something startled me out of sleep and I woke with fear coursing through me. Dark shadows crawled over my body in the hazy twilight. The deck was lifeless. I was cold, and cowered into my fur, back against the bulkhead. I felt a touch and heard myself exhale.

A winged female materialized from the night. "I remember you," I whispered, my voice trembling.

She approached me, seeming to float over the dark, yawing deck. She moved through the greyness like a burning ember whirling in the darkness. She was radiant and her light twisted into a beautiful being of light.

"Where did you come from?" I whispered, feeling a little tipsy from mead.

"Shh, you mustn't wake the crew."

"You are beautiful," I said, reaching out to her face, struggling to touch it. "Are you real, or a dream?"

"I'm as real as you are," she said with a smile.

My mind swam with the movement of the boat. She touched me and instantly removed the harshness of the world, and my lonely fear of the darkness.

"I know we've met, but I can't remember where." I shook my head in frustration. "I can't remember my name."

"Your name is very important," she said. "I will give you a name and I will give you a gift with your name."

"If your gift is not your heart, I don't want it."

"Your name . . . is Helgi."

"Helgi," I echoed. "Yes, my name is Helgi."

She moved closer. Her arms protected me and her body warmed me. My cheek rested against her feathered gown; her heart beat in my ear.

"Please stay with me," I pleaded. "Keep me safe." I cowered away from the stinging loneliness of the dark night, riding the wind; I surrendered, feeling sheltered and protected in her embrace.

"Helgi, you must go to Sigarsholm," she said, releasing me from her embrace. "There are many swords lying in the hóf, but there is one there that is best of all. It is the Shield Destroyer. Down the blade is engraved a blood-flecked snake. It shines like gold. In the hilt is fame; in the haft there is courage and in the point resides fear. Take the Shield Destroyer; it will make you strong and keep you safe. Now, Helgi, sleep . . ."

"No—no," I frantically protested, feeling myself drifting away.

I burst gasping from sleep. I crept myself to my knees and leaned over the gunwale to stare into the fog and catch my breath. Though merely a hazy disk in the sky, the morning sun warmed my cheek.

I recognized by the ship's movement that we were in shallower waters. I looked around for someone to query, but saw no one. Steadying myself, I struggled to stand, rasping and grunting with the effort.

An island emerged from the fog. I recognized the coastline: Sigarsholm. "Gudrid," I called, struggling to remain on my feet. "It's Sigarsholm!"

Longships were approaching us. More and more images were flooding my mind; a story was emerging, but there were still gaps in it.

Gudrid and Thorfinn joined me. "You look a little better," Gudrid said.

"Thorfinn," a woman called, "can I speak to you?"

"Gudrid," I said as Thorfinn walked away. "My name is Helgi."

She beamed.

"I recognize them." I pointed at the approaching longships. I searched the faces of the crew on the nearest ship, then brightened. "Isung!" I called.

"Helgi!" Isung called back as the oars were withdrawn and the longship coasted alongside us.

Thorfinn had rejoined us. "These are Gudrid and Thorfinn," I told him, indicating the couple beside me. "They rescued me."

After a cursory nod, Isung reported, "Hunding's forces have fled back across the water; a scout saw their boats on the peninsula connecting to Logafjoll, Hunding's land."

"We're hunting him down and finishing him, once and for all," I said.

"There is no way to approach the peninsula without being seen. The floes moving toward us are close; it's too dangerous to enter Hunding's land from the norðr."

"Isung, take me back to Sigarsholm. You," I yelled to the other longship, "escort this boat to the cave port."

At Isung's order, his rowers reached for the *Hringhorni's* gunwale and pulled until their ship thudded against its side. I carefully stepped into the longship, leaning on the shoulder of a rower to steady myself.

A storm cloud moved over the sun, instantly changing the sky to churning pewter; misty air whipped past me. The ocean began rolling.

As we headed to the beach, Isung gave me an update. "Helgi, we drove Hunding's men off the island. Longships and dragon boats from Hundland rescued as many of their clan as they could, while the rest fought us on the beach. Thør, Hrafn, and Atli returned to help us finish them off. Your brother is nowhere to be found."

"He's probably dead," I said, feeling a little numb from the cold.

"We've been meeting with some delegates from a völva colony. There's a Lady Frigg waiting for you in the hóf; she says that she's a messenger and brings a letter from her husband, for you. She comes with Queen-mother Borghild's consent."

"Any news of the queen?" I asked.

"No."

I hoped she was successful in gathering information from her Hundland allies and from Hunding's clan. The information would probably help us kill Hunding. "Hunding got away. I'm going to Hundland to finish him off once and for all," I said.

We were silent for the rest of the trip through the choppy water until the bow of the ship braked on the stoney beach. I hang-dropped over the side and headed to the hóf.

"Thør," I yelled.

"Helgi, it's good to see you," he exclaimed, arms open. "We we're worried."

We met and grasped wrists. "I'm back from the dead, I suppose—I still have more lives left," I joked, and waved to Hrafn and Atli to join me.

"I was rescued by people going on an íViking. They said they were returning to a land called Grœnlandia from a place called Vinland. Come with me," I said. "Isung say's Lady Frigg is waiting for me in the hóf." I glanced at Thør; his eyes lit up at the mention of Lady Frigg.

The temple's front entrance was still barricaded, so we walked around and entered through the cave tunnels and made our way to the cavern housing the port. The

Hringhorni had docked; its mast towered over us. An ornate metal ring the width of the *Hringhorni* was attached to the ship's stem.

Thorfinn walked toward us; Gudrid followed him with a baby in her arms. "I'm afraid that my son won't sleep unless he's kept moving," she said, smiling. "At least until he gets used to being on land."

A veiled female appeared in the entrance of the tunnel leading to the temple. The covering did little to conceal her silver hair and pale skin, but it was her piercing blue eyes that captured all of my attention. As I approached her, I saw the faintest curve of her mouth. "All of you, follow me into the temple," she said.

"Us, too?" Gudrid asked, referring to her and Thorfinn.

"Yes, Gudrid. You too."

Lady Frigg turned and led the way along the dank tunnel, moving at a measured pace up the tunnel's sloped floor. She turned to us when we entered the main hall of the temple.

"How did you know my name?" Gudrid asked, rocking Snorri in her arms.

Lady Frigg ignored her. "Everything that you need to know is in this letter," she said, producing a parchment scroll and handing it to me. "Please—you must follow its instructions implicitly. And you must do so immediately."

I looked around at the stunned and faces looking back at me, then I unrolled the scroll and read:

My beautiful boy,
If you are reading this, I am dead.
I knew when you were made that we did right.
You have the strength of your mother and the majesty

of your father. My son, you are our redemption. Your integrity is as present as the Norðr Star. You are ready to fulfill your destiny.

The goddess Freyja is about to give birth; the father is Loki. They have a powerful union that will allow them to rule both the gods and the Jötunn. The disparaged Æsir is powerless to resist, and the Vanir supports them.

Freyja is their living martyr; she was given to the Æsir as tribute to end the Æsir–Vanir war, a stalemated war that was impossible to win. Her sacrifice has given her immense power among the nine worlds. The dwarves have named her Goddess, Ruler of Nine Realms. They've promised her their allegiance.

You must not underestimate Freyja's power; she's my equal in seiðr sorcery. If you confront her, she will kill you. But with Thør's help, you can outwit her.

I want you and Thør to dress up as nursemaids and steal her baby. Thør has dressed up as a woman before; he'll give you some pointers, if you need them.

Take the baby to Hoddmímis Holt. It's a wooded glen that lies beneath the Great Ash, Yggdrasil. Gudrid will assist you.

Give my best to Thør.
Óðinn

"That rash old fart!" Thør yelled. "He knew how much I hated dressing up like Freyja. He did this just to irritate me."

Thør pulled Mjölnir from his belt, then angrily returned it to its place. He stomped up to the statue of Óðinn and lifted it off its pedestal.

"Thør!" Gudrid yelled as he lifted it over his head. "Put it back!"

Thør froze with the statue over his head, appearing unsure of what to do. He stared at her. His insulted look slowly hardened into anger, but he replaced the statue on its pedestal, turning it to face away from the statues of Thør and Freyr.

He turned back to the veiled woman. "Lady Frigg, you look familiar. Have we met?" he asked, sounding a little calmer.

"I don't believe so, Thør," she replied, then turned back to address Helgi. "Freyja's hall, Sessrúmnir, is situated on an ice floe norðr of here; keep the midday sun at your back and head toward the glowing sky at midnight. Take *Hringhorni*; Baldur's light will mask your approach from the sun, concealing you in the light. Good luck to all of us. And gods' speed."

She turned and walked away, quickly disappearing into the cave system.

"I'm going with them," Thorfinn said to Gudrid. "Before the alfather was eaten by Fenrir, he told me that Tostig will be reborn. I have to see for myself. Besides, they need me to sail the *Hringhorni*."

"Well then, we'd better get you three dressed in maidens' outfits," she said, and lifted a hand to wipe sudden tears from her cheeks. She forced a chuckle. "I'd better get started making one for you," she said to Thør.

∞   ∞

Sessrúmnir Hall glowed on the horizon like a second sun moving through the Norðr Sea, brilliant against the churning skies. The sheer sides of the ice floe protected it, as did the icebergs that crept around it. Its walls were the colour of white ice, its portals covered with sheets of quartz ice. Towers and spires floated in the wind, filling the sky.

Despite its grand majesty, Freyja's hall was dwarfed by the size of the moving floe, a moving island that the entire country of Sigarholm could easily fit within. Her fighting field, Fólkvangr, held her half of those killed in battle. The only movement on its white surface were a mass of black dots moving on one side, like ants training for the last battle at Ragnarök.

"Thør, how do we get into Sessrúmnir Hall?" Thorfinn asked.

He stopped and stared into the sparkling light on Fólkvangr. "Very quietly," he replied.

"We need a camouflage," I added. "Maybe a . . . white . . . one."

We looked up at the luminescent fabric of *Hringhorni's* sail flapping and billowing in the wind. Shadows from the churning sky passed over it; it glistened like snow and ice in the moving light.

We looked at each other.

We anchored *Hringhorni* to the ice floe and quickly undid the rigging. Minutes later, we were creeping up a sloped side of the moving island of ice with the sail covering the three of us.

Thør kept hogging the sail. Our white nursemaid's dresses and pinafores helped to camouflage us, but my tanned shoes kept peaking outside our covering and I was worried that we'd be seen by someone looking out of a spire window in Sessrúmnir Hall.

"Thør," I whispered harshly, "you have more than enough sail over there; my feet are exposed."

"We're almost there," he said. "There's a stable up ahead. We'll find a way into the hall from there; lots of places to hide." then he groused, "What is special about this baby, anyway? Loki and Freyja had a kid together—so what! The gods and the Jötunn have been having children with each other for eons."

We dug a hole in a top layer of snow and I buried the sail. Then we waited and watched, my mouth watering with the smells of cooking over open fires. The stables were across a yard. When I was sure it was clear, I signalled Thør and Thorfinn to follow and we moved in single file across the yard. My veil kept getting snagged on my stubble, so I had to keep adjusting it. As we approached the corral, I snatched up two pails I found against the fence and handed one to Thorfinn. No one seemed to notice us yet. I heard chopping and the smell of meat cooking over an open fire was stronger here.

"Hey, where are you going with my buckets?" a stable boy yelled.

"We're only borrowing them," I said, noticing that it wasn't a boy, but a dwarf.

The dwarf's eyes widened and he jumped, ready to turn and run.

"Dvallin," Thør said, his guttural whisper cutting through the sounds in the yard.

Dvallin turned and attempted to escape, but Thør's longer gait quickly closed the distance and he caught up with the dwarf as he sprinted away, grabbing the back of his collar. "Fancy seeing Freyja's dwarf here."

"I'll yell for the guards," Dvallin cried.

"You do, and I'll snap your neck."

Dvallin's body relaxed in submission to Thør's hold. "What do you want?" Dvallin squealed. "How can you feel like a hero in a pinafore, picking on someone who barely reaches your waist? Aren't you a little big for a maiden?"

"Did you get your night with Freyja after you forged her necklace, Brísingamen, little man?" Thør asked, shaking Dvallin as if trying to knock the sarcasm out of him.

"No," he barked. "She had a headache and has been putting me off ever since. I stay close to her, doing menial tasks, until *she's* ready."

"I will give you an opportunity to complete your contract with Freyja, but I want something in return," said Thør.

Dvallin looked at him, expression hopeful. "Oh Thør, I will do anything."

"Where is Freyja?"

"She's in her tower. She hasn't left since she announced the coming birth of our saviour. You are not going to harm her, are you? Because I will gladly forfeit my life to stop you."

"No. We only want something that she has. You will take us."

Dvallin practically swooned. "Oh Thør, touching my beloved might be the last thing I do, but I will leave Miðgarð with the sweet taste of my goddess on my lips."

"You will get your chance, I promise; but if you betray us, I *will* kill you."

"I vow not to betray you, Thør. And to prove it to you, I give you a gift: Tyrfing, a gold sword forged by my brother Durin and myself. It cuts through iron and stone as easily as it cuts through clothing; it will never miss a stroke and it will never rust. But be warned, once unscabbarded, it must be used."

"What happens if it is not?"

"It will strike its possessor and whoever is near, until its thirst has been satisfied."

"And where is the location of this sword?"

"It's on *Sigarsholm*."

I perked up. Sigarsholm.

Dvallin shuffled across the yard and descended an outdoor staircase into the hall's basement.

Thør turned back to me, frowning. "I don't trust dwarves," he said. "They're full of double truths and deceit."

"We don't have a choice," I said. "We have to go along."

We followed Dvallin, trying to blend in to the everyday behaviours of Sessrúmnir's servants. He wove around people and at times disappeared from sight. We passed a busy pantry and strolled into a flour cloud. Maidens rolled and beat dough, chatting, laughing, and coughing.

"Heather, do you have my smoking pipe—love? I need to get out of here for a bit. The flour is making me cough . . ."

". . . he was getting a bit to rump-bumpy with me. I told him that I thought he was a very nice man, but I had a pox—he believed me and ran like the wind. Hahaha!"

Behind them, I saw Thorfinn surreptitiously lift the lid on a wicker handbasket and look inside, then drop the lid and lift the basket by its handles. He saw me looking at him and lifted an eyebrow as he casually caught up with us, basket in hand. Before I could question him, Thør whispered, "Freyja will be in her tower, ready to burst. We're running out of time. The alfather's letter said that we didn't have much time."

Dvallin led us to the other side of Sessrúmnir's main hall, up to the entrance of what looked like a servant's staircase rising to the tower's apartments. As we passed through the doorway, a guard stepped out of the shadows with his hand on his axe.

"Hold it," he ordered.

"We are the nursemaids," Thør said.

"Yes—yes," Dvallin said, running to our side. "Freyja needs her nursemaids. Please, let us through. You see me running up and down the stairs all day."

"You three smell like the stables—especially you," the guard said, scanning Thør up and down. "Aren't you a little big to be a nursemaid? You can't go upstairs smelling like *that*."

"The smell is from the buckets—not us," Thør said as he swung it, knocking the guard's helm off his head. The man collapsed to the floor.

"Thør," I said.

"He wasn't treating us like he should."

"Wait for me," Dvallin said, running back into the main hall. A minute later, the dwarf retuned with a horn of mead, which he splashed over the guard's face and tunic. "When he's discovered, they'll think he passed out—drunk."

We opened the door and ascended a circular staircase that coiled up the inside of the tower wall to the upper levels. At the top, the floorboards were covered with rugs and the air was warm and comfortable.

"Take our buckets back to the stables," I said, handing them to Dvallin.

Farther down the hallway, a servant girl turned a corner. I moved quickly, determined not to lose her. When I reached the corner, I slowed and cautiously looked around it. The girl was speaking with two men, a tray in her arms.

"—better not. Loki doesn't like me being touched by other men," she snapped.

I heard the creak of a door opening and shutting

again as I drew back. "We're here," I said, turning around.

"What's next? Because at some point those guards will come down the corridor and find us," Thør warned.

I waved for Thorfinn and Thør to follow and boldly walked to the door. "We're with her," I said to the guards, pointing to the closed door. As they looked us over, I opened the door and entered the tower room. They didn't stop us.

A curved wall with a balcony towered over a guard seated across from the doorway. Another guard stood, along with three giant hounds, before a fireplace, flames snapping within.

"Oh," I said. "The mistress called for her nursemaids."

The guard looked us over, pausing on Thør. Saying nothing, he tilted his head toward a door beside the fireplace, and returned to his seat—along with the dogs.

Our feet scuffled up the stairs like those of hurrying servants, and we slipped into the apartment.

A servant girl fanned Freyja, who sat on a couch on her balcony overlooking Fólkvangr. She was watching as her half of the slain warriors—no longer able to exercise free will—mindlessly fought and killed each other. Once the weapon that had killed a warrior was wrenched from his body, he rose and began the butchering again. Until the final battle, her half of the slain were eternally imprisoned in their repetitive behaviours, subject to the will of the gods.

She kept two dead ravens strung by their feet from the balcony ceiling, their black feathered wings blowing in the icy wind. Their limp bodies swung back and forth, their movement watched by her cat, which sometimes rose on its haunches as if ready to strike, then lay back down. "Look at how they swing in the wind," Freyja said, one hand stroking her bulging belly and the other stroking her cat. "The wind blowing through their limp wings almost gives them the illusion of flight."

Her other cat chased mice, momentarily disappearing and returning with a rodent in its mouth to offer to Freyja, or sauntering back in, breathing heavily, without a bounty in its mouth. The rest of the clowder rubbed up against the hems of our dresses; I kept nudging them away with my boot.

My shoes were killing my feet, my hair itched under the bonnet, and I had a sneaking sensation that I was being gawked at.

Freyja turned and saw us. "You are finally here. My . . . my baby is about to be born."

"Oh, we must get you to the stool," Thorfinn said, gesturing to Thør to take her other arm and lift her off of her couch.

I grabbed a stool and placed it underneath her. She squatted on it, supported by Thør and Thorfinn. They raised the hem of her gown to rest on her thighs.

"Rub the mistress's belly," Thorfinn instructed. "Gentle, circular motions."

"Where are my midwives?" Freyja yelled.

"Go see what's keeping them," I said to Thorfinn as I walked toward him and Thør.

Her boar woke up from its nap and slowly sauntered out of the room.

"Make sure that my baby is alright," she said.

"Your baby will be fine," Thør said, gingerly taking her hand.

"You are quite a large woman, aren't you," she commented, eyeing him. "Well, I guess you'll do for the heavy lifting."

"Oh, I wish my beloved husband Óðr were here, by my side," Freyja said, and closed her eyes as if attempting to *will* him to her.

"Yes, Mistress, that is a shame," Thør said, patting her hand. "He's off—somewhere—with *his* . . . soldiers, isn't he?"

Three women entered the room. "Oh, my völvur! Lynza, Griet, Lyana, please come to me," Freyja pleaded, dropping Thør's hand. "My baby is coming."

I quickly looked away when I recognized two of the women, suppressing my anger and clasping my hands to hide their shaking. Lyana! And Lynza. What are they *doing here*? I decided to do nothing and wait till they revealed their traitorous purpose.

They scurried around the room, preparing it for the birthing.

"Make our goddess a bowl of tea." Lynza ordered.

"Which herb will I use?" Griet asked.

"The blue cohosh."

Griet walked to the hearth and ladled water into a bowl. Moments later she returned with the tea. "Your Highness, please drink this," Griet said. "It will help to promote labour."

"*Shoo*," Lynza whispered, pushing us away. "And the same to the rest of you. We'll call you to take the baby and clean up the afterbirth." She poured oil scented with chamomile, rose, and lavender into her palm, then reached up underneath Freyja's gown. The fabric rippled and moved as Lynza massaged the oil into her belly.

Lyana danced around them, chanting and rattling stringed shells over Freyja. Griet returned from the fire with a smoldering bowl of herbs. She joined Lyana in the circle dance, leaving trails of smoke spiralling in the air. We stepped back.

Lynza raised her arms into the air over Freyja's belly button. She closed her eyes and tipped her face toward the ceiling. Her expression twisted and shuddered; her forehead tightened. Her mouth opened and she coughed up an oozing glob of phlegm. She reached for the hem of her pinafore and cupped the material in her palm, then spat the glob onto it. She slowly opened the material and peered into the mucous.

"Do you see anything?" Freyja asked frantically, struggling to speak through her contractions.

Lynza slowly closed her hand and regarded Freyja, looking shocked and disoriented. She slowly shook her head as if concealing something.

Freyja inhaled a slow and controlled breath and pushed. Lynza knelt, ready to grab the baby. The rest of us looked on. Nothing in the room stirred, except for the crackling of the fire and the cats walking along the wall, avoiding the birthing commotion.

Thorfinn ran to the fire and ladled boiling water into a tub; he placed it on a table and placed linen next to it. "We are right as rain, Mistress," he said excitedly. He ran back and stood next to me and Thør.

"Loki!" Freyja yelled. "Where are you?"

"Freyja, I'm here," a soft voice replied behind us. Loki, the Light-walker, drifted into the room. His head-to-foot black leather armour shimmered as he walked. He passed me and grabbed my ass. I squeaked.

Freyja smiled at him. "*My* Loki, set free from bondage."

For killing Óðinn's second son, Baldur, I remembered.

Loki stood behind Freyja's stool and held her other hand.

"Loki, will you grant me one request?"

"On this day, of all days—the birth of our saviour—yes."

The light filtering in surrounded him. His face and hands turned to light. It faded and Loki had changed.

"It pleases me to see the face of my lost husband, Óðr," she said, closing her eyes, waiting for the next contraction.

I looked at Lynza; her expression was haunted. She tried to conceal it, but it momentarily burst through her mask of calm before she regained control.

The next contraction hit and Freyja's back arched; her fingers gripped the edge of the stool and she screamed and pushed.

Strained silence followed, interrupted with a loud intake of air, panting, and coughing.

"Get this out of me," she yelled, pounding on the stool. "I want to be free of it!"

Loki lay his chin on her shoulder and whispered into her ear, then kissed it.

"Get away from me. You're too warm," she snapped. Rivers of perspiration streamed down her face and ran underneath her gown. "Just stand there Óðr—I mean Loki."

Another cycle of inhaling, pushing, and panting started.

"I see the child's crown," Lynza cried, reaching between Freyja's legs with a shaking hand to touch the baby's crown as it pushed through into Miðgarð.

Lynza startled, retracted in fear. I looked at the protruding face. The baby's eyes had opened. It was smeared with placenta, peering at Lynza.

"Mother. . . please consecrate the crown of the child," Lyana yelled.

Lynza dipped her fingernail into a pouch of salve and touched it to the child's forehead. Her hand appeared to move uncontrollably, scribbling in detail. She leaned back and brought her hand halfway to her mouth. "I . . . I consecrate this child ruler and heir to the nine worlds," she stammered. She covered her mouth with her trembling hand, suppressing an emotional reaction.

Freyja kicked Lynza away, and used her anger to overcome the pain. As the next contraction came she pushed, and reached between her legs to grab the baby and lift it out, dripping. The afterbirth splattered to the floor. "It's a king," she screamed, shaking with hysteria. The newborn cried out with her. Griet reached out to take the baby, but Freyja raised the baby into the air, its umbilical dangling and splattering blood on us.

"Praise to Freyja, mother of our saviour," Griet announced as she cut the umbilical, then bowed in submission and backed away.

"You have done well," Loki said to Freyja, changing back into himself.

She cradled the baby in her arms, looking down at it. The baby started to settle. Freyja gently wiped the afterbirth and blood off his face and stared down at him, her face momentarily softening into peace. She remained like that for a moment, then handed me the baby without looking at it.

As I stepped around the afterbirth and took it, I noticed that a part of the fluidic mass twitched. A snake slipped out of it and slithered away. One of Freyja's cats jumped out of nowhere and chased it into the next room.

A few moments later the cat returned without its prey and lay down next to the fire.

Thorfinn followed me to the table and helped me clean the baby, while Thør helped Freyja back to her couch and cleaned up the afterbirth.

"Thorfinn, did you notice the look on Lynza's face?" I asked, examining the scratch marks on the baby's head. "It looked like she saw something as she consecrated him."

"How is the baby? Is there anything special about him?" Thør asked, leaning over him.

The baby peed; the arc of piss hit Thør in the beard. The pressure dropped and a final spurt hit him in the mouth.

"He'll be a drinker of mead," I proclaimed and chuckled, watching urine drip off Thør's chin.

Thør slowly wiped his mouth with the back of his sleeve, then turned and spat on the floor. "What are you doing?" he asked when he turned back to me.

"I'm trying to see what Lynza scratched on his head," I said, gently stretching the skin on the baby's forehead. "It's an ægishjálmr," I said after a moment. "Is it homage to Freyja?"

"It could be. She consecrated the baby with a rune of magical delusion to deceive others so they can't see things as they truly are. That's seiðr magic. Only Óðinn and Freyja wield that power," Thør said. "So maybe it is homage to Freyja."

"Thør, I watched Lynza," I said, dropping my voice. "Her finger scribbled, as if someone else was controlling it."

"There's only one person I know that's capable . . ." Thør stopped and chuckled, shaking his head.

"There's more," I said. "Freyja also gave birth to a serpent."

"What?" His eyes widened peering at me over his veil in disbelief.

"I saw it in the afterbirth; it slithered away."

Thør glanced at the couch. "I have to get back," he said, and returned to Freyja.

"We have done well, Loki," Freyja said, her breathing calmer now, and even.

"Oh Mistress," Thør said. "Lynza consecrated your baby with an ægishjálmr. I'm sure it is homage to you and your seiðr mastery."

"Yes," Freyja said, drifting into a trance of triumphant fulfillment. "It can't be Óðinn's; he's dead. I know, because I killed him."

Her back arched and she straightened up on her couch; arrogance washed over her face, then pleasure. She leaned back onto her couch, staring outside.

"*You* killed him?" Thør said.

"I saw a wolf eat Óðinn with my own eyes," Thorfinn whispered, looking at me.

"As it was foretold, Fenrir will devour Óðinn," I said.

"The Æsir accepts things as they are, but the Jötunn do not," Freyja said. "The Jötunn create and transform. We forged Miðgarð with our hands and our hearts; we are constant and immortal. We shape its air, its land, and its ocean. I am half Jötunn and the Æsir pulled me from my world and kept me imprisoned in Asgard under the pretense that it will keep the peace. Being forced to accept eternity in Asgard was a living prison. Óðinn cannot understand.

"Finally the Jötnar overthrew the world of the gods. The water barrier that kept the ice giants out froze and we saw our chance—so we took it. The alfather fled, as did the rest, except for the Jötunn members of the Æsir; their allegiance lies with us.

"Óðinn was forced to flee," she continued. "He had no other place to go, except Miðgarð. I would've bashed my newborn baby on the rocks if it brought Óðinn to me. But I knew it was only a matter of time; he couldn't elude us forever." She frowned in thought. "I think I found him with humans at a place having something to do with wine . . . or wheat . . ."

Thør cocked his head; I could see his face reddening with his anger through his veil. He touched Mjölnir through his gown.

"I was taken from my mother along with my brother, Freyr, and *forcibly* given along with my father, Njordr, to the Æsir as tribute for the truce, to use for the Æsir's purpose; not as equals—that came later. My mother, Skadi, is a giantess; she warned our father about the Æsir's idea of a 'truce'—just another word for subjugation. They used me as their whore.

"First they tried to marry me off to Hjordith, as his payment for building the wall around Asgard. Then they tried to marry me off to Thryrm, so Thør could get his hammer back. But I sabotaged their plans by getting the old flaccid-farter drunk; I knew Thør would hear of it, and he did, before the Æsir knew what he was doing, Thør dressed up like me and slayed him." She smiled. "I was free and clear of guilt."

Her smile disappeared. "I would've been able to live with everything that was done to me in the splendour of Valhalla, but the final curse came from Óðinn. He wanted me to teach him the mystery of seiðr magic, and promised to protect me and make me his equal. I had something that Óðinn didn't, a power that he wanted and a female form to create it with.

"I married Óðr and after our long honeymoon, Óðinn sent him away on a long expedition. And that's when Óðinn raped me and forcibly took seiðr magic from me.

"I buried my hatred for him, maintaining a false front. I even made an agreement with him, swearing on his spear, Gungnir, in the presence of Loki that I would not use seiðr magic to obstruct Ragnarök."

"Get me some mead!" Loki yelled to me.

I jumped, slid the baby to Thorfinn, and ran to the barrel. I dipped a horn into the golden liquid and sprinted to Loki, my gown jumping around my knees as I ran. Kneeling in front of him, I held the horn out in front of me, keeping my eyes on the floor. He took the horn and grabbed my wrist; I closed my palm into a fist.

"Thank you, my dear," he teased, his tone making me feel uncomfortable. "Such strong hands are an asset to us." His rough thumb stroked the vein on my wrist before letting it go.

I rose to my feet but remained crouched, walking backward to the table. I saw his shadow turn away.

"Where was I?" Freyja said haughtily. "Oh yes—so my handsome . . . Loki agreed to release me from my sworn vow, because, as he said—"

"Anyone who makes an agreement in the presence of a trickster isn't afraid of the odds," Loki added with a chuckle.

"We've been together ever since," Freyja said, smiling too.

"I changed myself into the likeness of Fenrir and devoured Óðinn; his delusion was fuelled by his male stupidity and his fear of the end. I stared into his eyes, knowing his fear would kill him. By the time he saw through my trick, it was too late; I tore into his throat, silencing him. Without his voice, he was powerless to use his seiðr magic on me. I took my time devouring him, relishing each sinew and muscle, devouring his organs and drinking his blood."

Now she appeared to be having a conversation with herself. "I am Jötunn, not Æsir. Don't you know what it is? It's the twilight of the gods. Their dwindling powers will not save them. It's a time of brute force. This is the day that the Jötunn forces rise; it's our time. Miðgarð is ours. The Æsir is diminishing into nothingness."

She belched, and lingered a moment before continuing. "The Æsir were quite taken with my powers, and sought my services. But soon their values—honouring kin, loyalty, and obedience to the law—were being pushed aside by Óðinn's desire for seiðr magic. I used their greed against them. Their only power lies in their methodical pursuit of knowledge and belief as doctrine. Óðinn believed I was Fenrir and believed that he would die—so he did."

She looked to Loki. "Loki, you're part Jötunn; you live the Jötunn value: *innovation* above all."

"I do," Loki replied.

"And don't forget, my love . . ." she stroked his cheek " . . . the Æsir-Vanir war was never won. As part of the truce, the other half of the slain are mine. With Óðinn out of the way, our child will survive Ragnarök and the Jötunn will rise—again." Her matter-of-fact tone carried her story like moving gears in her plan.

"You tell it with the poetry of a worshipped goddess," Loki interrupted.

"And the mother of a god." She giggled. "Loki, you

gave me everything that I had hoped to gain. To finally get revenge for being used as Jötunn tribute, their whore to end the Æsir-Vanir War. Now that Óðinn is out of the way, I have no adversary versed in seiðr. Our reign will save the Jötnar and the humans. The Ragnarök will be our resurrection."

"Hail Freyja, saviour of humans!" Þør squeaked.

"H-hail!" Thorfinn and I echoed awkwardly.

"The final battle on Vígríðr is won."

"We're a bit full of ourselves," Thorfinn mumbled as he passed us with a bucket full of clean water.

Þør finished cleaning Freyja and the floor and took the buckets to leave outside the door to be picked up, returning with a bulging sack that he casually set in a corner near the table.

Freyja sighed, clearly enjoying the sound of her own voice. She slumped on her couch and her skin lightened and her stomach morphed into sculpted curves.

"Don't forget about me, Freyja," Loki said. "Without my help, you could not have found Óðinn. I was on Vinland stealing that baby, remember?"

"I don't deny it, Loki." Her tone was defensive. "It's just that your tricks do not compare to the power that's needed to create a world order."

"You need me," Loki said, peering into Freyja's eyes.

"Your tricks can't affect me," Freyja retorted.

I picked up the baby and glanced at Þør and Thorfinn. It was time to go. I handed the baby to Thorfinn, and Þør lifted the squirming sack from the corner. He glanced behind him to make sure no one was watching and rested the sack in the crib. Tipping it, he dumped out Dvallin.

"Take this key," Dvallin said without preamble before

lying back in the crib. "It will get you into the lower catacombs: ice tunnels dug out by the fire Jötunn. They lead back outside."

"Where's the door?" Thør asked.

"It's in the stables, a trapdoor in Sleipnir's stall."

"Sleipnir—Óðinn's horse?" Thør could hardly contain himself.

"Freyja captured it to train as her steed. I was the one entrusted to care for him."

"You stink, little man," Thør said, taking the key and pulling the swaddling blanket over him.

Thorfinn opened up the lidded wicker basket he'd appropriated to reveal that it was filled with enough blankets to keep the baby warm. I gently placed the baby inside and wrapped his head and body in more blankets, keeping his eyes and nose free. Then he closed the lid and gripped the handles.

"Is there enough air getting into the basket?" I fussed.

"Yes, there is," Thorfinn replied. "He won't smother."

"Let's get out of here," Thør said.

We left the tower room and descended the spiral staircase. The guards stationed at the base of the tower ignored us, and we entered the bustling corridors of the hall.

We weaved in and out through the crowd of servants, trying to blend in to the everyday madness of working in Freyja's hall. The heady aroma of bread, wine, and roasting venison carried by domestics filled the air around us. We knew that Dvallin could be discovered at any time, or do something stupid and get himself caught, but we had to keep to the measured pace of those around us. We squeezed through the queues of people ascending the stairs as we descended into the kitchen. A cold wind blew into the room from an opened door; the hearth flames cracked, stretched and roared. It was as if safety beckoned to us, showing the way.

We walked through the door and into the yard, then headed for the stables. Thorfinn hugged the basket, protecting the baby from the winter wind. The yard was empty, except for stable hands taking the horses inside.

Inside the stables we split up, searching for Sleipnir's stall. All around us, stable boys looked up, saw us, and jeered. "Yoo-hoo!" several called, leering and beckoning for us to join them.

Thør and I met up and looked down the last row of stalls. Thorfinn stood in front of a stall door partway down. He waved us over. We joined him and looked into the stall. A beautiful grey steed lay at the back of the cubicle, partially hidden in the shadows. Thør and I looked around, making sure that no one was watching as Thorfinn carefully opened the door. The horse didn't move.

When we sidled into the stall, the horse jumped to its feet, startled, and paced from side to side. Its head reached out to Thør's face, the chain attached to its collar going taut. The horse appeared agitated until he sniffed the basket; then he calmed down again. When the stallion turned and moved into the corner, we saw the red stripes of bloody lacerations on its flank.

"Shh . . . shh . . . I won't hurt you," Thør whispered, raising his palms and slowly cupping them under its jaw. "What have they done to you?" He slowly stepped forward and removed the chain at the collar.

Sleipnir trotted out of the shadows.

"It's not eight-legged," Thorfinn said, looking

surprised.

"Whoever heard of an *eight-legged* horse?" Thør said.

"It is said that Óðinn's horse has eight legs."

"Don't you know what a kenning is when you hear one?" Thør said sarcastically, rolling his eyes. "*Eight-legged* means that Sleipnir is *fast*, because it looks like he has eight legs as he runs; it doesn't mean that Sleipnir *has* eight legs."

"I guess it's all in the interpretation," I said.

Thør chuckled to himself as he brushed aside hay with his foot, looking for the trapdoor. He found it and inserted the key, turning it several times. A mechanism clicked and he fished up a ring set into the wood and lifted the door. A glowing white tunnel of ice waited for us at the bottom of the ladder.

I stepped in and Thorfinn handed me the basket. Looping the handles over my wrist, I slowly descended the ladder. Thør and Thorfinn followed.

"They carved through solid ice," I said, looking around in awe.

"Dvallin told me that Surtr burned through the ice to hollow out the tunnels," Thør said.

There was a splinter in the ice above us and light bled through from the surface. Large fractures glowed blue and white. Hay covered the tunnel floor. As we walked down the sloping tunnel, I heard a *clop* and looked behind me. Sleipnir had somehow stepped down into the tunnel. His ears touched the roof as he trotted toward us.

"Here comes eight-legs," Thør quipped.

I shivered. A cold wind whistled through the network of tunnels. My cotton dress rippled in the breeze, sending the cold up it.

Sleipnir poked his head in between Thorfinn and me. His body heat felt nice on my skin.

Thør stayed in front, scouting ahead a bit and listening down tunnels as we approached intersections. Thorfinn and I slowed to Sleipnir's pace to stay warm.

Thør raised his fist in the air. I heard a horn blast, muffled by distance but increasing in volume as it approached us. "We're found out!" Thør yelled, running back to us. "Thorfinn, get on Sleipnir. Take the baby out of here. Find the boat." He helped Thorfinn onto Sleipnir's back and I handed up the basket containing the baby. I watched as they trotted down the tunnel and turned a corner. Suddenly I felt a whoosh of air, and looked at Thør.

"Eight-legged," he said, nodding.

"Maybe we should've left on Sleipnir, too," I said, creeping around the corner.

"No, the baby is more important than you and I. Besides, something tells me that Sleipnir knows where he's going."

We heard the heavy footsteps of troops coming down the tunnels. It sounded like they were coming from all around us.

"That tiny-turd squealed," Thør hissed through his teeth, pounding the ice wall with his fist.

"Maybe to save his own life," I suggested. "This way!"

I headed in Sleipnir's direction with Thør following. We didn't have weapons save for Thør's hammer, and despite the damage that could do, he probably wouldn't use it against the humans that he was supposed to protect.

The hollow echo of shouts and footfalls chased us through the tunnels. It sounded like they were closing in.

"I see their shadows," a voice behind us shouted.

Thør turned and stood his ground. Three soldiers turned the corner, with more heads popping up behind them. Thør lifted his dress and took out Mjölnir. "Stand back," he said, glancing back at me. "And cover your ears."

Thør lifted Mjölnir, hitting the ceiling and splintering a section of it. With all of his might, he slammed his hammer on the floor; the tunnel shook. He lifted his hammer and slammed it down again. The tunnel floor splintered. The split widened and crawled along the tunnel floor.

"Retreat!" ordered the soldier in the lead, seeing the crack heading toward them. They turned and ran.

Thør walked over to me, a wry smile on his face. We continued on.

We stopped in an intersection and looked down the tunnels. "I'm a little disoriented," I said, hearing more soldiers approaching from behind us.

Suddenly a cacophony of yells burst down another tunnel, cutting off a second route.

"Let's split up; I'll try to get them to follow me. You go that way," Thør said, pointing.

I ran.

The tunnel looked like it was frequently used. Straw and gravel were ground into the ice, giving me traction. I ran around a curve and the voices began to recede a little. I noticed something lying on the floor a short distance ahead, when I drew closer I saw that it was a scrap of cloth. I looked up the tunnel. There was another scrap a little farther ahead. I scooped it up when I got to it. *Thorfinn, you old sea conqueror.*

"Thør, I found them!" I yelled back the way I'd come,

hoping that he heard me and had time to turn back and follow.

I chased the pieces of cloth till I saw natural light seeping from beyond a sweeping turn in the tunnel. I ran into the light and stopped. Loki waited at the cave exit, backed by six soldiers.

"Come closer, *nursemaid*," he commanded. "You don't want to anger your master." His eyes were dark holes; his form seemed disembodied, a dark ghost against the paleness of the tunnel walls and the snow beyond the exit.

"I don't have your baby," I said.

"Who said anything about the baby?"

Loki's body blurred. My head tipped, feeling like it rolled backward. My personality seemed to split—I felt like two Helgis, one violating the other; one fearing and hating the other.

Confusion tore through my head, one gusting thought desperately trying to catch the other. Rage thundered through me as if I were a drugged berserker, with thoughts only of killing and maiming anything within arm's reach. And all the while I wanted to kill what I couldn't capture inside of me.

I stumbled backward, hitting my head on the ice wall and feeling as if the wind had been knocked out of me. I felt the pull of a bolting horse and terror; something was violently taken from me and then two hands grabbed my shoulders from behind and my stomach felt like I'd leapt off a cliff.

Loki stood in front of me, next to his men—again. Thør stood over me. Time appeared to restart.

"Kill them," Loki said, before vanishing into the white of the blizzard behind him.

Fighters descended into the tunnel. They calmly passed around a calfskin pouch.

Drugged mead.

They didn't rush; they knew the effects of the drug would heighten the pleasure of their massacre.

"We're trapped," I said, looking at the massed soldiers. "Are we fighting the living, or Freyja's half of the slain warriors?"

"I don't think it matters," Thør replied. He hesitated. "Helgi, there's something that I have to tell you. I'm . . . not like you. I—"

Suddenly the ground thundered with the pounding of hooves, and the storm winds wailed, carrying a baby's cries. Thorfinn, with the baby under his arm, rode into the tunnel. The fighters at the entrance turned. Sleipnir reared and knocked them to the tunnel floor before they could raise their axes and swords.

Thør picked me up and we ran for the exit, followed by the sound of clanging axes and shields. When we reached Sleipnir, Thør lifted me up and put me on the horse's broad back behind Thorfinn. I heard his hand slap the horse's rump and I instinctively grabbed Thorfinn, who was holding onto a fistful of Sleipnir's mane. We bolted into the storm. The impact of Sleipnir's hooves pounded in my head and beat into my chest. The storm wiped away Sessrúmnir Hall, Frejya, and Loki. The sloped ice field disappeared in the whiteness.

"Thør," I yelled, turning.

Thør was holding onto Sleipnir's tail, his feet braced, and the horse dragged him through the snow; he slid along behind, occasionally bouncing into the air like a blanket on a windy day. The wind of our passage split his beard and curly hair down the middle to stream behind him, and stretched the skin of his face. "Eight-legged!" he shouted, grinning.

Sleipnir slowed to a trot and then stopped, chest heaving and flanks lathered beneath my legs.

"Umph!" Thør shouted, skidding to a stop. "I guess, there's just no comfortable ending to that."

"Thør, are you okay?" I asked.

"Yes; just let me rest."

"How's the baby?" I asked, turning to Thorfinn and shouting over the child's wails and the wind.

"He's fine; he's against my torso. I think he's hungry—he's squirming and wants to be unbundled."

The storm broke—a little—and more fighters advanced, blocking off our escape route. The glint of shields, metal blades, and spears flashed in the air. The warriors' pace quickened when they saw us over the fold in the hill.

"More soldiers!" I yelled.

Sleipnir neighed and angrily shook his head. He dug his hind hooves into the snow and bolted toward the advancing army.

"Shouldn't we be heading away from them?" I yelled.

My heart pounded in my head as Sleipnir picked up speed, though the pounding in my chest lessened. Snow whipped around us and seemed to lift us.

"Helgi," Thør yelled, giggling somewhere behind me, "you and Thorfinn—get down and hang on."

"Hang on for—"

Grey masses grew—no, *unfolded*—on either side of us. Sleipnir leapt into the air and before my face was pushed into his back, I saw the feathery grey tips of wings flapping up and down.

I squeezed my knees together, hugging Sleipnir's

back as I felt myself slipping a little. My knee rested in the fold of a moving wing. The air moved in my ears as the horse's massive wings began beating up and down. "Oh my gods, he can fly!" I yelled.

The baby stopped crying and I thought I heard excited squeals blowing away in the storm.

"Here we go!" Thør laughed.

My stomach went weightless; we were airborne and climbing upward. Spearmen lifted their weapons, but they were toppled by the soldiers falling in Sleipnir's wake. The archers' arrows scattered, blowing off target, and Sleipnir's wake blasted them to the ground like a forest of twigs.

From the air, I could see that Loki and Freyja had mobilized a third of her troops to look for us. The storm concealed our ascent. Sleipnir banked left and then right, varying our flight path, making it difficult to figure out our direction.

As Sleipnir turned downward, I turned. Thør bounced up and down on Sleipnir's wake, content and smiling. "Thør, where is he taking us?" I shouted.

"I wouldn't worry; Sleipnir probably knows where he's going. This might be the Old Man's doing. If he doesn't land, we'll try to coax him down. Until then, enjoy the ride."

Thør looked down. "I think . . . he's taking us to *Hringhorni*. That's where I get off. You two take the baby back to Sigarsholm."

Minutes later, we landed. The storm blew around us, concealing us in its flurries as Sleipnir hit the ground and galloped to a stop. I turned, but Thør was nowhere in sight.

"Thør!"

"I'm here," he yelled back, appearing through the storm. "I jumped off." He walked past us and Sleipnir followed. Up ahead, the boughs concealing *Hringhorni* appeared to be undisturbed. "Right where we left it," Thør said. "You two take the baby to Sigarsholm. I'll take *Hringhorni* back and meet you there."

"Why don't we all go with you?" Thorfinn said.

"No, there's no time. I don't know why this baby is so important, but we need to follow Óðinn's instructions. I won't be far behind. See you on Sigarsholm." Thør disappeared into the swirling snow, heading in the direction where we'd buried the sail; moments later he returned with it folded under his arm. He found the anchor chain and lifted it out of the snow, boarded *Hringhorni*, and began rigging the sail. The boat bobbed away from the floe.

We heard a horn blasting in the wind behind us. "It's time for us to go," I said.

"You take the front, and I'll hold the baby," Thorfinn said.

We switched spots and I grabbed Sleipnir's mane.

The bukkehorn blasted in the wind once, then again, followed by another one. "The troops are converging. They'll be here any minute," I said, noticing distant torches flickering in the storm. "Okay it's time to fly," I said, bobbing up and down.

The trumpeting bukkehorn grew louder.

"Take us to Sigarsholm," I pleaded, rubbing Sleipnir's neck. "Bad people are coming to hurt us." I turned to Thorfinn. "I can't make him move."

"Giddy-up," Thorfinn shouted.

Sleipnir trotted forward, but made no move to lift off.

Suddenly three scouts appeared through the sleet;

seeing us, they lifted their horns and blasted out their location. The baby squealed and Sleipnir turned and bolted across the snowy plain. Then he leapt, his wings unfurling and reaching for air. I felt the push of air underneath us as his hooves skirted the heads of the frightened scouts and took us higher and higher. He seized the air and glided on top of it like a fish gliding through currents.

We climbed, touching the bottom of the churning clouds. Sessrúmnir Hall and its floating island shrank in our rear. The Norðr Ocean lay below. Drifting icebergs clustered together, creating large bodies of calm water. Sleipnir descended, swerving around the mountains of ice and skimming over the sky reflected in the water. I leaned over and saw our reflection shimmering on the glassy surface. The wind wasn't as harsh over the water. Sleipnir's body heat warmed me and I hardly felt the cold. We turned, heading suðr.

"How's Baby?" I yelled back.

"He fell asleep again," Thorfinn said. "I think he's grown since this morning."

"That's impossible," I replied.

My eyes were glued to the incredible wonder surrounding us. From here, the water, earth, and sky ceased to be separate. The air and the water moved together and when I closed my eyes, I didn't know if I was flying or gliding through the water. "I'm flying on Óðinn's horse!" I yelled, feeling my stomach and head whirling with the air currents surrounding us. I could see the world from a new perspective. Cloud banks, distant and dark, flashed and boomed. Rain fell in places, morphing into snow as the hidden wind caught it and swirled it into funnels and rolling crests. Birds flocked around us and herds of humped giants leapt out of the water and shimmered out of existence beneath the surface again.

Miðgarð flowed around me as I flowed over it and through it. The land and the ice moved through the thin, wispy clouds. We were all moving through Miðgarð as time moved through us. I wondered if the gods had these same thoughts as they looked down. I felt like a god myself, riding the air, looking down at the sea Jötunn jumping in and out of the water. They were the size of mice scurrying across a deck. On the ocean, they were giants next to our ships. Now I felt like the giant.

I grinned, thinking of Thør sailing *Hringhorni*. He was an interesting character, the way he always imitated Thør. Maybe he sought to honour his deity by protecting us the way Thør did.

I wrapped my arms around Sleipnir's neck and let my mind drift with the moving scene below. My eyes started to get a little heavy, and I slept.

I woke with a start—my head had tipped forward. The baby was screaming, his cries rising louder and louder. I turned in time to see Thorfinn place his hand in the basket and gently pat the baby, trying to quiet him. "I can't stop his crying," Thorfinn said.

"Maybe he needs foooo . . . !"

Sleipnir dived, plummeting toward the open sea. I ducked as we picked up speed. He flapped his wings in front of himself, slowing our descent. My stomach lurched into my chest. I could make out a forested and rocky island. The horse banked toward it and I saw the grey slanted sides of the temple rising out of the treetops. *Sigarsholm*.

Relief rushed through me as I saw people congregating across the snow-covered surface, looking like ants crawling on a sand hill.

Sleipnir's back tilted slightly and I grabbed his neck tightly. I felt Thorfinn grab onto me as an updraft *whoosh* of Sleipnir's wings flapped near my ears. Sleipnir's back tipped up and down, making our vertical descent a bit rocky. I waited for the thud of landing, but felt only a forward push as he landed, the horse galloping then slowing to a trot.

The world stopped again. The only thing I heard was the baby crying. I sat up and lifted my leg over Sleipnir's broad back, preparing to drop to the ground. "*Ow, ow, ow!*" I yelled. Stiffness changed to aching and then to pain as I brought my legs together for the first time in hours. It felt like I was stretching them back into place. I froze on the horse's back, unable to straighten my legs.

Sleipnir shook his body and I slid off. The ground rushed up to me. I held my breath, waiting for the pain. I hit the snow on my feet. The pain tore through my legs and into my stomach and my jaw. I sank down in the snow, trying to breathe the pain away. "Son of a . . ." I growled, then, noticing the people running toward us, holding out furs and boots, finished with, "he's quite the ride."

"Helgi, take the baby," Thorfinn yelled.

I staggered to my feet. Snow stuck to me and water dripped from my sweaty brow into my hair and down my back. I touched my hair in pained confusion, worrying that my headscarf had blown away during the flight. I slowly limped bowlegged to Thorfinn, stepping gently into pain with each step through the snow.

Gudrid ran to me and wrapped a fur pelt around me. "Here, put your feet into these," she said. I kicked off my clogs and shook the strap off my toe as Gudrid bent over and held open the boot for my foot to slip into.

"Are you still nursing, Gudrid?" I asked, handing her Baby when she straightened.

"When was the last time he ate?" she asked, putting the baby underneath her pinafore.

"Too long," I replied.

She appeared to be unlacing the top of her dress under the covering, and occasionally peeked down her collar. She reached in and tried to get Baby to feed.

"We have contact," she said, sounding relieved. "He smells like he needs changing, too."

"Sorry; there was no time for that, either."

She gazed down at the mound under her pinafore, and her brows pinched together. "He's large for a newborn. When was the baby born?"

"It's been only one dægur."

She looked up at me, brows raised now. "One dægur? He looks much older."

"Take it slow, old man," I joked as Thorfinn hobbled over.

"Thorfinn, I missed you," Gudrid exclaimed, careful of the baby at her breast as she rushed over to hug him.

"I missed you, too," he said, returning her embrace and kissing her.

"Take the horse to the stables and feed him," I ordered my men.

"Where's Thør?" Gudrid asked, looking around.

"He's sailing *Hringhorni* back," I said.

"Thorfinn . . . and Helgi, I know that you just returned, but we must settle the matter of Freydis; she has invoked her right to a speedy hearing in front of the althing," Gudrid said.

"Helgi," Thorfinn said, "as prince you have the right

to refuse leading the althing, but I'd like your impartiality on it."

"I'd be honoured," I said. "You choose the other four representatives and we will use an outside altar; there's a hörgr in the forest. We'll convene once Thør returns."

I turned toward my navigator as he approached. "Isung, my friend; it's good to see you,"

"It's good to see you, too," he replied.

"Tell me what's been happening."

"We heard reports from the völvur that Hunding is back in Hundland." He paused before adding ominously, "We think he isn't acting alone."

"Does he have an ally?"

Isung shrugged. "We don't know. The völvur are helping. They are here with your mother, Borghild."

I perked up. "Where?"

"She's with the colony in the caves. They live underground. You'll need to hurry, because she is leaving for home. Hunding is trying to eradicate the völvur colonies. As our allies, they may give us an advantage against Hunding and the other clans. Hrafn and Atli haven't found Sinfjötli," he added. "We don't know where he disappeared to, nor if he's still alive."

"After the althing, I leave for Hunding's fortress," I said decisively. "Prepare a ship for me."

"Helgi, there's no need," Isung said, and stepped aside. Behind him an ice floe had drifted between Sigarsholm and Hundland. It was the size of a fighting field and provided a temporary land bridge to the other side.

I nodded once in approval. "They'll be gathering forces," I said, thinking ahead.

"So have we," Isung replied. "The völvur are massing

to our side with your mother's sponsorship."

ℭ ℭ

I stood in front of the hörgr, facing the setting sun. It was little more than an outcropping of ancient rocks that had served as an altar and a place of outdoor prayer for the wisdom of the gods for thousands of years. The horizon glowed, but the churning sky hid millions of shining lights. Below the vault of the night sky, assembled Vinlanders stood facing us, their flickering torches providing the only light.

"Gudrid," I said, "are there direct witnesses to the accused transgressions that can serve on the althing?"

"Yes, Prince. Arnora escaped. She wasn't part of the original crew and so went unnoticed. The only other one who escaped was Tostig; he later died."

"Did Tostig die at the hands of Freydis, or did he meet his demise some other way?"

"His death is not related to the defendant's charges," Gudrid replied.

I nodded and turned to the assembly. "Arnora, step forward to the hörgr and serve on the althing."

Arnora nudged through the crowd and stood next to me.

"Gudrid, who are the remaining three?" I asked her.

"Thorfinn and myself, and Thør, as an impartial member."

Hearing their names, the pair moved from the sidelines to join me at the hörgr.

"Bring in the accused," I ordered.

Two warriors escorted Freydis, shackled at the wrists and ankles, through the crowd. The Vinlander community parted, their faces and body language radiating disgust. The warriors stopped in front of the hearth where a fire burned and turned Freydis to face the rest of her community. She stood with her head down, her dishevelled hair hiding the shame she wore on her face.

"Gudrid, what are the charges?" I asked.

"Freydis and her husband, Thorvald, are charged with the wanton slaughter of the *Mímir's* crew: thirty-four of her kin and countrymen, including the unborn.

"You betrayed your community and sundered the mutual trust required to live among us. But greater than these things, you carry the seeds of conflict just as your father Eirik the Red did; his blood is on your hands." I paused. "Do you have anything to say before we sentence you?"

Freydis lifted her head, although her hair still curtained much of her face. "I am innocent of these crimes," she said, her voice breaking. "Although my hands committed the crimes, the will was not mine. I was overtaken by a madness; it was a *possession*."

Startled murmurs rippled through the audience.

"Arnora," I said, "what is your testimony?"

"I witnessed Freydis's slaughter. I heard the pleas from her victims and the cries of pain from our kin. I saw family members in their death throes, and brothers betraying sisters and sons betraying mothers."

"Arnora, what is *your* punishment for Freydis?" I asked.

"Banishment, like her father."

I turned to the other woman. "Gudrid, what is your testament?"

"Freydis is my sister," she said, then sighed. "Not unlike the sisters she murdered. I was married to two of her brothers. We have travelled and fought together, keep our community—Grœnlandia—together. But I can no longer trust her."

Freydis began weeping uncontrollably. Gudrid's face softened with sympathy, but she said in a subdued voice, "My judgement is banishment."

I nodded and looked to Þórr. "Þórr, what do you decide?"

"Like the son of Óðinn and Jörð, my sworn duty is to protect. I am not only of the booming sky; I am also of the earth. Our first duty is to defend our kin, so the community will continue. Protecting one's kin and community protects our future kin and teaches them to protect and direct theirs. Freydis's killing has forever put into question our ability to do that. She has bloodied the pages of our saga; she has opened us up to the judgement of future generations. A future that will be built on the instability that she's created," Þórr said. Then he drew a deep breath. "But I know of the possession that she speaks of."

The murmurs rose to derisive and angry shouts.

"Who are you?"

"How do *you* know—"

I raised my hand for silence.

"My judgement," Þórr shouted over the interruption, "is clemency. But she will have to earn back your trust."

The crowd didn't react.

"Thorfinn?" I prompted.

"I stand with my wife: banishment. Gudrid has the sight and if Freydis was possessed, Gudrid would've known—"

"Gudrid wasn't at Hóp," Freydis cried. "There is no way that she—"

"Silence!" I roared. "Freydis, your peers on this dais

have judged you. Future generations *will* learn from your actions; your crimes go beyond killing. Your act is an assault on the social order and you have taken the crime of your father and used it against your kin in the same way. For the same crimes as your father, you will be banished from the safety of your community. You will be taken to a habitable island. One where you have a chance of a life. In the end, we all share the same chance."

Gudrid collapsed; the conflict of love against duty must've weakened her. Thorfinn swept in to catch and support her.

Freydis had to be dragged away, stumbling and resisting, refusing to move. She no longer had the support of the community for survival. She would have to survive on her own, or find another community that would take her in.

Gudrid sobbed into her hands. "There is no other decision that I could've made," Gudrid cried. Like all of us, her mind knew what had to be done, but her heart struggled to accept it.

Arnora drifted past Gudrid and silently placed her hand on Gudrid's shoulder. She joined a group of opened armed Vinlanders.

"Gudrid, you are correct; there was no other decision," I said. "You fulfilled your duty despite familial ties. Your greatness today will be spoken of in the sagas."

"With Ragnarök coming, nothing will survive," Thorfinn said solemnly.

"Yes, Thorfinn, I've heard that rumour, too."

"With all due respect, Helgi, it's not a rumour. The alfather told me on Vinland. He said that his reason for wandering Miðgarð was to usher in the Ragnarök."

"Óðinn visited you?" I said in surprise. I looked at his

wife. "Gudrid, did you see him too?"

"Yes," she said. "I sensed that it was the alfather too."

"Where is the alfather, now?"

"He's dead. Killed by a wolf—Loki's son, Fenrir," Thorfinn said.

"And you witnessed his death, too?"

"Yes!"

"Gudrid, did you witness Óðinn's death?"

"No, I was on *Hringhorni.*"

"It's the boat that Óðinn arrived on," Thorfinn explained.

"Óðinn arrives on *Hringhorni*, so named because of a circle on the stem. Baldur is Óðinn's second son," I said.

"Baldur is dead, killed by Loki," Þór supplied. "Without Baldur, the summer sun no longer shines. It's why we have the Fimbulwinter."

I frowned. "Þór, do you think Óðinn is behind what's happening?"

"Helgi, I think we all want to know what that old man is up to," Þór said, shaking his head and laughing. "He weaves our events and writes *his* saga."

I looked to the sky. The days were darker and the sun didn't go far above the horizon. But it was like that at every solstice. The skies always darkened, but eventually they lightened again. "We *are* in the middle of a Great Winter. We've fought other clans for food stores and livestock," I said. "There was a rumour moving through our lands of the Fimbulwinter."

"Our soothsayer, Grimhild, said that she saw Óðinn's hand in this," Gudrid said, glancing at Thorfinn before turning back to me. "Helgi, there is something that I have to tell you. I've heard about the events in your life; they've happened before."

"Yes, Gudrid; my life and those of hundreds of other warriors. Maybe my reputation precedes me." I laughed.

"No, Helgi. In our and the other Vinlanders' time, the Norse people have travelled farther east and west than have those in the time you are from. Our ancestors have travelled and conquered hundreds of kingdoms, and we far outnumber your clans."

"Gudrid," I said, "what you say is too . . . miraculous. You live the saga that I began."

"Yes."

I frowned, perplexed. "Where is Vinland and these other places you speak of?" I asked her. "And how do we get there?"

Gudrid looked into the night sky. Occasionally the constellations sparkled through breaks in the overcast sky. "Helgi, I wish I knew. I don't recognize these night skies."

"Helgi, I'm going with you," Gudrid said suddenly.

"Then I'm coming too," Thorfinn said. "You'll need help with Snorri and Baby; they're both still breast-feeding."

"We'll make slings to carry them," Gudrid said.

"I can help, too. I like babies—most of the time," Thør said.

"Isung, what are our numbers?" I asked as he arrived and handed me a sword and shield.

"Not enough to wage a war, but we might have enough to hold them off. We'll keep them busy on the floe's top side, so you can get through undetected. We'll lure Hunding's field warriors to the front and back sides of the floe where archers in dragon boats will attack them with flaming arrows," Isung replied. "We've sent scouts onto the floe. There is a system of ice gorges and caves through the centre of it—rivers of meltwater are hollowing it out. The scouts returned just before you got here. They couldn't get all the way to the other side, but we think they got through most of the way. They marked their path"

"Good," I said. "With most of them focusing on you, we should be able to slip by them. I don't want them retreating and reinforcing Hunding's camp."

"Hunding's men got a beating at our first battle," Isung said. "I don't anticipate a large, or even a powerful, force."

"Once I raise his severed head by his hair in front of his fighters, they'll follow me," I said confidently. "I'll see you when I get back, Isung."

ဆ   ಣ

Gudrid walked up to me with Baby slung on her back like a sack of potatoes. She was carrying a longbow and a quiver under her arm. Thorfinn followed her with Snorri sleeping in a sling on his back. Baby squirmed and wriggled in his sling.

"Gudrid, how are your combat skills?" I asked her

"Improving, Helgi."

Thør and Isung joined us, and we set out.

Isung led us down a narrow ravine. We stepped through ankle-deep water. I waited for the cold sting, but the water was tepid. "Are there hot springs on the island?" I asked.

"Yes. The völvur are masters at harnessing its heat."

He pulled aside a curtain of vines and vegetation and I felt warm air wafting past me as it escaped. We entered a dark cavern illuminated by torches that flickered at the entrances of several tunnels. Cloaked women moved around this main chamber. My eyes jumped from face to face, looking for my mother.

"Son!"

I turned and saw Mother approaching, accompanied by her body guards. I hugged her, suddenly a boy again, needing the security of her arms. "Mother, it's good to see you," I said, and drew her aside.

"You as well, my son." She quickly changed the subject. "There's little time to lose. Hunding is slaughtering our völva sisters. He is chaining their bodies to skerries so that they drown with the incoming tide.

"As well, I've heard stories of disloyalty and treachery against King Volsungsson. I have sent Lynza back to Borghild Hall to warn him."

"Mother, Lynza, Griet, and Lyana are working with Frejya and Loki."

"Then I may have sent my loving husband to his death." She looked at me and I could see that this revelation unsettled her. "You must find Hunding and kill him. Hunding has incited civil war."

"Against Father! He betrays his family and his clan. But I should go with you, to protect you."

"No, Helgi. You must kill Hunding. He is hunting down my völva sisters and killing them. Hunding sees us as a threat, because we ally ourselves with no one. We are losing not just lives, but our heritage. You have to stop the destruction of völva skills and knowledge that will be lost to future generations."

She gestured behind her and I noticed several völvur dressed as Mother was, waiting. "I take my staff-carriers with me," she said. "With them, I'll infiltrate Borghild Hall. Don't worry; they should keep me safe. You must lead my sisters to safety. They bestow favours upon those who are worthy."

I looked into her face for a long moment, then kissed her cheeks, hoping this wasn't the last time I'd see her alive. If my father was in danger, the treachery would be coming from within the hall, and my mother would be caught up in the danger. She gave me a quick smile and lifted a hand to my cheek, and then she turned away.

I watched her disappear into the cave, trailed by her guards.

℘   ℭ

The floe had crawled close to the island peninsula, ripping into a section of it. We leapt onto it, our boots sinking into the porous ice.

"Thør, lead us in," I said, feeling safer with him along. "The floe waits for no one."

"The flow of time?" Thorfinn asked, looking at me. I shook my head. "Oh, you meant the ice floe. Sorry. Gudrid has my head spinning, talking about time flowing all the time and the flow of life. Lately she's been talking about destiny a lot, too. Destiny this and destiny that."

"Thorfinn, it's nice to hear that you're still listening after all these years." Gudrid chuckled.

"I love you, Gudrid," Thorfinn said, "but your sight still scares me a little. Probably because I don't understand it."

We dropped to our hands and knees as we approached the crest of the hill and crawled the rest of the way up to observe what lay beyond undetected.

Huge rocks dotted the surface, ripped away from land to sink into the floe. Beyond those, a vast, shimmering blue gate rose higher than our heads. Icicles the length of javelins hung from the top of it, glistening in the light.

"It looks like the gates of Jötunheimr, the home of

the Jötunn," Thør said. "Hopefully we'll cross a few of their paths."

"Have you crossed paths with Jötunn?" Thorfinn asked him.

"I've crossed many Jötunn: frost, fire, water, and wind. The frost ones are particularly slippery." He flashed a lopsided grin. "They took Mjölnir from me—once. Never again."

"Helgi, it looks like the scouts got in over there." Gudrid pointed to an opening that had been knocked through the gate.

We descended the slope toward the entrance, our feet sometimes sinking shin-deep into snow that crunched underfoot in some places and sloshing through slushy pools in others. More rock was exposed in these places. When we reached the gate we passed through the opening single file and entered a large ice cavern, where the walls danced with blue or shimmered to white as light from without penetrated the layers of thick and thin ice forming the cavern walls. It was quiet here, the silence broken only by an occasional echo of water dripping into a pool.

"This is incredible," I said, hearing the power of my words echoing along the walls and across the ceiling. Let's keep moving."

"Wait!" Thør's voice said behind me. I turned to see Thør trying to squeeze through the opening. A trunk-thick icicle blocked him. Knocking through it might collapse the rest of the gate and alert Hunding's men in the area.

"Thør, try sucking in your gut a little more," I said, trying to be helpful.

"My stomach isn't the problem," Thør replied

indignantly.

"Try giving it a few taps with your hammer," I said.

"Come here and hold onto the bottom of it," he said, reaching for Mjölnir on his belt.

"Gentle taps," Gudrid advised, taking advantage of the delay to feed Baby. "You might bring the ice ceiling down on us." She covered Baby up and moved farther away from the entrance.

"Thorfinn, you'd better stand back too," Thør said, lifting his hammer.

I braced the bottom of the icicle while Thør grabbed it farther up and gently tapped with his hammer. The icicle splintered and cracked off. He let it go, leaving me with the full weight of the huge icicle. I tipped over under the weight of it.

"Oh no!" Gudrid shouted.

Seeing me falling, Thør grabbed the icicle before I hit the ground. He tossed it aside.

Nodding my thanks to Thør, I got to my feet and went looking for the first marker while Gudrid finished feeding Baby. Thorfinn followed me.

We stepped carefully across the ice blue cavern floor. Our hide boots provided some traction, but travelling could be treacherous if we encountered steep slopes in the passageways.

"The ice will slow us down," Thorfinn said, then added, "There," and pointed at the first marker.

"It will slow down the Hundings, too," Thør added as he and Gudrid joined us.

There was enough exposed rock in the glassy tunnel to provide firm footing, and we made good time. It funnelled into a network of smooth and curving passages that looked like they'd been formed by flowing water. We moved in stunned silence, occasionally gasping in awe as the shifting light shimmered off the different angles and thicknesses of ice. The frost Jötunn world was being transformed into something magnificent right before my eyes.

Suddenly the floor shifted. "What was that?" I said apprehensively.

"It's just the ice," Thorfinn replied.

We walked deeper and deeper, passing towering walls of ice that looked like waterfalls frozen in time.

"Hey, look!" Thør said, laughing. He stood in front of an ice sheet. The light danced and bounced off it and reflected Thør's wobbling frame across it. His enlarged and deformed reflection gave his body the illusion of monstrous proportions. "Look at me, I'm a hideous ice Jötunn," he said, raising his arms and shifting his weight from side to side.

"I didn't think you could appear more menacing," Gudrid said.

We slid down tunnels and crept up again, looking for the next marker. The ice bulged in places and rocks punctured the tunnel walls. We chipped off the ice and climbed over them

"I haven't seen evidence of Hunding's men," I said. "They must not have gotten this far, or maybe they're being kept busy topside. Has anyone seen the next marker?" The others shook their heads and we trudged on for a few more minutes, until I stopped dead and said, "I hear rumbling." I placed my hand on the wall.

"It sounds like a river," Gudrid said. "It's probably meltwater."

I scouted farther ahead and looked through a fallen section of the cave wall. Rushing water was slowly melting the ice. A river of water flowed somewhere underneath us, taking chucks of ice with it. It fed a pool of water below us that looked like it drained into the sea.

"The floe is starting to break apart." I said, returning to the others. "We'll have to find another way around"

"Let's find someplace up ahead. Snorri needs to be fed," Gudrid said.

We stopped when the tunnel opened up into a chamber. Gudrid sank to sit cross-legged on the floor and began feeding Snorri and Baby.

"The rest of you wait here," I said. "I'm going to check what's up ahead."

I turned into a tunnel and walked through a mist that hung in the air like fog. After walking in it for a few minutes, my feet felt damp. The tunnel wormed up and down, never seeming to go in a straight line. The ice crunched, grated, and squealed all around me. A strong, cold wind blew around me. I approached a portal that opened onto an ice valley peppered with mushroom-shaped cliffs. I barely made out a chiselled ice ledge underneath the curvature of the icy cliffs through the blowing snow.

I stepped farther down the tunnel. The walls were composed of thick, greyish black ice. My eyes slowly adjusted to the dimmer light and shadows began taking shape around me. Gigantic slabs of slate protruded from the walls, disappearing into the murkiness of the wavering ice. Large gaps in the ice, made by the stone, widened into tunnels farther in.

"Helgi, are you alright?" Thør's voice boomed down the tunnel.

"There's a tunnel that I'm going to check out," I yelled.

I crouched, entering the opening on my hands and knees. It led to another chamber. Light shimmered through the ice, bathing the chamber in a pearlescent glow. I stopped. A large female form clothed in a dark gown stood frozen in the ice, her arms outstretched. A cloak floated behind her, frozen in mid-ripple.

I stepped back to study the distorted beauty of the woman's face. Sightless eyes stared back at me. Strands of her long, flowing hair fanned out around her head in a long-gone breeze. Large raven wings, bent and misshapen, stretched out behind her.

She's a Valkyrie. I felt a cold surge of panic. *I have to get her out.* "Thør," I yelled through the opening, "I need your hammer."

"Helgi, what's happening?" Gudrid asked, her head appearing at the opening. I watched her crawl through the tunnel and push to her feet to stand next to me. "Helgi, what is it?"

"A Valkyrie, trapped in the ice," I replied, jerking my thumb over my shoulder at the frozen form.

"Helgi," she said, looking into my face, "there's no one there."

I turned. She had disappeared! I spun around, looking at the walls of ice surrounding me. She was gone, but there were others, their limbs flung wide, bodies contorted, suspended upside down and diagonally in the ice in everlasting death. I flung my hands up to my face and rubbed my eyes with the heels of my hands. "Oh Gudrid, what is happening to me?" I groaned. I dropped my hands and looked again. They were still there, frozen in the ice, their swords and shields floating around them, just out of reach. Their dishonour was eternalized in the ice and their final ascent to Valhalla restrained—forever.

"Helgi?" Gudrid lay her hand on my shoulder.

"It . . .was her—again. I keep seeing a beautiful woman with magnificent wings. Gudrid, I think it was the same woman that I saw on your ship. Every time I see her, time seems to stop and I'm lost in her stare."

"When we rescued you," Gudrid said, "you couldn't remember your name. It could've been the shock from the water. Maybe the female is from your past and your mind shapes her into a being of the skies."

"I think I love her," I said, struggling with the feelings in my stomach and the thoughts in my head. "I know she's real. Gudrid, she gave me my name back when I couldn't remember it. She's my first waking thought. And I hold onto her—somewhere in my head—during the dægur."

Suddenly the chamber shook, shifting the stone slab. We crouched on the floor. Gudrid crawled through the opening and I followed. We rejoined Thorfinn and Thør, tending the babies, and we all retreated back down the tunnel. Behind us, with a deafening report like a lightning strike, the ice wall started to crack. I looked back to see sunshine streaming through the crevice from the other side. "Part of the floe is giving way—run!" I yelled, pushing Gudrid along with me.

The floe tipped as its weight shifted, taking Gudrid and me with it. We slid back down the sloping tunnel. Behind us Thør and Thorfinn, still clutching the babies, slid down as well.

The floor shifted back again and we stopped. "We have to keep moving," I said, standing. "The floe is breaking up. We don't have much time."

I helped Gudrid to her feet. She took Baby back from Thør and put him in his sling. He was awake, but not crying; his eyes closed and he drifted back to sleep.

The shifting ice had moved the boulders that we'd passed farther back, and a gap had opened up in the ceiling. "That looks like it goes to the surface," I said, studying the dim light filtering in. I climbed onto the rock to get a better view. "The rocks have shifted. They'll be easy to climb to the surface."

I helped Gudrid tie the sling closer against her chest for the climb. Then, with her following, we climbed over the boulders. I chipped away at ice sheets to create footholds and found handholds on jutting rocks, always buffeted by a cold wind blowing past. The entrance lay ahead, opening onto the icy surface.

I peeked out of the hole when I reached it. Snow blew across the surface, partially obscuring it. I couldn't see any sign of Hunding's men. "It's all clear on the surface," I called back, dropping back inside again to take Gudrid's hand. "Careful; some parts might still be slippery," I warned her and Thorfinn and Thør, who followed.

I stepped onto the surface and looked around once more as I helped Gudrid, Thorfinn, and Thør out of the hole.

"Do you hear that, Helgi?" Gudrid said.

"Yes," I said. "It sounds like people screaming and wailing."

We trekked through knee-deep snow. The wind confused the direction of the voices and we stumbled around, listening for them. "It's this way," I yelled, pulling my fur tighter around me against the wind. I gestured for them to follow. We stumbled through fields of white, eventually ending up at the edge of the floe.

"Look," Gudrid yelled, pointing through the blowing snow at a skerry.

People were chained head to foot in long lines along the length of the small, rocky island. Metal rings around their necks and ankles were fastened to metal rings bolted into the stone surface and their hands were tied behind their backs. All but immobile, they squirmed, trying in vain to escape the ocean that splashed over the edge of the skerry.

"We have to rescue them," I said. "The tide will drown them—if the cold doesn't take them or the shifting floe doesn't crush them first."

I ran down the sloped side of the floe to a path along its edge that angled down to the water. The skerry lay just below an ice cliff. It looked scalable. Pulling out my axe, I dropped over the side, dug the axe into the ice, and used it as a brake as I slid down the cliff. I landed on the skerry.

A shivering old woman looked up at me with terrified eyes. "Hold still," I said, lifting the axe.

"Wait!" Grimacing, she closed her eyes and turned her head away, her body tense with fear.

I raised my axe and swung down hard on the link that held her collar to the rock. It hit with a piercing clink. The woman flinched, but otherwise held still. I swung again and the link broke apart under my axe blade. I helped the old woman sit up, and untied her wrists.

"Thanks be to the three deities, Óðinn, Þór, and Frejyr, for freeing us," she said as I helped her to her feet. "And thanks to you, too."

Þór ran past me, heading to the other end of the skerry to start freeing the others.

"Here," I said, giving her the axe. "Help us free your kin." She took the axe, looking like she didn't know how to hold onto it. "Hold onto it halfway down the handle,"

I instructed, "and make short, light taps to help with targeting, then strike as hard as you can." I pulled my sword from the scabbard strapped to my back. "Where do you come from?" I asked. "Why were you chained here?"

"We are völvur. I am Skuld. My people are not held in high esteem, as they once were. In these times, our services are sought out by the *good* men who wish to do evil. These are the very same ones who chain us to the skerries. Our deaths are their escape from the evil that they do; we are murdered for wielding our staffs and wands for them."

Skuld stepped over the next prisoner and used her arm to shield the trapped völva's head as she tapped the chain a few times and then hit it harder and harder until it finally broke. She glanced at me and grinned.

I jumped to the next prisoner and swung my sword, breaking the ring anchoring the collar.

"Hunding believes that he must have the heads *and* the souls of his people, to lead them to victory," Skuld continued.

"How can the people prosper without the contributions of the völvur class?" I asked.

She nodded. "We are priests and priestesses, prophets and shamans. Some call on the spirits and command them and others foresee future events, see things how they will be." Skuld chattered on as she repeatedly hit the link.

"You're doing very well," I said, watching.

"Helgi," Thør yelled. "We have to hurry—the tide is rising."

A woman jumped into the cold water, risking death. "Bring us back a boat," Skuld yelled to the swimming woman.

"I need *your* help," I told Skuld when she turned back to me. "I'm here to kill Hunding for betraying his kin. You and your people can help me succeed."

She stopped in mid-swing and looked at me. "Elimination of *your* enemy will take care of ours, too. His heirs—"

"Heir—the others are dead."

"You have *this* information on good authority?"

"As a matter of fact, I do," I replied.

"His remaining son, Hæming, isn't a strong leader," she said. "It will fracture Hunding's clan. Some will see him as the heir and leader; others will see his inexperience in battle and leave to join cousin clans. Logafjoll will be ripe for conquest."

"I promise that once Hunding is dead, I will protect you and your völvur sisters and brothers," I said.

"Very well, then, I swear allegiance to you. Once this deed is known, we all will follow you," Skuld replied.

We continued freeing the völva from their chains. A small boat approached the skerry. When it had moored alongside, the freed völva boarded it.

"Gunnr and Hildr, good work," Skuld said to the two völvur who had brought the boat. "Any sign of Hunding's men?" They shook their heads. "His forces might be engaged in battle." Skuld said.

"Yes, we took Sigarsholm from them; they're probably engaged with us," I said, adding, "I am Helgi."

"Prince-son of our beloved Borghild?" Skuld asked. I nodded.

Their pink lips curved and their cold white faces lit up. "The oceans are rising. The prophecy is unfolding—"

"*Unfolding*," Hildr whispered behind Gunnr.

"The hero of a völva-born will save us," Gunnr

intoned.

"*Völva-born,*" Hildr repeated.

They exclaimed and we all stepped back as water suddenly flowed onto the skerry.

"Take the boat and pick up Thorfinn and Gudrid," I said to Gunnr and Hildr. "We will finish freeing the remaining völvur."

Skuld nodded and immediately leaned over the nearest völva, raising the hammer. As she struck the chain, a piece of metal chipped off and hit the trapped völva on the cheek. Blood trickled and disappeared into the water now seeping around the back of her head. "Sorry sister," Skuld said.

"Just—get me free."

I helped Skuld free the last one as the boat returned and sidled alongside the skerry. Thør and I were the last two to board it. The small vessel turned and headed toward the shore.

"Take us to the caves," Skuld told the rowers. "Hunding has found a few of our cells, but the shoreline caves were left untouched by his men because they were thought to be impassible," she told us as the boat followed the shoreline past a forest on the edge of the peninsula. "It is our most secretive community. I will take you there."

"We have tunnels between here and Hunding's fort that will get you past their stations and patrols," Gunnr said.

We sailed in silence, the only sound the dip of the oars and the heavy breathing of the rowers. My eyes darted across the water and over the land, looking for signs of Hunding's men or forest-dwelling allies. Then what I'd thought was distant thunder faded to the rumbling of distant battle: axes thunking against wooden shields and the shouting of men and women.

The shoreline remained quiet. But I felt a subtle fear growing into panic. My breath shortened as fear rushed into anger.

A hand shocked me into the present.

"You felt it too," Skuld said.

"Yes. What was it?" I turned, feeling the frantic pangs fading in my chest.

"You extended your consciousness across the land," she said. "In time, as you explore more and more, your journey will reveal itself to you. Don't turn away; it's not as unusual as it seems."

The waves lapped against the shore. Völvur jumped out and held the boat stable while the rest of us disembarked.

We ascended a hill where völvur stood with torches raised in the waning light. They met their rescued sisters, hugging them and laying their hands on them and dancing around with them, celebrating their liberation. I moved through them and they turned and laid their hands on me, touching my shoulders, my back, my head. They led me up the hill in a torchlit procession. I noticed I didn't feel cold, and sensed there was something beneath thought permeating the group. They led me through a dark opening.

"Trust them to guide you in," Skuld advised as Thør, Gudrid, and Thorfinn were also led through the opening.

We stepped into a pitch-dark tunnel. The floor felt like it was lined with flat stones. Suddenly rumbling surrounded me. "What's that?" I blurted.

"The portal is being closed. Don't be alarmed; you are safe."

"Where's Gudrid?"

"I'm here, Helgi."

We walked through wafts of smoke from burning lemongrass and air thickened with the perfume of scented oils. The smells intensified, seeming to pierce my head. A light moved through the darkness, leading us into a large cavern.

Hundreds of völvur sat in groups around fires. As we approached they stared, then stood and reached out to me. My company of völvur blocked them, but they lingered as we walked by.

"They sit with the Reverend Mother, our leader and spiritual guide, waiting for the prophecy's fulfillment," Skuld said. "And to witness our debt being paid."

We walked around stone pillars that curved up into the chamber's ceiling. On a rock overlooking the entire chamber, a tiny female sat. She was the size of a girl, though her features were those of an adult. Her eyelids were shut and her pale pink lips smiled. As we approached she rose and turned, staring at the cave ceiling. Her head jerked around the room, sensing we were there.

"The hero, the killer of Nidhogg—the dragon slayer is here," she said, sniffing the air. Her mouth opened and her dark teeth bit her bottom lip.

"Forgive me, Reverend Mother," Thorfinn yelled. "I didn't slay Nidhogg."

She raised her head higher and squealed with loud laughter. "Thank you, Thorfinn," she said, "for clearing that up. Ha-ha; hee-hee!" She tipped her head back and wheezed, laughing more after each inhalation, exploding with hoots that prompted the völvur around the chamber to laughter.

She calmed and looked up at me with pink eyes gleaming in a porcelain face. "Helgi, you were given life—*again*—to finish what you started."

Life . . . again. "I am sorry, Reverend Mother, but I don't understand."

Her pewter lips split in a grin. She scrutinized me, ignoring my confusion. "You have rescued my daughters and you have earned the alliance of the völvur. We will be with you, watching over you, hidden but ready to intervene. If you look up, you'll see us in the forest trees looking down, ready to protect you. We'll be cloaked in white as you move across the snowy plains, ready to fight and die alongside you."

"Reverend Mother," I said, kneeling on one knee, "I pledge to give you safety and protection on our lands and abroad. And to fight your persecutors and shield you on the battlefield. I will wear holly as a symbol of my pledge to protect you and your people."

The room exhaled in weeping and hands covered falling tears. The Reverend Mother raised her hand and the room fell to whispers.

"Reverend Mother," Skuld said, "I will accompany them to Hunding's fort."

"Go! Eradicate Hunding and the rest of his family line," the Reverend Mother said.

Arms turned me, and we were led down another tunnel. Overhead, a raven fluttered past us and landed on top of a barrel. Its beak opened and closed and it cocked its head, its eyes following me.

Skuld led us into a small cavern. Fire burned in a hearth; food and a steaming bowl of water were laid out on white pelts. We sat, relishing the break from the cold.

Gudrid and Thorfinn unstrapped Baby and Snorri.

She laid them on a pelt and undressed them one at a time to bathe them. "Baby is growing," she noted. "He looks like he might be ready to eat solid food."

"How is that possible?" I asked, looking at Thør and Thorfinn.

"I don't know," Gudrid replied. "Maybe it has something to do with Ragnarök."

As Gudrid washed Baby, he kept pointing to the ceiling and making sounds that were strangely close to words. He squealed and kept rolling away as Gudrid struggled to keep him still.

Gudrid mashed some berries in a wooden bowl and fed them to Baby on her index finger. "He's eating," she announced, before unbundling Snorri with her other hand.

"We have heard reports that Hunding is looking for you," Skuld said, "for annexing Sigarsholm."

"How did you know about, that?" I asked, a little surprised.

Skuld flashed a smug smile. "Believe the Reverend Mother when she says that we see all."

Yes. . . the fine line between prophesy and spying, I thought. *A human web must disappear in places.*

"I've been consulting with the völvur," Skuld said as she sat down next to us. "Our knowledge of the northern lands surpasses that of your best scouts. They could take you to unseen places beneath the earth, and through mountains via tunnels through rock and ice so high up that summer never comes. We can move your armies, unseen." Her pupils were dilated, as though she spoke of a vision. "It will give you immunity that no other clan has ever had. You could gain and hold territory of a size that will dwarf that of your kin."

I looked at her, tempted by the proposition. All I needed to do was reach out and grab it. "For now, Skuld, we'll use the tunnel to hunt down Hunding. Mother said that there was more to this than capturing territory. The alliance with the völvur has only begun; I'm sure we'll find other pursuits that will benefit both of us. But it's always good to think ahead," I added with a grin.

"Thorfinn and I will make the trip to Hunding's fort," I said, turning to the current problem. "Gudrid and Thør remain here. Sorry, Thør; I think you're a little too large for a stealthy approach."

He grimaced, then nodded.

We rested and ate in silence.

Baby, lying on his stomach, looked at me and squealed in delight. He flailed his arms and tried to push himself off the ground. I stared in amazement, finally realizing just how rapidly he was growing. Maybe Gudrid was right and this was Ragnarök's effect.

Skuld entered the chamber. "Are we ready to go?" she asked.

I picked up my fur pelt and swung it over my shoulders, then strapped on my sword and axe. Thorfinn held Gudrid in a hug, kissing her and whispering to her and Snorri. In wordless agreement, Skuld and I turned and left the chamber to give them their privacy.

Moments later, Thorfinn and Gudrid walked through the door. Gudrid dropped Thorfinn's hand and stopped, while Thorfinn strode forward to join us. "Good luck," Gudrid wished us.

"Don't worry," I said, handing Thorfinn his pelt. "We have protectors watching over us."

Skuld beckoned Thorfinn and me forward and led us toward the light—a different cave opening than the one we'd entered through. We moved in silence, our breath hanging above our heads. Thør held a rope ladder steady where it dangled from an opening in the ceiling. I gave him a nod as I passed, then started climbing.

I scrambled through the opening at the top and came up short, seeing a cluster of thorn bushes surrounding the opening, which acted as both cover and a deterrent to keep people and wildlife away. To one side, an earthen panel braced with twigs rested—clearly meant to disguise the hole when not in use.

Thorfinn and I followed Skuld through a cedar forest where the boughs gradually whitened with falling snow. Crouching, we scuttled around rocky escarpments, using our axes to clear away the underbrush in front of us.

"Hunding's men normally hunt us in the forests; usually no more than six travel together," Skuld said. "We have sentries high in the trees. If the Hundings get too close to the caves, we drop satchels of the Devil's Breath. It's a hallucinogen that leaves them without will or control. We guide them away from the area. When they recover, they have no recollection of what happened."

"I don't think, we'll encounter many of his men," Thorfinn said. "All of his forces are out trying to engage you." He looked to me. "But we can't be too careful."

We stepped onto new snow; it fell from the tree boughs in wet clumps as we brushed past. As we walked up the sloping floor of a ravine, our eyes constantly scanning the forest, Skuld looked up at a raucous, squawking flock of birds perched in the trees high above. I remembered my mother doing that, too, reading their behaviour, looking for restive behaviour that signalled danger ahead. She led the way up to the top of the ravine. Towering cedar trees reached to the sky, their boughs dropping clumps of snow—and hiding our footprints—as we brushed past them.

My head jerked up at the sound of a branch snapping and my body tensed, ready to dart for cover. Boughs parted and a völva peered out from the top of a swaying cedar, her legs wrapped around its trunk. She looked at me and smiled like an angel watching over me. Skuld looked to see if the coast was clear and waved to her. The lookout let go of the boughs and disappeared into the cover of the tree.

"Hunding's hall and fortification is up ahead," Skuld told us. "Several garrisons protect it."

"Is Hunding in his hall?" Thorfinn asked. "A forest attack might be simpler."

"If he isn't there, I'll wait for him," I said. "Skuld, I don't expect you to risk your life. Hunding is my job."

"I'll cover your escape from the outside. And the völvur in the trees are prepared to cover you from the heights," Skuld replied.

We headed deeper and deeper into the forest. The only sound was the wind blowing through the boughs and the snow dropping with soft, susurrating thumps all around us. Thoughts of finding Hunding and feeling my sword's blade pushing through his flesh played over and over in my mind. I wanted to take all the agony that my brothers had inflicted on me and carve it into Hunding's heart.

My thoughts drifted back to the beautiful Valkyrie in the sky, an angelic being that might someday take my cold corpse to Óðinn's hall. The thought of her touch made me almost wish for death.

Suddenly I heard a bird whistling an unfamiliar tune. I looked up to see another scout signalling us with strange hand movements.

"Hunding's men are coming," Skuld whispered, pushing Thorfinn and me deeper into the underbrush.

We heard voices and the hollow clang of shields against belted weapons. Through the thicket of bare branches we lay behind, I saw feet marching by and pressed my face close to the ground until they passed, heading deeper into the forest.

Skuld waited for the all-clear chirp from the treetops before leading us from hiding. "It's a patrol," she said. "There might be more."

"How will you get us past the battlements and beyond the gate?" I asked.

"We have an ally on the inside—a völva sister. She can get us beyond the fence wall."

"Can we climb over it?" I asked, thinking about sneaking in during the night.

"No," Skuld replied, shaking her head. "The fence is constructed of tall slabs of slate sunk into the ground."

As we climbed up a rock escarpment, I saw the slate fence rising in the near distance and understood Skuld's point. It would take three men standing on one another's shoulders so a fourth could climb up them and over the top.

We stopped and looked for patrols before proceeding, then followed Skuld down the length of one wall. Detecting a distant booming that was growing louder, I looked ahead and saw the rising mist of a waterfall. The sound rose to block out the birdcalls. One side of the fortress was protected by a cliff that overlooked a waterfall on the other side, Skuld told us.

She led us to the trunk of a towering cedar. I ran my hand along the bark, chunks of which were torn away, running up all sides of the trunk. "Here, put these on," Skuld said, handing each of us an odd pair of metal sandals. I flipped one of them over; sharp prongs stuck out from all around the bottom of the sole. "They will help you climb the tree."

Copying Skuld, I slipped my boot into one and pushed my heel into the curved cup on the back, then closed a hinged iron band over the top of my foot and clasped it with a cotter pin.

Skuld went first, grasping a branch above her head and then lifting her knee high and pushing her sandal into the trunk. She pulled herself up with a grunt, lifted her other leg over a branch, and dug that sandal into the other side of the tree. Using this technique, she climbed higher and higher, disappearing into the blowing boughs.

I followed her, grunting as I climbed the tree. Skuld made it look easy; she climbed the tree like a bird fluttering from branch to branch, as if she was meant to be in the trees and the air. I awkwardly plodded up the tree, wiggling my stuck sandal out of the tree each time until I realized that I was pushing the blades too far into the bark. I applied less pressure and climbed faster, finally stopping underneath Skuld. I looked toward the fortress.

Smoke rose from the other side of the wall. I was able to see over the wall; Hunding's men huddled close around their fires, keeping warm in the wind. Hunding's hall sat in the centre of the fort. Attached to the great hall were two other structures.

Thorfinn settled on a branch below me and also looked toward the fortress.

"We wait until we're given the signal," Skuld said. "It shouldn't be long."

Several guards stood around a large fire near the gate. An older one moved over to a barrel next to a cookhouse door and filled his horn with mead. Then he waved his arm in the air, appearing to order the younger guards still close to the fire to patrol. They reluctantly strapped on their scabbards and headed for the gate.

The door of the cookhouse opened and a young handmaiden walked out, eyes on the ground to avoid the guards' looks. She carried something wrapped in a cloth. One of the younger guards who had not left reached for her bottom. Anticipating this, she sidestepped his lunge, silently kicking wet snow in the air as she hurried away.

"Come here," the young guard yelled. "I want to talk to you."

"I must get the master's meal ready," she called back, not taking her eyes off the ground and not slowing down. She entered the great hall and returned moments later empty handed. She headed toward an animal pen on the other side of the wall, immediately in front of our tree.

As her arm reached out to an unseen door, she rolled her eyes up and looked directly at us.

"That's it," Skuld said.

There was a scuffling on the other side of the wall and chickens squawked. She reappeared, holding two chickens in each hand. She headed back to the cookhouse. As she did, she passed the old guard and others who had not gone on patrol, now slumped around the fire, their mead spilt across the snow.

"You old drunks." the hand-happy young guard said.

"Why don't you bring that basket into the cookhouse," the handmaiden said, her tone flirtatious.

With a last glance at the sleeping guards, he followed her into the cookhouse.

Skuld stepped onto a branch hanging over the camp's yard, and leapt onto a bough above it. I clutched the trunk as the treetop bent over. She let go and dropped the short distance to the ground. The tree swayed upright again. I followed her, and Thorfinn landed next to me seconds later.

"I don't think the patrol saw us," I said as we were showered with cedar needles.

We jogged across the yard, looking in all directions. The camp appeared to be empty. The few people wandering on the other side of the yard didn't seem to take any notice of us. As we walked past the gate, I heard it rattle, and held up my hand in warning to the others. We pressed ourselves against the wall as the gate opened inward. Carefully drawing my dagger, I flipped it, pinching the tip of the blade between my fingers.

A helmed head moved past the edge of the gate. Taking quick aim, I threw my blade at the man's neck. His face froze in an expression of terror as the blade penetrated his throat. He collapsed, and the wet snow absorbed his blood.

"Watch for the other one," I said, closing the gate before dragging the body out of sight around the cookhouse. Thorfinn followed me, kicking snow over the bloodstained trail.

"I'm surprised that Hunding has left his fort so undefended," he said, looking around. "He must have lost a lot of fighters."

Shouts and rustling inside the cookhouse broke the silence. The door slammed open, hitting the side of the house. "Get out!" a voice yelled, and a guard was propelled out the door. He fell into the snow, his trousers around his knees. As he turned and saw us, Thorfinn drew his axe and threw it; it flipped through the air and plunged into the guard's chest. He dropped to the snow.

"Our sister, Göndul." Skuld said, happily holding her arms out to embrace the handmaiden who emerged next through the cookhouse door.

"Come quickly," Göndul urged, waving us into the doorway.

Thorfinn dragged the limp body out of sight, concealing it with the other one behind barrels at the rear of the cookhouse. I erased the blood from the snow. We followed Göndul into the building.

"Göndul, where's Hunding?" I asked.

"He's not here."

My stomach sunk into my boots.

"His son Hæming is in the great hall."

"What of his guards?" Skuld asked.

"I drugged the mead; they'll be unconscious for the rest of the day," she said. "We've received word that Hunding is returning by land. He is returning via the Norðr—"

"Yes, we met him on the water; his crippled fleet probably made it to his Norðr territory," I interrupted. "I'm here to finish his clan and return his men to their rightful leader, King Volsungsson." I thought a moment. "Göndul, I need to look like a handmaiden."

"Me, too," Thorfinn said.

I shook my head. "No, I do this alone."

Thorfinn looked at me, disappointment in his eyes.

"I need you and Skuld to plan our escape and to delay Hunding and his men. Take my sword." I unbuckled my scabbard and handed it to him.

Göndul had slipped away. Now she returned and handed me a bundle of clothes. "These are the largest I could find."

I put the clothing on over my leather armour. The dress was snug, but workable. I removed my bracers and made sure the hem dropped to my ankles to conceal my legs. I strapped daggers to my thighs and tucked one into my boot, again checking that everything was concealed above the hem of my dress and didn't show telltale bulges in the pinafore.

"Helgi," Skuld said, holding out a pair of satchels, "here are some Devil's Breath bombs. To release the powder, you must throw it hard, or have an object press on it, like a boot. Don't be near it; if you are in close contact with it, hold your breath until you are out of its lingering cloud."

I concealed them in a hidden pocket of my pinafore.

"Hæming is waiting for a meal in the great hall," Göndul said, wrapping a headdress around my head. She left enough linen to wrap around my cheeks, concealing the straggling blond hairs of my growing beard. "It's fortunate for you that Hunding's maidens must wear a veil in his and his son's presence," she added as she pinned the veil to the headdress. Then she looked at me and pinched the tops of my cheeks still visible above the veil.

"Ow!" I protested, drawing back.

"Young maidens are supposed to have rosy cheeks. And put these gloves on," She said, handing me a pair of gloves. I tugged them onto my hands and flexed them, eyeing them critically. "You must wear them," she insisted. "Your hands are too masculine."

Turning, she handed me a basket smelling of freshly baked bread from the table. "Follow me," she said, picking up the platter of venison and striding over to the door. "Try to keep your head down and do not look Hæming in the eye," she instructed. "He will have us beaten and you would be exposed for sure."

"We'll be ready with the escape," Skuld said.

I lifted the basket onto my shoulders, using it to partially conceal my face and lack of a bosom, and walked out into the yard.

The wind numbed my cheeks and I felt the veil sticking to my bristled chin. My mouth and chin were soon wet with condensation caused by my quickened breathing underneath the veil.

"Hæming won't be armed, but his personal guards will inspect your basket and my tray before they'll let you approach the head of the table," Göndul said as she struggled to balance the covered tray while trampling through the knee-deep snow. "Do you plan to kill Hæming?" She asked.

"Not until I get information about their clan's betrayal. I suspect that Hunding isn't working alone."

We entered the great hall. Hæming sat by the fire. Two wolfhounds lay on either side of him. Their black eyes peered at us, and they sniffed the air.

His guards raised their hands, signalling us to stop. Göndul set her tray at the end of a long banquet table and backed away. I did the same with the basket and stood staring at the floor, trying to avoid their gaze. The guard looked over the food, then signalled us to approach the head of the table. As I passed him, he glared at me. I held my breath and kept my stride short, striving for daintiness as I picked up the basket and held it between us to distance myself from him.

The oak floor creaked. The wolfhounds remained alert, but didn't leave Hæming's side. I surreptitiously scanned the room for weapons. The family shield and two lances hung behind Hæming, over the fireplace. The guards wore swords and axes for two-handed combat. They didn't take their eyes off of me.

The dogs sniffed as I approached Hæming. One stood and sauntered toward me. The other rose and followed. I steadied myself and held out my hand. One dog sniffed it and then the other. I felt its tongue lick my cupped palm as I turned it up.

A sign.

The wolfhounds turned and sauntered into the adjoining room. I wiped my hands on my pinafore before uncovering the basket and placing the loaves on the table.

Hæming's eyes burned into me. He was Hunding's youngest and I sensed that his immaturity, coupled with the laxer constraints imposed on the last in line, would make him act out. I'd heard he was an unseasoned leader and he'd demonstrate it by being unreasonable and demanding.

"You, girl. I don't recognize you. Who are you?"

"Your Grace, I am . . . uh . . . am . . . Sigrún, Göndul's—"

"You could be a spy!" he yelled.

"Oh, no! I give you my word, Your Grace, I am no such thing, I said, giving him my best performance of a young and nervous handmaid.

"There are spies *everywhere*," he said, sounding like he enjoyed my discomfort. "Have you seen people acting suspiciously?"

"Uh, no, Sire. I don't think I have."

His lip curled. "I don't think you're intelligent enough to be able to tell the difference."

I swallowed my pride, suppressing a retort on its way

up and forcing it back down into the pit of my stomach.

Göndul set the tray of venison on the other side of the table and unfolded the cheesecloth. I caught a whiff of burnt flesh.

Hæming seized a leg and ripped it in half at the joint, then attacked it with his teeth. Göndul lifted a pitcher of ale from a side table and filled his horn, then stood next to the hearth, waiting for instructions; I walked to the other side of the hearth and stood still, staring at the floor.

The door burst open with a thud and a blizzard of snow blew into the great hall. A bloodied fighter dashed in behind it. "Sir, King Hunding is on his way. There are two guards missing at the front gate," he yelled.

Hæming tossed the leg aside and half rose. "Where are the captains?" he yelled.

"They're drunk, Prince. Passed out next to the hearth."

"Seal the building; call for reinforcements," the hall guard ordered, before leading the others outside to sound the alarm.

"Go see to my father's safe return," Hæming ordered his personal guards. "I'll be fine here."

"Barricade this door," a guard yelled to us before they left.

Göndul and I lifted the beam leaning behind one of the heavy wooden doors and slid it across the width of the double doors. I pushed a metal bolt into the floor.

"Hey, you move like a man," Hæming slurred at me. His eyes narrowed. "Gua—"

"Oh, Your Grace," Göndul said, intercepting him, "my sister has walked bull-legged since birth." She picked up the mead jug, glanced at me, and refilled his horn.

She drugged it.

As he lifted the horn to his mouth, I circled around and slipped one of the lances off the wall. Now just to watch and wait for the drug take effect.

Hæming ripped off the end of a loaf and threw the other half toward the basket. He missed.

"Ask him questions before he passes out," Göndul whispered as Hæming mumbled out orders to himself; he was shifting into his own little world.

I grabbed Hæming's bobbing neck. "Who is plotting against King Volsungsson?" I said, putting my mouth to his ear.

"We *all* are," he said, and giggled as he reached for his horn again. He struggled to lift it out of its holder.

"Who is *we*?"

Hæming gave an elaborate shrug. "My father and Hothbrodd. Högne is joining the alliance by offering his daughter to Hothbrodd."

"Granmar and my father fought side by side for their lands. They are like brothers; he will not allow it," I said.

"Granmar doesn't know." He giggled again. "Hothbrodd will kill King Granmar and break the alliance with the Volsungssons. Högne's daughter is a Valkyrie— or so *he* says. She will give Hothbrodd great power and powerful heirs." Hæming started to drift off.

"Helgi, hurry," Göndul pleaded. "They'll be back any minute with Hunding." She scurried to the door and put her ear to it. She looked back to me, her expression urgent. "Helgi, we must go."

I let go of Hæming's shoulder, letting his head thump on the table.

"Helgi!" Hæming exclaimed, finally processing who I was. He tried yelling to his guards, but he was unable to lift his head off the table, and his voice became more and more slurred until he drifted into sleep. "Her progeny . . . will rule Miðgarð," Hæming managed to slur out before his cheek slipped into a pool of spit.

"I remember my father speaking of a plague moving across the land," I said. "Children are not being born; Miðgarð is starving itself of life."

"Sigrún can bear children," Göndul said. "She is our saviour; she will cure the land of its plague."

"What did he call Högne's daughter? A Valkyrie. I wonder if that is the same Sigrún—"

"Helgi, he didn't know what he was saying," Göndul said dismissively. "Maybe he was hallucinating."

"Will the drug finish him off?" I asked, looking at the back of his head.

"I didn't measure the dose, so I'm not sure."

I raised the lance and pushed it through the back of Hæming's neck. As I pulled it out, blood bubbled up through the puncture and flowed onto the table, the growing pool spilling over the edge and onto the floor. Watching Hæming's blood spill across the table, I knew this washed away the hope of Hunding's heirs and the future of his family line. Despite the plague's outcome, the final link in the chain was Hunding. Once he was destroyed, his kingdom would fall.

Fists pounded on the door. "Open up in the name of the king!" a guard yelled.

While I dragged Hæming into the other room, Göndul cleaned the scraps from Hæming's plate, wiped up the blood, and threw the rags and food into the fire. I drew Hæming's sword and ran to the door. I lifted the floor bolt, then slid aside the beam far enough for Göndul to open one door. Hiding the weapon behind my back, I stood beside Göndul and we both bowed.

Hunding bolted in, one body guard before him and another following him.

Göndul quickly forced the door closed with her shoulder, pushing out anyone else who sought to enter. I slid the beam back into place, then whirled to drive the sword into the nearest guard's side. The blade slid through him and he fell to the floor. As the second guard turned to attack me, Göndul leapt forward and drove a dagger into his neck.

Hunding was thrust forward out of harm's way— toward me. I tried sidestepping him, but he caught my elbow on its backswing and threw me on the floor with him. My veil dropped; I leered, happy that he knew who I was.

Pushing him off of me with my shoulder, I rolled, swinging my sword above my head, then dropping it like a guillotine toward his neck. Hunding rose to his knees and the sword passed through the point where he'd been. I jumped to my feet, but the heel of my boot caught in my hem and I landed back on the floor. I managed to untangle myself and jump to my feet again, slightly disoriented.

Hunding was still kneeling. I ran toward him, sword extended. He dropped onto his back and lifted both feet to hit me square in the chest, pushing the breath out of me and throwing me backward onto the banquet table. He scrambled to his feet and turned to face me, regarding me with eyes sharpened by long years of battle and longer days of running. Hunding was much larger than me and I didn't have the advantage of the stormy waters to turn our fight into a fairer one. I needed to find a way to use his larger size against him.

I pushed myself off the table, turning pain into rage. Hunding swung his axe and I dodged it easily, realizing he had a weakened shoulder. I swung, hitting his leather shoulder pad. A roar of erupted from his mouth and his axe clanged to the floor. I pulled my sword back and swung again, missing him as he dodged to my left.

"Your last heir is dead by my hand," I taunted, trying to unsettle him.

I stumbled backward and sidestepped as he barrelled at me. The rage and hate in his face caught me off guard. Being cheated out of his legacy fanned his rage. With that immortality threatened, his instinct for survival made him desperate and dangerous. For the first time, I was scared for my life.

I swung at Hunding, the tip of my blade slicing through his side. He dropped his axe and I kicked it across the floor, out of his reach. Drawing his long sword, he swung it in front of me again and again, shifting his weight, forcing me to back away, toward the hearth, knowing that any attempt to block it would unsword me or knock me to the floor.

I kicked a chair at him. He stumbled onto it. I leapt for his family shield and pulled it from the wall. Holding it up in front of me, I baited him to hit it. He swung and I sidestepped, kicking the back of the chair in between us. He stumbled over it, giving me enough time to grip the shield handle on the inside of the boss.

He swung again and I stepped around the corner of the table, deflecting his blade with the shield. I aimed for the blood trickling down his shoulder, and my blade sliced into him as if he were a plump sausage. My mouth curled as I heard his agony and pain. He fell and I stepped back, watching him hit the floor. I kicked him in the head with the heel of my boot.

Hunding tried to get up, but collapsed, then rolled away. I waited for him to face me. There was no satisfaction in winning an unfair fight.

Göndul ducked into the other room.

Hunding rose to his feet and turned to face me, swinging his weapon. Again he used his weight to his advantage. I tried deflecting another blow with the shield and was thrown into the wall, hitting my head.

The impact jarred a horn-shaped oil lamp out of its sconce and splashed oil ignited on its way down. The floor, the wall, and the table between us burst into flames. Hunding didn't notice it—or he didn't care. He barged through the growing flames and swung his sword, avoiding my shield and trying to unarm me. I dodged it and swung my blade up, hitting him in mid arm, just above his bracer. I felt the blade slice through flesh and bone. I bashed the shield against his chin. His sword flew out of his hand and he dropped to the floor.

I pressed the tip of my blade through his leather breastplate and partially into his chest. Hunding's breathing grew harsh. He stared at me, his eyes declaring defeat.

I pulled out a Devil's Breath bomb and dropped it next to Hunding's head. I held my breath and stepped on it. A small cloud whiffed out; Hunding inhaled it and coughed. I stepped back and waited for his eyes to glaze over.

"Hunding, before I split your chest in two, I give you one chance to renounce your treachery against the clan— our family."

He looked at me with defiant eyes. "Your father is dead, murdered by your brothers," he said.

I leaned on the sword and pressed it farther into him.

"Sinfjötli will kill your mother, but not until after he uses her to pull your strings; until he has an opportunity to get rid of you. *Whose family betrays the clan?*"

"No!" I yelled, pushing the blade farther into his chest. "You're lying."

Hunding squirmed as blood spurted from the wound. "What have *I* to gain?" he rasped. "Helgi, open your eyes and look around you. The world is dying. "There is a plague upon us; Miðgarð is barren; the sons and daughters are no more. But Sigrún is not of this world. She will save us; she will bear our children. We don't fight for land, we fight for life. There is a weakness in the male heart that interprets possession as love and ownership as desire." He stopped and stared off at the ceiling. Presence left his eyes, leaking out in a teardrop.

"Where is my mother—where is Borghild?" I yelled, shaking him.

The flames were growing behind me and the hall was turning into Hunding's funeral pyre.

There was pounding on the door.

"Reinforcements," Göndul yelled as she lit a torch from the hearth.

The flames now filled the hall with acrid smoke.

"Into the other room," she ordered. "Hunding has tunnels under the settlement. I'll hide you in the flour mill. Quickly! If they alerted Hunding's men, they'll try to cut the tunnels off. We don't have much time."

I turned and followed her into the room. The dogs sat in the shadows of the corner, shivering. "Hold this," she said, handing me the torch.

I felt a draft across my ankles as she moved to the corner and lifted a trapdoor. The wolfhounds immediately leapt into the opening. Göndul dropped in after them and reached up to take the torch back before crouching down and moving away from the opening. I followed.

We crawled through a tunnel for several long minutes before it opened into a cave. "The mill is that way," Göndul said, pointing down a rough tunnel with a light at its far end. "Here," she said, beckoning me closer. She removed the remnants of my torn headscarf and veil and replaced it with hers. I handed her the sword and shield and turned, running toward the light.

As I ran, my mind turned. *Sinfjötli convinced Father to come with me so he could find mother and take her back to be killed. Her travels were kept secret, so Lynza must have been his accomplice.* Figuring out their plot didn't matter. I could do nothing until I returned to Borghild Hall.

I slowed and walked into the basement of the mill. Water rushed underneath the floorboards, turning a mill wheel. I walked to the other side and looked down at a river.

I picked up a sack of flour and walked up the stairs. The workers and maids had their mouths and noses covered to avoid breathing in the thick clouds of powdery white flour all around us, kicked up off the floor by the workers' constant movements. *I fit right in.*

I was desperately looking for something to do when three maidens walked past me, each carrying a sack of flour. I turned and followed them.

Footsteps pounded up the stairs and two guards burst in and scanned the room. "Oh, what do they want?" a voice whispered, its owner obscured in the cloud of flour. "They should be finding out why the sea levels are rising."

"Probably out looking for the new girls, the filthy bastards," another voice answered.

I set my sack down on a stack next to the others and followed the maidens while keeping an eye on the soldiers. They were moving from one maid to another and pulling aside their veils. I fought panic as I realized how vulnerable I was. *I gave my sword to Göndul!* I reminded myself that I still had my daggers and the Devil's Breath.

"You there," a guard yelled, pointing at me through the haze. "Stay where you are."

I looked around me, anxiously seeking an opportunity to slip into the crowd. There was no way out.

"Lieutenant, we've captured a völva spy," a voice shouted.

The lieutenant's gaze lingered on me. The seconds slowed. Then his head snapped away and he stomped back down the stairs.

I ran to the window with the other maids to see who they'd captured.

They have Skuld!

Two guards were dragging her by her arms; at some point she'd lost her footing because she was on her knees. "I'm not carrying this load back to the barn," one of the guards yelled, dropping Skuld on the snow. He lifted his sword and brought it down, striking her across the back of the neck. Blood splattered across the snow.

They were about to walk away when her headless body suddenly sprouted wings. Her head and body turned to stone. The guards backed away in terror and confusion. A gasp went up from the spectators inside the mill.

A gale blew past the guards. The stone statue started turning to dust that blew away in the wind.

"Look!" one of the maids yelled.

Hunding's great hall was burning in the centre of the compound. The blasts of norðr wind blew smoke and embers into the air, spreading the fire onto the longhouses and barn roofs nearby. Hunding's fort would soon be engulfed in flames.

I turned and ran down the stairs, taking advantage of the diversion to slip out of the mill. Walking over to the wheel, I stepped onto a spoke and held on as it took me down to the river. I stepped onto a support beam underneath the mill and descended to the boulders on which the mill rested over the river.

I was out of the fortress, but I needed to find my way back to the underground caves, or get rescued by one of the völvur in the trees. And before that, I needed to get back on dry land. I looked up through the grid of mill supports. Seeing a bucket swinging in the wind, I climbed toward it.

There were small skerries dotted along the river parallel to the cliff. Farther down, the waterfall thundered beyond the turn in the river. I looked for völva scouts in the trees, but didn't see any.

I untied the bucket and tossed it into the river. The rope was coiled around a spike just outside a mill window; I lifted it off and tied a quick slip knot around the highest support, then climbed down, hoping that I could slip it off once I landed safely on the skerry. I walked along the beam to the river side of the mill and looped the slack over the water bucket hook and around a post, hoping that the added tension would slow the knot from slipping. Then I leapt outward, swinging over the river.

The rope went taut and I arced back toward the cliff

and the skerry. I looked down at my feet, watching the background swing by. I felt the knot slipping a little. I slid down the rope as it arced over a young bush and let go, landing feet first in the bare boughs. I flipped, wriggled, and tugged the rope until the knot slipped the rest of the way. Then I coiled the rope, looking for a way to the next skerry.

I spied a line of immersed boulders. Glassy water continuously flowed over them. Gauging the distance, I leapt toward the first boulder, adjusting my balance so I wouldn't slip in the ankle-deep water. Again gauging the distance, I leapt to the next rock, and then the next. My final leap to the last boulder brought me adjacent to the skerry—but it tipped toward me and then rolled on top of me, dragging me underwater. I pushed myself out of the way before it pinned me to the bottom of the river and swam to the surface, coming up beside the small island.

Pulling myself onto the skerry, I jumped into the river on the other side and made the short swim to shore, finally climbing up to the forest floor. I was shivering, at times uncontrollably, but I was outside of the fortress. I ran through the forest, scanning the trees in search of allies, and hoping I'd see Thorfinn. I felt safe, even without seeing anyone. I knew I was being watched from the treetops.

The air was cold and my wet body was cooling me down—rapidly. That would make my breathing heavier and slow down my running. I was feeling my clothing beginning to freeze. My veil began to stiffen and I wasn't sure if I could feel my toes.

Something moved in the bushes up ahead. I couldn't tell if it was Thorfinn, a völva, or a patrol. I whistled, remembering the treetop völva's bird call. Then I waited,

ready to run. I heard the call whistled back to me.
"Thorfinn," I whispered, "is that you?"

A head peeked over a rock. It was Thorfinn.

"Am I glad to see you," I said.

"Göndul helped me escape," Thorfinn replied. "When
Hunding's men couldn't find you, Göndul came back
and said that you'd escaped. So she snuck me back to the
forest. She said you killed Hunding."

"Yes. His burning hall has erased him. Not even a
body remains." I paused. "Skuld is dead. She transformed
into a Valkyrie and turned to stone."

I looked around for the entrance to the caves. "I
have to return to my home. Hunding told me of a plot to
murder my father and mother. It's being carried out by
my half-brothers."

We found the entrance to the cave and scrambled
down the ladder. A guard posted on the cave floor
recognized us and ran to notify the others of our return.

"I might be too late, but I wouldn't underestimate
my mother's survival abilities," I said, then noticed I was
rambling—nerves.

Gudrid appeared. She ran to Thorfinn and hugged
him. Thør followed, carrying Snorri under his arm. "Are
you going to keep wearing handmaiden's clothes?" he
joked, seeing me.

"Good to see you, Thør," I said, taking off the dress
and what was left of the veil. "Your excellent instruction
has saved me—again."

His smile slowly faded and he looked confused,
uncertain whether to take it as a compliment or a friendly
jibe.

"Helgi, look," Thør said and nodded toward a small
hand holding onto his finger. Baby tottered from behind

him, just beginning to take his first steps.

"Is that Baby?" Thorfinn asked, taking Snorri from Thør. Thør nodded.

"Did you take him to see the Reverend Mother? Does she know what's going on?" I asked.

"Yes; she came to see us," Thør said. "She said that there is a powerful magic disguising the boy. She can't penetrate it. It might be seiðr."

Baby stumbled over to Gudrid. She caught him as he was about to fall.

"Does he speak?" Thorfinn asked.

"No," Gudrid replied. "But he is very expressive. We know what he wants by his gestures. Don't we?" Gudrid looked down into his upturned face.

An attendant approached. "Your Highness, the Reverend Mother would like to see you."

"Take me to her."

The attendant nodded and turned to lead the way.

We entered the main cavern. The fires were extinguished, except for the one in the centre. I approached the Reverend Mother. She wore a black veil over her head. I looked around and noticed that all the völvur were wearing black veils.

She looked up and I could see her light pink skin through the veil. "Helgi," she said. "We mourn the death of our sister, Skuld. The future is dark, veiled in the end of time." She paused. "And we honour you for eliminating our executioner." The Reverend Mother raised her staff and shook it in the air. Bones and luminescent stones strung together on its end rattled. She waved it in circles.

"Prince Helgi, kneel before me," she said. I obeyed. "Hear me, Týr. I beseech you to acknowledge the feat of Helgi, Slayer of Hunding. In your name, I bestow to him the name of Hundingsbane. Prince Helgi, rise and be reborn as Helgi Hundingsbane."

As I rose from one knee, the dark occupants of the cavern rose, chanting and yelling.

"Reverend Mother, can your völvur network warn my mother and father of Sigird and Sinfjötli's betrayal?"

"I'll dispatch more völvur to assist Borghild. I fear that we might not get to her in time," the Reverend Mother replied. "Now go! Return to Sigarsholm and go to the hóf. Make an offering to Týr."

I was led back into the tunnel. Gudrid and Thorfinn led me back to our cavern.

Thør was there, with Baby wrapped in a pelt on his lap. The boy stared up at him, listening to a bedtime story. "Now, after Óðinn, the god of war, attacked the Vanir, they rose up and fought back. The war went on for eons. When the lands of the Æsir and the Vanir were both destroyed, the war ended in a stalemate. They decided to stop killing each other.

"To keep both sides from fighting again, they exchanged hostages. Your mother, Freyja, was one of them. But something went wrong. Mímir, one of the exchange hostages sent to the Vanir, *accidentally* lost his head."

Baby squealed and laughed, clapping his hands in the air.

"Yes, that's right," Thør said, chuckling along with Baby. "One of the Vanir, accidentally decapitated him. No one admitted doing it, but I think it was *your* mother. The Vanir demanded the return of Freyja, because they said that with one of the hostages dead, the exchange was now out of balance. Óðinn refused, so the Vanir sent Mímir's head to him.

"And to show the Vanir how smart he was and how stupid they were, Óðinn took the rotting head and stuffed it with herbs so it wouldn't rot. And then Óðinn spoke charms to it and asked it questions. It told him many things, including things about the Vanir that he did not know. When the Vanir found out that they had been outsmarted, they went into a rage and demanded Mímir's head. Óðinn told them no, adding, 'It's not worth losing your head over.' There has been peace ever since." Baby squealed some more.

Thør bundled him up tightly and set him down. "Go to sleep," he said, then rose and walked over to us.

"'Not worth losing your head over'?" Gudrid teased. "I've never heard that version before."

"I'm returning to Borghild Hall," I said. "There is a plot to murder my mother and father. I have to try to stop it. Once the clan knows of my brothers' plot, they'll rise up against them and follow me. But I must make one stop in Sigarsholm. I must return to the hóf."

"Isung is waiting on a dragon boat to take us back to Sigarsholm. It's moored outside the first entrance we used," Thør said.

Thorfinn picked up Baby and followed Gudrid, Thør, and me to the boat. I wrapped my fur around myself and left the comfort of the cave. The sky was dark and the air was still.

"Hail, Helgi Hundingsbane," Isung said from the bow of the dragon boat. Behind him was a full complement of twenty-four rowers.

"It's good to see you, Isung. I must return home, but first take me to Sigarsholm."

"Aye!" Isung yelled, and signalled to the rowers.

"Atli and Hrafn, I'm returning home. I want you

to stay here and recruit what's left of Hunding's men. Tell them that I need brave men and women to defend our lands. And that any man or woman who follows me will get part of the plunder and a barrel of mead. Their families will get protection from outside invaders. Gods' speed."

I boarded the dragon boat. We left the cove and headed away from Logafjoll.

"Helgi, when your brothers capture you, they will kill you, too." Thorfinn said.

"That's a chance I'll have to take. The Reverend Mother said that she sent völva to assist my mother and I have to believe that they're watching over me and will protect me, too."

"Helgi, you'll be outnumbered," Gudrid said.

I shrugged. "I'm outnumbered anyway."

The constellations lit the sky and the water was calm. I welcomed the break from fighting and the time it gave me to plan my next move. The boat made great time getting back to Sigarsholm. Bonfires dotted the shoreline and shone in the calm night air.

"What's your plan to save your parents?" Thør asked, stepping closer.

"I'll have to find a way to sneak them out of Borghild; the hall is full of secrets. I don't know if they've implemented their plan. Sigird won't allow Sinfjötli to murder my father—yet. Unless the clan leaders are involved in the plot, which I doubt; they usually know the whereabouts of the king at all time."

"The greed for riches and glory goes beyond loyalty and glory," Thør commented.

"His leaders are richer with my father alive, because my father has made them rich with lands and gold.

They're better off following father. No, I think Sinfjötli coming along was to remove suspicion from him, so his ascension to king will not be hindered by scandal. And to find my mother and capture her. They're not in it alone; Granmar's son, Hothbrodd, is with them.

"Hothbrodd will kill his father and break the alliance with our clan. But Hunding confessed that Hothbrodd is secretly in league with my brothers to take his father's throne, while Sigird and Sinfjötli murder Father and take his."

"It will take the suspicion away from the princes and put the suspicion over Granmar's murder onto Volsungsson in retaliation for dissolving the alliance," Thør said.

"And once Granmar is killed, Volsungsson will fall and suspicion of a revenge killing will fall on Hothbrodd," Gudrid added.

"Under clan law a revenge killing cannot *be* avenged. It's a perfect murder that only the gods could conceive," I said.

"Here, take this." Thør draped a pouch over my head and shoulder.

"What's this?" I asked, feeling the pouch fit comfortably under my arm.

"A few things that the völva gave me, and one or two additions of my own."

"Helgi, someone should travel with you," Isung said. "Once the clan knows of your victory over Hunding, it will make you their hero and leave Sinfjötli and Sigird desperate. And they can't risk fracturing the clan, because they know that you, the next in line, could gain a much larger contingent of followers; more land owners and more land. Killing Hunding has given you that power."

"No, I have a chance to get my mother and father out of danger and I'm taking it. Hunding said that Sinfjötli will use my mother to pull my strings. I plan to turn that against him."

The dragon boat headed to the beach. My father's First Fleet oarsmen were the best in the clan. It felt like we glided above the water. I stood at the top of the bow holding onto the dragonhead, watching the rapid approach of the stony beach.

"I'm heading into the hóf," I said. "Do not disturb me. Post guards at the entrances."

"Helgi, we opened the front entrance; you can get in through there," Isung said, then turned and ordered, "Rowers, 'way oars!"

I grabbed the masthead, preparing for the keel to brake on the smooth stone beach. "Hang on!" I yelled as the boat bumped onto the shore and slid to a quick stop. I leapt out and walked up the beach to the hóf. My fighters cheered as I passed, but didn't approach me.

I walked through the front entrance. It had been tended to: unlit torches were piled at the entrance and the sconces on the walls were lit, returning it to a functioning place of worship.

I headed down the hall and stood at the intersection leading to the hóf.

Helgi.

My torch flickered in a draft coming from farther down a dark corridor, the direction I'd heard the voice calling my name came from. The damp breeze must've put out the oil lamps in the sconces, I reasoned. I relit them with my torch as I passed.

I rounded a curve in the stone wall and saw a grey light ahead. I walked into a chamber with a sloping floor. At the other end was an altar, illuminated by the dim blue light that found its way down a cylindrical vent shaft in the ceiling above it. Dust motes kicked up by my footsteps clouded the blue light; dust coated the altar and the statues to Óðinn, Thør, and Freyr around it. Time had taken the room from a place of devotion to a place of indifference.

The grey stone of the wall here was smooth beneath my fingers as I moved around the perimeter, lighting the oil sconces. The tiny flames struggled, then finally burned into life, bathing the chamber in a flickering glow. I touched the torch to the hearths on either side of the stone altar, igniting what fuel was left in them.

I looked around me. Swords lay scattered on the floor, piled on the altar, and leaned in stacks against the wall nearest the altar. Above it, a figure—also coated in dust—hung on the wall. The hilt of a scabbarded long sword on her back stuck out behind her head. Her hands and feet were bound. The woman looked so real that I wanted to touch her. I reached out and touched one of her feet, then drew back with a gasp.

She's real!

I jumped onto the altar and reached up. She was hanging by a golden belt that had been wrapped around her. I wrapped my arms around her legs and lifted, hoping I could somehow unhook her. I felt her weight fall forward and I slid her down my body and into my arms.

"What have they done to you?" I murmured as I held my ear to her mouth, hoping to feel a breath. Feeling the merest brush of warm air, I lowered her down to the altar and jumped off to arrange her more comfortably. I undid the golden belt around her and unbuckled the leather scabbard. Cradling her head in my arm, I searched my pockets with my free hand for the vial of Baldur's brow elixir Mother had given me. I hastily uncorked it and tilted her head; her lips parted slightly and I was able to pour the syrupy elixir between them. Carefully extricating my arm, I gently wiped the layers of grey dust powdering her face, arms, and legs away with my palm. Her beauty returned from grey death.

Her hair fell over the end of the altar; I stroked it, feeling the strands sliding between my fingers and watching the falling dust trails hit the floor. Each stroke slowly changed her hair back to a silvery blonde. Impulsively, I leaned over and touched my lips to hers, feeling in the pleasure of the touch a nervous shame. I pulled away when I felt her lips move against mine.

As I backed away, she opened her eyes and looked around. She looked a little dazed, but remained calm. As her eyes fell on me, I stammered, "You . . . you're the Valkyrie in my visions on the ship. Are you the daughter of Högne that they speak of?"

She nodded. "My name is Sigrún. We've met many times . . . Helgi."

"Sigrún, your belt imprisons you."

"The belt is a gift from Loki to my father. It keeps me under control—tied to my father. I can't ride the lightning when it's tied around me."

"You are free; I freed you," I assured her.

"Yes, you did, but eventually you will misplace or lose the belt and—like everything lost—it will fall back into Loki's hands." She sounded resigned. "I will be imprisoned—again."

"You can keep the belt and run away from your father and Hothbrodd," I suggested.

"I can't; the torc around my neck is Freyja's:

Brísingamen. It was also given to my father to keep me captive. When I marry Hothbrodd, it will be given to him." She lowered her eyes in shame. "The torc can't be removed."

"Thør's stolen belt keeps you earthbound and in line," I summarized, hating Högne for the way he treated his daughter.

"Helgi," she said, turning her eyes to me, "you must kill my father and Hothbrodd. Rescue me from my imprisonment. If both of them are dead, I might be able to remove Brísingamen and be set free."

I looked into her eyes and saw the innocence of a caged bird. One that was meant to fly, but instead was confined to do others' bidding, against her will. "I will kill Högne and Granmar's sons for you," I told her. "What of your brother, Dag; won't he avenge your father's murder?"

She grabbed my head and kissed me, so long that it seemed her mouth didn't want to let me go. I was getting aroused. I climbed onto the altar with her and my body pressed on top of hers. She wrapped her arms around my trunk, pulling me closer. Pushing my arms underneath her, I pulled her up to sit on top of my loins. I kissed her chest, inhaling her scent, finding my way to her lips. She kissed me back. I pulled up her gown and struggled to unlace my pants. Finally I tried to force them down while lifting her.

"No—wait," she said, tearing her lips away from mine. "We mustn't; we can't. Not here and not now."

I lowered her back down onto the altar, releasing all of my expectations with a sigh. I rolled to lie on top of her and looked into her eyes. She pulled me away from my thoughts and I was able to briefly feel warmth in the darkness of my fighting and struggling. It took me away from my violent world—the unseen Jötunn within me that couldn't kill itself and so lashed out and slaughtered others. It gave me clarity to see that my fight could be won by surrendering; I could surrender to Sigrún.

She stroked my hair and face. I felt safe in her arms. Her wrists brushed my nose and I could smell her again. Her body touching mine warmed me in the cold chamber. Firelight flickered on the walls and ceiling; the air sparkled with floating dust motes and time slowed. I felt weightless, suspended in the air and unburdened by my battle-worn body.

I slid off of her and lay on the cold altar next to her. Where our bodies touched, they vibrated with an electric energy. I squirmed closer. I closed my eyes and my skin felt a soft, feathery down touching it. I felt light wings brushing over me, calming me. I drifted.

I imagined that her wings cocooned us together, insulating us from the outside world. I dreamed that Sigrún could change me into something that could love her without possessing her, and give her a reason to love me.

I drifted away . . .

80   03

Suddenly I was jarred out of sleep as the hóf shook. A blast of light and heat hit me, knocking me off the altar to slam onto the cobblestone floor. "Argh!" I yelled as my sore shoulder struck.

I rolled to my feet, ready to fight, confused. The wall sconces and hearths were out; the room was in complete darkness. The only sound I heard was my ragged breathing.

"Sigrún?" I whispered, feeling her despair trickling

down my cheeks.

I stretched my hands out in front of me and groped in the blackness for the wall. I smelled the oil of the sconces in the darkness and a moment later touched the cold, hard surface of the wall. Working from memory, I turned and followed it with my fingers until I passed through the doorway into the dark corridor—the blast of wind had extinguished the sconces here, too.

"Guards! Guards!" I yelled as my hands found the dark, stony threshold.

Seconds later an orange glow grew into a lit torch in the hands of a guard.

"Give me your torch!" I grabbed the torch and whirled back into the chamber, the torch trailing smoke and light behind it. As the light pushed the darkness away, a black-winged shadow climbed the wall above the altar and disappeared.

A sword lay on the altar, marking the locus of our embrace, and the black silhouette of our bodies had been left in the dust surrounding it. A dimming light moved up the shaft. I stumbled backward onto my knees, dropping the torch and the sword, feeling her breath leave my body.

I lost her. She's gone.

I don't know how long I crouched there. I felt heavy and my heart despaired. I searched for the gold belt. She must've taken it.

I pulled the sword partway out of its scabbard and looked at the blood-flecked serpent along its blade, and the serpent's tail wrapped around its flat, just as Sigrún had described it. I strapped it on next to my scabbard and looked for Tyrfing, the sword that Dvallin mentioned in Sessrúmnir Hall. I searched the floor, wondering how I'd recognize it amidst all the other swords.

Dvallin had warned that when drawn from its scabbard, the sword had to be used. I looked for a sword in a scabbard. There was only one, in a leather scabbard. Someone had tied its hilt to its case, probably to prevent it being accidentally unsheathed.

"Helgi!"

"Down here," I yelled, picking up the sword and my torch.

Thorfinn met me partway down the corridor; Thør and Gudrid were following him.

"What was that?" Thorfinn asked. "It looked like a bolt of lightning shot out of the hóf."

"It was Sigrún. The Valkyrie," I said, looking at Gudrid.

I walked past them and left the building. They followed me to the beach.

"Isung!" I yelled.

"Yes, Helgi," he said, approaching me with Baby trailing behind him and Snorri asleep in his arms.

"Assemble the fleet and send a scout to Hrafn and Atli. We're going to war."

"Against who?" he asked, handing Snorri and Baby to Gudrid.

"Granmar and Högne."

"Both at once?"

"Yes. Recruit the völvur."

"Wand-carriers? Helgi, with all due respect, they will go up against hardened killers with chain mail, shields, swords, and axes."

"Who says we'll use them for hand-to-hand combat? We need their talents for delusion, deception, and *especially* projectile weapons. Their potions can affect the

minds of a group of fighters with one shot. Arm everyone;
there are swords in the hóf.

"I'm taking *Hringhorni*;" I said, heading into the
cave port. "It should get me to our shores. From there I'll
get into the castle. Isung, if I time it right, your arrival
will divert their attention, giving me a chance to rescue
my parents. If I'm alive, I will signal from *Hringhorni* to
proceed with the attack. If they're already dead, or if I'm
captured, fight the good fight and don't attempt a rescue;
we'll see each other on the final fighting field, Vígríðr at
Ragnarök.

"Focus your attack on Granmar and Högne's forces,"
I continued. "If you make it that far, Sinfjötli and Sigird
will be sending ours. I'm hoping that once my father's
forces recognize our boats, there will be hesitation. I hope
we can use that to our advantage. If news of my victory
against Hunding has reached home yet, I might be able to
split their forces and recruit more fighting men."

"We won't let you down," Isung said.

"Thør, tow me out," I yelled as I boarded *Hringhorni*,

I raised the main sail as Thør towed me out. I passed
him with my hand in the air, looking out the port to the
open water. Then I set the steer board and *Hringhorni's*
sail toward home. Despite the wind and water conditions,
the boat didn't waver from its intended course. The stars
seemed to be going out, one by one. The water calmed to
a rippling glass that *Hringhorni* easily traversed. I knew
that I'd get there before morning.

I unsheathed the sword that Sigrún had given me.
It was perfect, like her. I had never seen an edge that
was so sharp and a haft that was so balanced. I grasped
its hilt and raised it in the air, feeling her strength in
it. The serpent carved into its blade shimmered and

its neck embraced my hand, the teardrop-shaped head resting in the centre of the back of my hand, just below my knuckles. The sword felt like it was part of me, an extension of my arm. *She is a part of me.* I waved it around in the air, hearing it slicing through the ocean gusts; listening to its cut in the wind.

It's wrath; it's Gramr. It's the sword of my forefathers come to me, to lead by taking and defending what's mine. I understood its strength and the weakness in me that it could exploit. And I saw its beauty, standing tall in front of me, as if I saw Sigrún, floating in the air and wind above me.

I tied off the rigging and slumped on a bench, staring into the night, wishing and hoping that Sigrún would come to me. The open water didn't feel as cold as I'd expected it to be, thinking of her.

Hringhorni headed into a mist that covered the deck, crept over the hull, and wrapped around the mast. Dark forms appeared above my head and move into and through the mist. They enveloped my body and I smelled their moist breath as it brushed my skin and lips.

Helgi.

I turned. Sigrún stood next to me on the deck. She was naked. I reached out and pulled her closer to me, then felt her on top of me. Our arms twined together and my lips touched hers, pressing harder and harder.

She tore my leathers off and lifted my tunic partway over my head, tangling me in my sleeve. Her skin was warm and soft. I lifted my tunic over my head. Her arms touched my shoulders. I lifted them around my neck and kissed the skin on her breasts, feeling my hot breath on my face. She turned her head down to meet my lips with hers and I looked into her pearl blue eyes.

Her nipples poked me and I closed my mouth around one, then the other, and kissed the cleft between her breasts, inhaling her scent. She smelled like the cold norðr wind.

She pulled my pants down to my knees and sat on me. I felt myself going into her. She bent over and kissed my lips. I surrendered as she pulled me into her body. Our bodies bobbed in time with the boat and panting, we pressed our mouths together.

I couldn't breathe . . . I couldn't take another breath . . . Then I was yelling into the wind as I erupted, feeling the pain of loneliness rush through me and out the other side.

I'm empty.

The terror hit. My insides shuddered; I lost myself. The images went mute in front of me and the words became meaningless. Then my insides contracted and I found my breath again.

She lay on top of me, our chests heaving together, our hearts pounding into each other, our sweat slick on my torso. We lay together in the moment. I couldn't let her go, fearing that she'd take my breath away with her. I wanted to feel her beating heart on top of mine—*forever*.

I could feel the mist touching my skin as it flowed around us and between us and around us. I touched her back with the palm of my hand. Her skin was soft, like the down of a baby bird. I pressed her body tighter against mine. I could see the stars through the mist. In that moment, I didn't care in which direction the boat was headed, because I was already *there*. It wasn't a feat to accomplish, or a task to complete. It was lying on top of me.

She lifted her chest off of me and leaned on her

elbows to look into my eyes. "Helgi, remember our promise."

"Yes, I haven't forgotten," I said. "I will free you."

"You might want to turn away," she said.

"Why? I see your naked body."

She laughed. "No. When I take off. Some men have found it a little intimidating."

"*Some* men. Other men?"

"Oh, no." She chuckled again. "I mean my father and brother, Dag, have said that it could be uncomfortable for men."

"Oh." I swallowed. "I would love to watch you fly." I leaned on my elbow with my head in my hand. "Sigrún, I love you."

She tiptoed toward me and held my face in her hands as she kissed my cheeks and then pressed her lips against mine. "Helgi, I love *you*."

My breath caught in my throat.

"I won't be too far away," she said, walking to the other side of the deck.

Sigrún folded her arms in front of her and hunched her shoulders forward. She transformed—wings grew out of her back and unfolded, turning her body into a perfect cross. She stretched and her face revealed her enjoyment at freeing herself.

"You're the most beautiful being I've ever met," I yelled.

I felt a charge in the air, like the air just before a lightning storm. White light flashed across the deck. I covered my eyes, then looked up into the night sky to catch sight of her, but she was gone. I pulled up my pants and lay there, staring into the dark. The rush of emotions pulled me back to Sigrún lying close to me.

I stood and finished doing my pants up, staring over the bow. Even in the dark of night, I recognized the coast of home. I looked along the coastline, figuring out how to infiltrate Borghild Hall.

Fires burned in the signal towers, marking the archipelago. If ships approached without instruction from the signal towers, they risked catching their keels on sharp rocks jutting up just below the waterline. I approached the archipelago and turned the sail to the first of the sentinel towers. I lowered the sail and tied down the riggings. I felt the boat start to drift, but knew that at any moment, I'd be spotted. I sliced through the anchoring rope with my axe and dumped the anchor into the water, then knelt in a relatively concealed area in the stern and pried up a deck board with my axe, creating an opening big enough to crawl through and hide in the space below.

I heard the alphorn signalling that I'd been spotted. Unstrapping my sword, I slid it into the opening along with my axe and Tyrfing, then slid in and put the deck board back in place above me.

I needed to find an ally on the inside. Hamund was one of Father's trusted jarls. He was my blood cousin, but a distant cousin of Sinfjötli and Sigird's mother, too. I had to trust that his allegiance would be to Father.

I lay with my eyes closed, listening. I heard the water breaking alongside *Hringhorni* and then the sound of hands and feet scaling the side.

"The deck is empty," a voice yelled. It was followed by footsteps pounding on the deck.

"The rigging is intact," another voice said.

"Oh, here . . ." Footsteps crossed the deck. "It's been torn away from its anchor."

"Sir, we believe she's a derelict," the first voice shouted. "We'll rig her up and sail her into the cave port for further inspection." There was a pause. "I don't think I've ever seen a boat rigged this way," the voice said again. "It's easy enough for one person to navigate it."

Hringhorni moved. I smiled in anticipation. Soon I would be moving through the safety of the hall's passageways.

"She'll be a good ship when we go after Granmar's fleet. It's a shame about the old man. But it looks like Sinfjötli arrested the killer."

There was a grunt of agreement. "That wife of his. Didn't expect that."

"They said that it was a crime of passion. Volsungsson was ready to move on to his fourth wife and Borghild couldn't live with it."

"That last part is still a rumour," the other voice replied. "As for naming Helgi as her ally, I don't believe it. What does it benefit Helgi to kill his father? If he wanted to advance himself, Sinfjötli would've been the target. Besides, he's off fighting to keep our lands out of Hunding's greedy grasp."

Another grunt. Of agreement? "We will honour Volsungsson as a great leader and fighter, but we must turn our attention to the present. Can Sinfjötli lead with his lack of battle experience?"

"I've heard that there is uncertainty there. That he has not been proven a leader in battle. He has not earned his leek to lead and his rune to fight. Helgi is the more experienced fighter, despite being far younger."

"I fear that the reservations about Sinfjötli could be used to divide the clan."

I smiled, listening to the family clan chaos that

Sinfjötli was bringing upon himself. But the smile was bitter. My worst fears had been realized. My father had been murdered and my mother and I were being falsely accused of it.

Their talk returned to the present with, "She's an easy ship to navigate; she'll make a fine addition to the fleet. Take down the sail."

The sound of the water on the sides of the ship changed; now I heard the echo that signalled entry into the cave port. Sounds of the outside world were replaced by voices and the thuds and creaks of ships being loaded.

I heard the two men who had boarded *Hringhorni* disembark over the side, this time descending via the ladder. I waited a moment to make sure no one came back aboard, then quietly moved the deck board and slipped out, leaving my swords behind. Crouching low, I tiptoed to the rigging and picked up the excess rope and lowered it over the side in between the dock and *Hringhorni*. Lifting my head carefully over the gunwale, I got my bearings, then slipped over the side and lowered myself into the frigid water. I took a deep breath, and dived. Swimming through the murky water, keeping the wharf on one side of me and coming up for air only in the shadows, I headed for a submerged drainage tunnel that would get me into a tunnel system within the hall.

At last I pushed myself through the opening and entered the tunnel. Just as my lungs started screaming for air, I burst through the surface, then kicked my feet vigorously to slop onto the tunnel floor. From there I sloshed into the drainage system chamber that I'd passed through what seemed a lifetime before. There I paused, shivering, and caught my breath. Arms wrapped tightly around my torso, I peeked into the tunnels leading in and out of the cave port. I had to get to the connecting tunnel without being seen.

I watched the flow of traffic through the grate in the drainage tunnel. Sinfjötli was getting ready for something. Warriors, many whom I recognized, were shuttling back and forth, carrying armfuls of axes; oxen pulled carts filled with spears and shields. It appeared that the entire clan was preparing for battle.

"I've heard reports that they've captured Prince Helgi in the Outerland," a voice said on the far side of an ox cart that was passing by. "He has confessed to his crime and is coming home to face his punishment."

I smiled grimly, recognizing a smear campaign when I heard it. *The work of a madman*, I thought. Only Sinfjötli would lie to his people.

". . . his mother will stand next to him."

Mother is still alive!

They passed by and I chanced it, emerging from the tunnel and following the shadows to a door in an alcove. Voices approached in the dark; I pressed up against the door and held my breath as they passed.

I peered cautiously around the corner of the alcove, then ran to a drainage gate in the floor. Careful to work silently, I pulled it open and lowered myself through the opening, swinging a bit so I'd land on a ledge that ran along the wall of the drainage tunnel. The stench of the castle's sewage hit me like a brick. I tried taking small breaths through my mouth, not knowing what inhaling it would do to me, and flicked mice off the ledge into the sewage below with my foot. After reaching up to pull the grate back over the opening above me, I looked around, trying to see through my watering eyes. This would get me into the hall, although there would be only one way out. Determined to focus on the end rather than the means, I moved grimly forward.

At last I crawled up into a privy and listened for activity. Hearing nothing, I pushed the wooden toilet seat out of its hole and climbed out, wiping my streaming eyes and taking deep breaths.

Peeking around the privy's privacy screen, I checked the sleeping rooms and the corridor. All clear—not quite! There was movement in the corridor. I ducked back behind the screen as footsteps approached. Someone entered the privy and I leapt at him, knocking him to the floor and wrapping my hands around his neck. Then I froze.

"Hamund."

Father's advisor stared back at me with terror in his eyes. I loosened my grip around his neck.

"Helgi," he whispered. "I'm happy to see you alive."

I slowly climbed off of him and removed his dagger as I helped him to his feet. He pulled his pants down and sat on the toilet.

"Helgi, you cannot be here. If you are caught, they will kill you. Sinfjötli has outlawed you and your mother for the murder of the king."

"Hamund, where are they holding Mother?"

"In the keep," he said, pulling up his pants. "But you can't be around here. It's fortuitous that Sinfjötli has the men working in the cave port, or we'd be overrun with fighters. They can return any moment," he warned.

The keep was strategically located close to the barracks, to defend it. Its entrance lay at the end of a curving corridor around the exterior wall that attached to the corridor into the barracks.

"I must free my mother."

"Helgi, there is only so much that I can do for you. How are you getting her out?"

"A ship is docked in the cave port," I said.

"I'll find a way to keep them away from the barracks and divert as many of the fighters away from cave docks as I can. Stay here till I see if it's clear."

"Here," I said, handing his dagger back to him. "If I'm caught, I don't want it traced back to you."

"You would've made a most excellent king," he said, turning and entering the corridor. Moments later he signalled the all clear and I headed to the keep door.

I knew two guards were stationed on the other side of the door. And the only way in was through them. I ducked back into the doorway and dug my fingers into the pouch that Thør had handed me onboard *Hringhorni*. He'd mentioned völva items and I hoped he'd included Devil's Breath. As soon as my hand touched the linen, I grinned. I pulled out a handmaid's dress with a head covering, veil, and pinafore. And a fur-trimmed pouch with the symbol for Devil's Breath burned into the hide.

I dressed over my leather armour. I slipped the small pouch into a front pocket of my pinafore and hung the shoulder pouch around my neck, bunching and folding it under my pinafore to even out my lopsided-looking chest. After wrapping the covering around my head, I strolled to the end of the corridor. I held my breath and reached into my pocket and pinched some of the Devil's Breath between my thumb and fingers as I opened the door.

The two guards were seated next to the door. "Is there something we can do for you, love?" one said as I shut the door with my back to them.

I turned and stepped toward them, then tossed the powder into their faces. They scrambled for their weapons but the drug was quickly taking them over—by the time they stood and drew their swords, they were tilting sideways and thudding into the wall.

I grabbed their keys and fumbled through the ring, trying to find the right one, then opened the gate. I wiped the residual powder on them and dragged their bodies out of sight, then relieved them of their daggers, which I concealed under my pinafore. At last I breathed.

Mother could be kept anywhere, but she'd probably be in the treasure room on the lowest level. I moved quietly down the circular stairs, pausing every so often and listening for activity below me. I followed a trail of lit wall torches, noticing that most of the keep was in darkness. This lit path would probably take me where I needed to go.

I reached the bottom of the stairs and walked down the corridor to the locked gate of the treasure room. "Yoo-hoo," I said in a high-pitched voice, deciding to announce my approach. "Are you boys, hungry? I have some food." I lowered one hand to one of the daggers underneath my pinafore.

Silence.

The light from a lantern glowed behind the locked gate. I fiddled through the key ring, looking for a key that matched the lock and unlocked it.

Beyond, a figure lay on the floor. I couldn't tell who it was in the dim light. "Mother?" I whispered, pulling down my veil.

She stirred, looked around, then sat up. "Helgi?" She squinted through the dark.

"Mother," I said, hugging her. I saw faint bruising on her cheek and neck. I pulled up her sleeve; her wrist was bruised from restraints. "Let's go," I said, taking her hand

and helping her to her feet.

"Are their more guards in the keep?" she asked.

"I don't know; I only saw two." I gave her the dagger and we headed up the stairs, back to the guard room. I locked the entrance gate and peeked into the corridor. The barracks were still empty. We returned to the head and I lifted the seat, tossing the keys in.

"I didn't know about this route," Mother commented.

"It leads to a tunnel grate in the cave port," I said, warning her.

I stepped in, lifting the hem of my dress, and crawled back to the grate in the corridor. Mother followed.

I looked through, waiting for a break in the foot traffic. When it was clear, I removed the grate and peeked down the tunnel, looking for approaching shadows. Seeing none, I jumped out and pulled Mother out, half dragging her. We ran to the next grate and crawled through the tunnel down into the drainage system, then entered the tunnel leading underwater.

"We have to swim from here," I said, taking off my dress. "I have a ship that will get us away from here. Isung is bringing a fleet to face Granmar, Högne, and Sinfjötli's ships."

Mother removed her cloak and stood in front of me with her underdress on, smiling. "It is good to see you, my son," she said, kissing my forehead.

"You too, Mother."

We eased into the hole and swam through the murky water to the rope hanging over *Hringhorni's* side. Mother went up first and I remained still, holding onto the rope and watching the port for activity. True to his word, Hamund had cleared the port. Only a trio of fighters on the other side of the cave were hanging around a doorway, talking.

I followed Mother up the rope and silently crawled over the gunwale. I saw that a jack with our family crest had been raised; Sinfjötli probably intended to use *Hringhorni* as his flagship.

"How are we going to get out of the port?" Mother asked, crawling across the deck with me.

"I'm roping off the mast. When *Hringhorni* gets out past the archipelago, the wind will take you suðr, to intercept Isung's fleet."

She looked at me with wide eyes. "Aren't you coming with me?"

"Yes, but I have to tow you out of the port first."

I crawled to the tow rope and peeked over the side. The warriors were still deep in conversation, but they had moved a little farther into the tunnel. I descended the ladder and grabbed the tow rope, slinging it over my shoulder. I needed only to get the ship moving, then its momentum would get it out to the archipelago where the channel winds would take it out to open water. I put the rope over my shoulder and heaved. *Hringhorni* started to move. I leaned forward and heaved harder and harder.

"Go get help!" I heard behind me. "Someone is stealing Sinfjötli's boat."

A commotion rose behind me, and it was approaching. I pulled harder and moved forward faster, but I was running out of dock. Fifteen strides . . . seven strides . . . two strides—I let go of the rope and turned.

A fighter had been barrelling down the wharf. He stopped, as soon as he noticed me. "Prince," he said, letting his guard down. "If I'd known—"

I wrestled him to the dock, trying to disarm him.

I saw Sinfjötli emerge from the tunnel. "Stop him!"

he yelled.

The guard I was grappling with tried to comply, but I punched him in the face and pushed him in the water. More fighters were heading toward me. I turned, ready to jump and swim after *Hringhorni*.

As I was about to launch myself from the end of the dock, I felt a piercing pain in my shoulder. I looked down at the arrow protruding from my flesh then dropped to my knees, hands gripping the arrow in my shoulder. I watched *Hringhorni* drift farther and farther past the sentinel tower with Mother standing in the bow, looking at me.

Move, I willed it.

Suddenly the wind began to gust, as if my will had manifested it. I sighed, happy to see that my plan to rescue Mother had succeeded.

I sensed soldiers standing behind me. Strangely, dying didn't feel so terrifying. If Sinfjötli wanted to thrust a sword through my back right here and right now, I wouldn't fear it. But I knew he wouldn't.

My head jerked back as a hand wrapped itself in my hair and yanked. "Welcome home, brother," Sinfjötli sneered, glaring down at me. He looked up. "Bring him," he ordered the guards. "And call the physician."

We moved through the corridors away from the barracks, avoiding the main thoroughfares of the hall. I suspected that he was taking me to Father's apartments, and that Sigird would be joining us, too.

The loyalties of the clan must be divided. Sinfjötli couldn't cover up my victory for too much longer. His story would fall apart and along with it, the unity of his followers. *It won't be easy getting rid of me.*

We entered Father's room. Father's physician

entered the chamber and looked at my wound. "It's a flesh wound, grazing the muscle. This will hurt a little," he said to me. He grabbed shaft and snapped off the metal arrowhead. I jumped as the shaft moved in my shoulder with the action. He pulled the rest of the arrow out of the back of my arm.

"Hold this," he said, wrapping a cloth around my bicep. I reached up and held it in place while he unlaced my armour and undershirt and bandaged the wound.

"Not much blood. It should start to feel better in a day or two," he said.

I rotated my arm, feeling the wound burning. The guards sat me in a chair and tied my wrists and ankles to it.

"Leave us," Sinfjötli ordered.

I noticed Sigird for the first time. He sat in a chair in the corner, partially hidden in shadow. He drank from a horn, appearing half drunk. He was barely old enough to grow a beard, but he was getting drunk. "Oh, look who's home," he said when he saw me looking at him. He staggered to his feet.

"And look who's drunk—again," I snapped back.

He sneered and staggered closer, then threw the contents of his horn in my face. "It looks like I need a refill," he said, staggering past me to the barrel by the door.

I heard the heavy wooden doors close behind me. The only sound left in the room was the horn dipping into the barrel, and the crackling fire.

"You've committed a noble act," Sinfjötli said, "by saving your mother."

I stared ahead, shaking the rest of the mead off my face.

"She'll run back to her völvur allies with stories of what we did," Sigird said.

"Don't worry; the stories won't travel beyond the pockets of resistance that are left," Sinfjötli replied.

"Did you kill Hunding?" Sigird asked me.

I nodded, knowing this would delay or interrupt their plans. "I saved the völvur, too. They've bestowed upon me the title 'Hundingsbane.'" I smiled, knowing the information would anger Sinfjötli, and his fear would start playing on his disturbed mind.

Sinfjötli grabbed the sides of his head and paced the floor in a fit of anger. "That stupid ox," he growled. "Hunding couldn't even do his part: eliminate the völvur."

"What can they do to us? They're mostly females, unorganized and scattered. Unless Helgi has organized them into his fighting force," Sigird said, laughing through his sarcasm.

"What happened to Father?" I asked.

"He foolishly challenged Granmar when there were insinuations that Granmar was making advances to *your* mother." There were lies in Sinfjötli's voice.

"And why did you hold her in the keep?"

"She was being questioned as a possible conspirator. It is not so out of the ordinary. In a situation such as this, we had to make sure that she wasn't inciting the advances and plotting against the king."

More lies!

"You just did what *we* were about to do: let your mother go," Sinfjötli said.

"Why are you holding me?" I asked.

"For the same reason," Sigird slurred, walking past me for more mead and squeezing my injured shoulder as

189

he passed.

I stifled a cry and looked at Sigird's empty chair, wincing.

There was a pounding on the door.

"What is it?" Sigird slurred.

"My lord, the ship is beyond the last sentinel tower," a guard yelled through the door.

"Well then, send out boats to retrieve it," Sigird ordered.

"You better go and make sure no harm comes to Borghild," Sinfjötli ordered. "Bring the boat back here."

The door behind me opened and I heard Sigird's heavy footsteps and his muffled grumbling as he left.

"You'll never catch it," I said as the door slammed behind me.

Sinfjötli walked to the door and banged on it. "Get me Jarl Hamund," he yelled.

I heard him fill his horn from the barrel of mead. He silently walked back to the fire, sipping while staring into the glowing embers.

"You called for me, Sire?" Hamund said as he entered.

"Yes. You will be a witness to my brother agreeing to give up the land decreed by our late king. I, as the current monarch, have overturned that decree. All lands will be returned to the head of the clan—me."

"King Sinfjötli," Hamund acknowledged. "I will gather the jarls."

"I will meet with them myself," Sinfjötli snapped. "You take care of *him*." Sinfjötli nodded at me. "Keep him away from the barracks. I don't want sightings of him spreading sedition among the fighters. Keep him under guard in one of the apartments. If he tries to escape, kill him."

Hamund bowed as Sinfjötli left.

"Take me to the tower room," I whispered to Hamund.

"Bring him and follow me," Hamund ordered the guards standing outside the open door.

They untied me and shackled my hands, then led me at spearpoint up the stairs to the tower bedroom.

"Prince," Hamund said, once the chamber door was closed, "I will find a way to get you beyond the outer wall. There is a growing faction of jarls who know that Sinfjötli is behind the king's murder. They have sworn their allegiance to you."

"Hamund, I need chain mail and a helm. I could use Father's, but it will be recognized."

"But, how will I get it past the guards?" he asked.

"You don't have to bring it to me, I will go to it," I said, walking to the wardrobe and swinging it open.

"Passages?" he said, smiling.

I nodded. "Hamund, my forces are on their way from Sigarsholm to meet Högne and Hothbrodd in battle. Have your allies meet our fleet. Isung is in command."

"I will. I'll have fighters meet you in the woods on the other side of the hall."

"Take the chain mail to my apartment," I said. "And bring a sword and an axe, too."

Hamund left and I scuttled into the passage on my hands and knees. I closed the wardrobe behind me and headed down the tunnel to my quarters. I climbed the rope to my bedchamber, using the chiselled steps and opened the passage door to emerge from behind the tapestry. My bedchamber was dark and cold. I entered the murky greyness and retrieved the dagger that I kept under my bed. Then I paced, waiting for Hamund. It felt like an eternity, but he finally arrived with my chain mail and weapons.

"Helgi, I won't let you down," he said. "Our forces will be there. I promise."

"Good luck and gods speed to all of us," I said, and he left.

I dressed and descended back into the passage. I moved through the tunnel carefully with my added armour and returned to the drainage room and entered the cave tunnel.

Hidden, I put on my helm and entered the tunnel to the yard. I marched across it and merged with the other fighters entering and leaving through the stone fortifications of the hall. Then I headed across the field to the forest.

"Where are you off to?" a guard walking the parapet yelled down to me.

"I'm on patrol in the King's Woods," I said, not looking back.

As I approached the forest edge, I saw a group of guards sitting around a fire. Using the trees as a screen, I crept around them.

"Look!" one of them yelled, pointing to the sky as a star streaked across it. The others stood, riveted by the event. It was followed by three more falling stars.

I passed them and disappeared down the hill into the ravine. I smiled, thinking of Sigrún's promise and the commitment to the Reverend Mother. In return, they had promised to protect me. Two ravens fluttered from tree to tree and I saw that as a good omen. It felt like I was being watched, as I'd felt in Hunding's land.

Hearing footsteps farther down the ravine, I took out

my axe and approached cautiously. A shadow stepped out from behind a tree and stared at me. "I am a friend of the late king's jarl," I said.

There was a pause and he stepped closer. "He is my friend, too," a shadowy voice answered. "Please follow me."

He led me down a path that sloped to the water. We quietly boarded a boat. As we departed, I noticed that the waterline had risen. Rowers took us out to sea.

Another figure approached me, wearing a cloak and helm. "Hail to Helgi Hundingsbane," a female voice said from under her helm. She removed it, revealing short blond hair. "I am Chieftess Eira the Merciful. I was one of your father's jarls and now I follow you."

"Eira, I need you to get me to the rest of my fleet," I said.

"Yes; we will find them." She looked across the water. "We had a sighting—Sigird's longship chasing another ship. We should see it as we clear the archipelago. Keep your helm on until we clear the sentinel towers."

"Eira, the water is rising, I said, noticing the height of the shoreline."

"Yes, it's been rising for a while. Soon the archipelago will be underwater. If the water keeps rising, Borghild Hall will eventually be underwater, too."

"Our fleet should've left Sigarholm by now," I said. "Where do you think they'll encounter Högne's fleet?"

"Probably near Drogeo."

I looked across the water, slowly making out the faint outlines of boats in the distance.

"We are getting more and more support with the news of your victory, but it is still being suppressed to avoid the rest of Volsungsson's clan jumping sides," Eira said.

"I'm recruiting from what's left of Hunding's clan; we might be able to match their numbers," I told her.

"It looks like you'll be fighting two fleets, but not at the same time. Högne's fleet is tiny compared to Hothbrodd's. You'll encounter Högne first. Despite his inferiority, you will be battle fatigued when you encounter Hothbrodd."

"I'm hoping by that time we'll have more jarls loyal to my father's memory fighting on our side, and Hunding's fleet will be joined with ours. Is that Drogeo and Vígríðr?" I asked, pointing to a red glow on the horizon.

"Yes. And a chain of volcanoes that have recently become active. The volcanoes are catapulting fire-rocks and boulders into the water, creating waves strong enough to destroy boats and high enough to submerge islands and large areas of land."

"That longship," I said, pointing ahead of us. "That has to be Sigird. Get us closer," I ordered.

"Taking him out could be a prudent move. He commands a part of your fleet. Killing him will leave his jarls in a difficult position; it will leave them uncoordinated with the rest of the fleet," Eira said as she signalled for her rowers to change course and prepare to attack. Their axes and swords lay ready at their sides.

We turned. Our oars moved faster and faster, and we quickly gained on the other ship.

"Bring us up along their port side," I ordered. "Watch for their oars."

I scanned the stern of the ship for Sigird's short body as our boat cut through the swells. Their coordinated rowing began to falter as heads turned and stared at us in the early pewter morning. As we closed within shouting distance, their confused faces scanned us. Eira's men stood, now holding their swords and axes, and let our boat coast. I slipped a shield onto my forearm on my injured side and pulled out my sword.

Those in the other boat prepared to defend it as the gunwales of the two ships screeched together. We engaged the first wave, trying to push them back, as rowers lifted wooden brackets and locked the two gunwales together. We jolted sideways. The floating fighting platform erupted in pushing, screaming, and yelling as swords and axes clashed, the mass shifting from side to side, moving with the bobbing boats.

Sigird and I stared at each other in the crowd.

Eira defended me as I fought my way through the fighters between me and Sigird, avoiding the swinging axes and the bodies struggling all around me.

Sigird's lieutenant swung his axe down at me. I blocked it with my shield, ignoring the pain shuddering through my shoulder. I jabbed my sword forward, felt a weak spot, and thrust hard. He stumbled back and a second fighter intercepted me. Eira's axe hit him in the helm and he stumbled to the side, disappearing under the moving mass.

I pushed through and faced Sigird. The fighting here seemed to thin a little. Sigird targeted my injured shoulder. I deflected his sword with my shield, feeling a shudder of pain through my shoulder. I pushed back with my shield, catching him off guard, and he stumbled backward.

I swung my sword and its tip sliced into his flailing arm; he yelled and his sword flew out of his hand and dropped into the water. Struggling to recover, Sigird tripped over a sword and landed on his ass.

"Helgi!"

An arm swung to my right. I deflected it with the rim of my shield, knocking the attacker's axe to the deck. I lifted my knee and kicked him into the water. His helm flew off and the weight of his chain mail sucked him under. I turned back to Sigird.

He had rearmed himself and swung his sword down on me. I sidestepped, but his sword cut into my side. I swung my shield and hit him in the side of the head, knocking him to the deck. He sprawled there, unconscious, his nose bleeding.

I turned, ready to deflect another hit, but the deck was empty of all but my men. Their soldiers were in the water, struggling weakly to stay afloat but slowly sinking below the surface. I turned back to Sigird. "Grab his other arm," I said to Eira.

She peered at me, brows high. "You cannot kill your brother."

I shook my head.

"Prince, your mercy is mightier than mine," she said.

"Killing him won't bring our father back. Keeping him captive will still disrupt their plans." She nodded. "Split up the fighters that are left," I said. "We'll take both boats and the injured and rendezvous with the rest of the fleet."

"Yes, Helgi."

"Offer mercy to Sigird's men if they join us," I added.

We split up our rowers. "Head to Drogeo," I ordered. We continued on course to join the rest of the fleet.

"Over there," Eira said, pointing upward, "the sky is soaked with blood."

I nodded. "So, Eira, do you think that this is the end—the Ragnarök?" I asked.

"Yes, that is what I believe," she replied. "It is the glorious end to our thought-forms and the opening to creativity."

"Chieftess," a fighter called.

"Excuse me," she said, and went to join the man.

I headed to the stern and found a quiet place to sit. I took off my helm and splashed water on my face and over my head. The cold ocean water numbed some of the pain away. *If the oceans are rising*, I thought, *those surviving the flood will take the boats they have and search for higher ground. They will naturally head to the highest known place on Miðgarð: Vígríðr's summit and Drogeo.*

I leaned against a shield and closed my eyes; the sounds of the ocean faded to a hum and the rocking lulled me, cradled as I was in the curve of the shield. As I nodded off, the red horizon exploded. The mountains turned to moving backdrops and the oceans turned to blood.

胉 ؒ

I awoke to a trumpet, like Gjallarhorn, blasting three times. I scrambled to my feet in shock. And looked to the sea.

Thør stood tall, holding the mast. He waved. Thorfinn and Gudrid, holding Snorri, stood in front of him, smiling and waving too.

"They're mine," I turned and yelled to Eira. "Take us over to them."

"Ahoy, Helgi." Thør's voice rumbled across the water.

Behind them came a flotilla of dragon boats filled with warriors and knarrs filled with völvur. The occupants lifted their hands in the air and cheered.

"You made it," Thør yelled.

"Yes. The queen is on *Hringhorni*."

The boats met and I leapt aboard.

"It's only by a miracle of Óðinn that we made it," I said.

"We were forced to abandon Sigarsholm," Gudrid told me.

"The oceans have been rising," Thorfinn added.

"We are heading to Drogeo to intercept Högne's fleet," I said.

I wondered if the prophecy was influencing our decisions, driving us to make decisions that in the end would fulfill what the prophets had been telling us; the saga that never changed becoming the truth by rote, echoing in our heads like ghosts from our collective past, influencing our actions and shaping our destiny. The rising of the oceans signalled the end, pushing us to fight the final battle on Vígríðr.

Baby walked out from behind Thør, one chubby hand hanging onto his outer coat. He looked up at me.

"Any changes with Baby?" I asked, touching his head and smiling.

"No. He doesn't talk, but he is a good listener," Thør said. "He likes me telling him bedtime stories."

"Where is Isung?" I asked, looking around.

"He's over there," Thorfinn yelled from a short distance away, pointing to a boat on a parallel course.

I turned toward the boat and shouted, "Isung!"

A figure standing in the bow of the dragon boat raised his hand. The rowers altered their course and closed on us.

"Óðinn's letter instructs us to take Baby to Hoddmímis Holt," I said. "It must be somewhere in the mountain chain; maybe Drogeo."

"The Great Weaver of our saga." Thorfinn nodded as

if he'd gained more insight into what the title meant.

"It seems that Óðinn has sent us down a path that has no turning. We have been coerced by events to obey his instructions," Eira said, chuckling to herself.

"Helgi, I am happy to see that you're still alive," Isung said as his ship pulled alongside. "Was your mission a success?"

"Yes—partially. I rescued the queen. It was too late to do anything for the king," I said.

"Ragnarök is nigh," Eira yelled. "A final chance to fight—again—and die in glorious annihilation."

"We will have our revenge before Ragnarök," Isung said.

"Have you heard from Hrafn and Atli?" I asked.

"Nothing yet," Isung replied. "We've received reports that Granmar is dead. So Hothbrodd will be leading it."

"Yes, we'll strike Hothbrodd, once we defeat Högne."

"Isung," one of his men yelled. "We've spotted *Hringhorni*."

I followed his hand to the small object on the ocean. "Take us toward it," I ordered. I looked to Gudrid. "Gudrid, you and Snorri must board *Hringhorni*. It's too dangerous taking you into battle." She looked like she was about to protest, but finally nodded. "The survival of Snorri is the most important thing right now. You are saving Miðgarð, too, by keeping Snorri alive."

I walked to the masthead and stared across the water. Silhouetted boats appeared from the lingering mist, converging on the same point in the blood-red skyline.

Blood swirled through the land and the sky. The sulphurous ocean wind stole my breath and streaking fireballs erupted from the volcanoes and hit the ocean, sending up clouds of phosphorus steam.

Mother's head poked over the gunwale as we pulled up alongside *Hringhorni*. "My son, I thought I'd never see you again," she said.

"You're getting company." I told her, guiding Gudrid forward. "This is Gudrid; she and her husband rescued me from Hel," I said as I helped Gudrid and Snorri onto the boat. Thorfinn boarded with her and hugged them both.

I followed them and walked to the deck board to retrieve my swords, strapping them onto my back.

"Goodbye, Mother," I said, hugging her. "I love you."

"Goodbye, my son. I will see you in the . . . hereafter."

"For the glory of Óðinn!" Gudrid said as I left *Hringhorni*. Her voice didn't reach the war-cry level that she appeared to be attempting.

"Wait," Thorfinn said. He turned back to Gudrid and whispered in her ear, then kissed her. He followed me back onto the dragon boat.

"It will be nice to have help steering," Mother said to Gudrid. "What a beautiful baby." She held Snorri in her arms and watched us depart. Baby waved goodbye to Gudrid as the distance between us increased.

"Let's check out Drogeo," I said. "Its summit might be where Hoddmímis Holt is located."

We headed into a mist, leaving *Hringhorni* behind us. It shrank with distance, turning into wisps of a boat glimpsed through the mist. The air held a sulphurous taint. The ocean swells deepened. We smashed through a crest, pushing the water over and around us.

The mist began to clear. A light on the summit of Drogeo shone through a break in the clouds, and the ice on Vígríðr twinkled in the light, its shining summit prominent against the flat red dawn. The wind bit into my skin, hardening my anger and making my eyes tear; I wiped away a stream running down my cheek and beard.

Drogeo was pulling me toward it.

Above it, bands of clouds were soaked in blood and fire. Yggdrasil took shape, consumed in stratus swirls. A volcano exploded in the distance. Silhouetted wings fluttered, brushing the light into the colour of fire and blood.

"We're taking you someplace safe, Baby." Thør said to Freyja's baby. "Away from all of this destruction."

Baby smiled.

ഐ   ക

We stepped onto the escarpment formed by Drogeo's shattered foothills. From there, a rough path ran up the side of Drogeo.

"It looks like the gods' footprints," Thør said, looking at the path.

I looked up and could make out forms through the sulphurous clouds, moving upward, their progress partially hidden by the blowing white snow of storms. Indeed, the blanketing snow covered their footprints, obliterating footsteps from the past, erasing their history from Miðgarð forever. The Norns were wiping out life as easily as sweeping snow across the surface of Miðgarð. I knew their tracks led to Iðavöllr, to the hörgr; the last dais where the gods would judge who among them would live in Gimli and who would die. We followed the remnants of their footprints up the escarpment to Drogeo's summit.

We climbed higher, passing Vígríðr. The ice field stretched 120 leagues in every direction. Serpentine gaps and icy blue crevices crawled across the field, splitting it in half. A blast of wind scraped across my face and stung my eyes.

And Hoddmímis Holt—I imagined Hoddmímis Holt as a green and yellow meadow, flower stalks waving in the ocean breeze, scenting the wind with lavender and tonka bean. A homestead would be silhouetted against the amber sky, with black smoke rising from a smithy and beyond, a twirling net hitting the water with a splat.

A memory tried to surface, but it remained hidden, fading into the sky, just as the lost landscape faded with it.

ဆ   ಚ

We reached the summit. Yggdrasil towered behind a woodland of ash trees. As we approached, Thør let go of Baby's hand and he ran to the edge of the forest, smiling and laughing.

"Don't run too far ahead," Thør called, smiling as he watched Baby gamboling about.

He ran into the forest and hid in the underbrush, enticing us to play hide and seek with him. I followed and pretended that I didn't know where he was, weaving around the tree trunks. Soon we were all laughing.

It was warm here. Brilliant sunlight tempered the cold wind. We strolled through the woodland as if we were out on a summer's day. The earthy scent of the forest's damp floor rose and mingled with the fresh, clean air blowing around us. The respite was pulling me into apathy for Miðgarð's plight. I didn't want to think about dying when life surrounded me.

"Helgi, catch him!"

Thør's shout jarred me back to the present. I looked around, thought I saw Baby's head bobbing through the shrubbery, but he kept disappearing, moving faster than I could keep up.

"Don't worry," Thorfinn yelled. "He can't hurt himself."

"Baby!" Thør shouted, frantically running through the woods. "Baby!"

I chased after Thør, joining his desperate search for Baby.

I burst through the trees into a clearing. A sheer cliff rose in front of me. As I approached its curved rock face, I looked up and gasped. It was the Great Ash—Yggdrasil.

Baby bolted out from behind a bush and ran across the clearing. "Come back!" I yelled, chasing him. He laughed.

He stopped at the edge of a sunken well and turned and looked at me. I heard Thør and Thorfinn approaching behind me. The forest shook and leaves fluttered to the ground. A shadow rolled over us.

"Come here, Baby," I said playfully, waving my arm, trying to entice him.

Baby turned and dropped into the well.

"No!" I yelled, leaping into a run. I dived in with my arms over my head. The water felt viscous. Someone grabbed my ankles as I tried pushing myself deeper and deeper, reaching desperately in front of me, trying to grasp anything.

He's gone.

I wiggled my leg, hoping Thør or Thorfinn would recognize it as a signal to pull me up. Soon enough, whoever had my ankles hauled me up and I burst from the sludgy liquid and flopped onto the forest floor. I wiped the goo from my face.

"Where's Baby?" Thør said frantically.

"I couldn't . . . didn't—" I coughed.

Thør dropped to his knees. The earth rumbled again. We stayed there. I didn't feel the warmth of the sun on my face, or the air filling my lungs. When birth was precious, this felt like a senseless loss.

I struggled to my feet, feeling heavy. My every movement was sluggish and I had to will my body to move. I couldn't shake off that I'd failed the alfather; I didn't fulfill his dying wish.

"Come on, Thør," I said. "I need you. Maybe the final battle will make all of this seem justified."

Thør staggered to his feet and we looked down onto Vígríðr. The ocean had risen and was approaching its edge. The ice floe that held Freyja's fighting field—Fólkvangr—had drifted down and become wedged on the submerged mountainside next to Vígríðr, creating a bay. Ships were landing on the floe and fighters were disembarking to march across to Vígríðr. Behind them, the volcanoes pushed plumes of black smoke and ash into the air.

"Helgi, look." Thør said, and pointed.

The waves were rising. *Hringhorni* tipped from side to side, tossed in the wind and the surf. Beside the ship, a huge tail lifted high in the air and slapped down on the water, pushing the boat farther out to sea.

ဆ ဆ

A bukkehorn blasted in the distance. The last vestiges of the bugle call from the Gjallarhorn—the yelling horn—reverberated with the dark thunder, rippling across the pallid sky. Its thundering booms struck the ground like the myriad hooves of charging herds of buffalo.

Vigriðr shook, cracked, and splintered.

A distant volcano heaved its guts into the sky,

changing it to churning pitch and blood. The black clouds parted and a pewter hole widened in the sky. Like stars in the distant constellations, points of light exploded into existence and plummeted across the bleeding sky, hitting Vígríðr and sending up plumes of ice-clouds. Seconds later their thunder echoed on the wind and black, smouldering heaps scattered across the icy glacier blew into human-shaped apparitions.

Fire erupted into the wind; silent flames shot into the dark sky and smoke billowed, extinguishing the starlight in its black cover over Miðgarð. The earth growled and shook and the ocean exploded into the air, showering hot water down on us

Fighters from every period in time, all the way back to the beginning of Óðinn worship, stared in confusion at one another, standing like toy soldiers in rows facing each other. I felt uneasy, frozen in anticipation.

The sky split, then wavered. Suddenly the figures moved, as a wave of consciousness moved across Vígríðr.

Deep in the ice, a pale, fiery glow bloomed. It churned through the eons of layers, bleeding into the ice and changing the glacier to blood. Miðgarð was slowly turning its insides out and drowning in a watery grave.

Jörmungandr writhed furiously through the water, stirring up the waves. It again raised its tail and hit the water near *Hringhorni*, trying to capsize Baldur's ship.

Two more ships headed for Vígríðr.

Thør's countenance withered; his hand, trembling, covered his brow. "I see my battleground," he said, and descending down the path to the water, gripping Mjölnir. He raised his arm and pointed his hammer at Jörmungandr's disappearing tail. "There's the Jötunn Hrym steering *Nagalfar*, the ship of the dead," he said, looking down at the rising ocean waves pushing it closer to Vígríðr. "And, there's Loki steering the boat filled with the Surtr and the fire Jötunn. I'll keep them away from Vígríðr for as long as I can."

"Thør," I yelled, "I'll never forget you."

You say the funniest things when you feel that the end is near, I thought. *No matter how corny or stupid it sounds coming out.*

A blood-red ring burned through the churning sky; Vigriðr glowed red. Humans, dwarves, and elves stood paralyzed in fear, washed in the glow.

A pair of hands raised a red shield rimmed with gold into the air. A sword banged on it, marking time. Their confusion changed to rage and they opened their mouths to shout war cries, their rage demanding slaughter without merciful thought. Their bodies exploded into life and their wrath whirled with their axes. Vigriðr erupted with screaming voices and swinging axes ricocheting off studded shields and hacking through arms and legs. Pools of blood stained the ice.

Projectiles struck the undead, turning their bodies into dust that vanished in the gusts blowing across the glacier. The living were trampled into nothing. Having lived to fight another day, they forfeited their glory to retell the sagas of humans and the gods, and then die without their saga being told.

The dead were forced to fight in retribution for dying heroically in battle to honour Óðinn. They'd had lifetimes of honour and now had to die in horrific glory one more time, to again face the pain and horror of the experience.

Ragnarök was not a battle of victors and losers; it was the honourable extermination of all living forms, along with the egos that created them.

Fiery lights rocketed through the sky to crash on the field. Volcanic fire broke through the clouds; blood billowed and flowed through them. The ocean was transformed into blood, and death's shadow floated across it. The wind howled like a wolf—or was that the wolf packs that ran across Vígríðr, leaping at the throats of their victims? The light shifted and they transformed into legions of völvur, volleying projectiles at the onslaught of fighters about to overtake them. Their fists gripped their staffs as they prepared to defend themselves.

Winged Valkyries wielding swords flew overhead. Völvur mounted on Valkyries rode the winds, swooping down and striking their enemies. They tore over the dragon boats, their victims cowering on deck, covered in a cloud of powder and reduced to hysterics. Some laughed and others scrambled across the deck on their hands and knees to cower in groups.

A group of völvur on the escarpment fired a barrage of arrows, taking advantage of their vantage points along the trail. Their targets were Högne's fighters battling with the surf to get to shore. When they exhausted their quivers, they advanced with slingshots and handheld projectiles, targeting the remaining men and women as they tried to step ashore. Drugged and injured collapsed down the slope and were swept away in the rising surf.

Boats bashed against the escarpment, carried by the ceaseless waves, tossing fighters into the water or onto the shore and smashing the boats into floating sticks.

We descended the trail to the shoreline. Scattered boats became log-jammed. I leapt into the first boat and kept going, jumping into the next one, boat-hopping across the water. I was headed for Högne.

Boats and longships filled with more of Högne's clan approached us. Thorfinn and I engaged his scattered fighters on the boats we boarded.

Isung pinned their longship between two dragon boats, fighting Högne's men from both sides. The rowers, split into two fighting fronts, began to weaken. The lines crumbled and Isung's fighters mobbed Högne's remaining fighters.

We leapt into a boat and rowed toward a mass of boats gathered farther into the bay between Folkvagner and Vígríðr. As we closed, the waters became calmer. Objects in the water thudded against the hull. They didn't jar us like growlers would. I looked past the masthead and saw bodies still soaked in their blood bobbing up and down. The sheer number of them slowed the boat down and we pushed and dragged them along with us until they stopped us altogether. The water between us and Isung was a mass of ballooning bodies—a never-ending, rolling landscape of death.

I scabbarded my sword again and leapt over the side, jumping from floating corpse to corpse, trying to distribute my weight as much as possible to stay upright. They bobbed as I leapt off of them, the bloodied-water soaking my boots.

"Isung," I yelled.

He turned, looking surprised to see me and smirking at my ingenuity. I leapt onto the dragon boat with a helping hand.

"I can't say that I've done that before," Thorfinn remarked, landing next to me.

"Have you seen Högne?" I asked, scanning the sea of helmeted fighters.

"No," Isung replied.

"He's probably cowering off in a corner of the battle, surrounded by his guards."

The air rumbled. A fiery rock flew overhead, lighting up the battleground.

"There he is," I yelled, pointing. "He's right through those two dragon boats."

"Port rowers, hold." Isung yelled. "Starboard, take it away." Then, as we turned: "Starboard hold. All rowers, go!" Our speed increased as we cleared the death-mass, and our keel sliced through the water.

"Rowers, reach!"

They reached forward, lengthening their stroke. I grabbed onto the gunwale, feeling the boat's shift in speed.

Högne's boats were scattered; fighters on both sides engaged each other in a mass of bashing boats, clashing steel, ripping bodies, and blood spurting into the wind. I couldn't see the difference between them and us anymore. We were humans inflicting pain and suffering on ourselves; we were already dead and out of control, incapable of saving ourselves.

"Rowers!" Isung yelled. "*Power!*"

Isung turned us into a battering ram.

As we headed into the mass of ships engaging one other, a sea creature leapt out of the water, crashing down across several boats and sinking them. The resulting wave tossed the fleet about. We crashed through it, the rowers undaunted, pushing through their exhaustion and straining their muscles. Sweat poured down their faces.

Högne and Dag cowered together. Fighters surrounded them. I reached over my shoulder and pulled out my sword. Arrows flew overhead and we crouched behind the shields for protection.

"Rowers, oars up!" Isung ordered.

We rammed through the water, intercepting a longship drifting in our path. Our keel hit their port side and we pushed them into Högne's boat.

I leapt over their gunwale and started swing my sword. I hit a standing fighter and knocked him over the side. Thorfinn joined the fight and we hacked and sliced our way through the rest of the boat; we were joined by more and more rowers, who abandoned their oars and picked up their weapons.

On Högne's dragon boat, he stood on deck with Dag, looking around frantically.

We pushed forward as more of my men poured into the boat. Those who remained behind fired arrows at Högne's men. They raised their shields to protect themselves.

A völvur-filled longship laid down covering fire so that we could attack. I led the onslaught, leaping onto their dragon boat, landing next to Dag and body-slamming him to the deck. His sword flew out of his hand.

I stood in front of Högne, in his pristine gold-plated armour, his golden helmet gleaming like the light of Óðinn's second son, Baldur. He looked like he was dressed for a parade.

As soon as he saw my face, he lifted his long sword and swung it at me. I stumbled back and hit his sword on his back swing, trying to force his body down, or to unarm him. His skill caught me off guard and the strike on his upward swing pushed me against Thorfinn. Two of his men tried to close in, but they were intercepted by more boarding fighters.

Högne tried to strike me with his shield, but I

sidestepped him and its edge brushed my shoulder. He swung his sword and our blades struck, throwing us into a struggle to unbalance the other. His larger size and the weight of his plate armour forced me back. A wave struck the ship and the deck tilted and we stumbled apart. I seized the advantage and jabbed at him awkwardly, but my sword swung wide. Another of his men toppled between us, his chain mail rattling, and the tip of my blade penetrated his exposed arm instead, nearly severing it. As he fell to the deck, I picked up an axe.

Högne's armour was splattered with blood. He'd taken refuge behind Dag, who was back on his feet and fighting. Dag swung at me and I deflected his blade with my axe. We dodged each other's blows, stumbling over the dead lying at the bottom of the dragon boat. Their empty eyes stared up at me as my feet stumbled over their chests and limbs, animating them grotesquely. I swung as I stepped on a head, almost slipping off of it.

"Ahhh!" Dag yelled.

Suddenly Högne's sword swung at me, hitting the mail hood that protected my neck. The blade didn't pierce my skin, but the blow temporarily dazed me and numbed the left side of my head. I stumbled back, trying to shake off the blunt pain ripping through my skull. Högne advanced and was preparing for another swing when, suddenly, the sky flashed and I felt the searing heat of a lightning strike charging the water. The charge reverberated through our bodies and we stood facing one another, shaking. My stomach jittered and my skin felt prickly.

Högne had been knocked against the mast, and apparently experienced the same aftereffects I did. He too seemed dazed—eyes wide, body tensed, frozen in fear. I pivoted my body and my arm swung. I hit him in the arm and he stumbled toward Dag. Stepping forward, I thrust my sword at the base of his neck, where his mail hood had come away. Dag's arm swung, deflecting my jab. I swung my axe at Högne, hacking into his exposed neck. He fell overboard, sucked to Hel by the weight of his armour.

Dag had been knocked off balance and was sprawled on the deck. I stood over him, pointing the tip of my sword at his exposed face. "You have one chance to spare your life. Follow me, or die. I do this out of love for your sister."

"I will follow you," he said.

I nodded once and took a step back. "Now disarm yourself, then pick up your horn and signal your surrender and order your men to fight for Helgi, son of Volsungsson and the killer of Hunding."

He stared, trembling, then released his shield and sword, dropping them to the deck. He drew his dagger with two fingers and dropped that to the deck as well. Then he rose and walked over to his horn, tied to the mast. He bugled a signal of a change of orders, then another to follow his lead. The same call was picked up by his other boats and transmitted to all of his ships.

Isung caught up and boarded, bringing some rowers with him. "Take up oars, men," I ordered.

We turned, leaving the watery battlefield, and headed out to meet Hothbrodd. Behind us, the fighting ceased.

I looked around to find Thorfinn on the deck, bloodied and heaving, but still alive. "How are you, my friend?" I asked.

"I'll live." He chuckled, then stood with a grunt.

"We're engaging Hothbrodd. Right there; see them?"

I pointed to approaching ships. "Isung, signal what's left of our boats to follow."

Isung blasted the yelling horn. Our vessels turned and followed us. There were only four ships left that were in any condition to follow. "Not much of a fleet." I commented.

Steam erupted off our starboard side from a volcanic vent just below the rolling water. *Nagalfar* approached. The longship had one passenger aboard. Thør, in *Hringhorni*, moved to intercept it. But though Jörmungandr remained farther out to sea, it appeared to be trying to redirect the course of *Hringhorni*. The world serpent writhed beneath the water, stirring up violent waves in an attempt to unseat its arch enemy, Thør.

Thør threw Mjölnir across the water. It spun through the air and knocked overboard several of the undead. The hammer struck disfigured dwarves and dark elves on its return trip to Thør. Before they closed to within firing range, Thør threw Mjölnir a second time. This time it punctured a fist-sized hole in *Nagalfar*'s hull. He threw it a final time and punched another hole in the hull, near the waterline. As *Nagalfar* dipped into the swell, it looked like it was taking on water. It turned around and headed for Vígríðr. Thør headed for the ship of the Jötunn.

Flames erupted and crawled along the ocean surface, swirling, pushed by the wind. A jet of sooty smoke pushed upward. As the flames moved I thought I saw the sons of Surtr sailing within the flames. Jörmungandr's waves pushed Thør's longship and ours toward the flames.

The hump of a sea Jötunn crossed his path, pushing him off course. Thør regained control of his boat and raised the sail. The bulge in the ocean marking the location of the sea Jötunn moved past, and he turned his ship toward shore, pursuing *Nagalfar*.

Hringhorni yawed and dipped, moving dangerously close to Hothbrodd's fleet. Gudrid and Mother tried to veer away from the fighting and away from Jörmungandr. They circled around, looking like they were headed toward the shore. Jörmungandr lifted his neck out of the water and wailed into the wind in a haunted, high-pitched tone.

"Isung, take over," I ordered. "Make sure that Dag fulfills his promise. I'm returning to Vígríðr."

Isung nodded curtly and turned to the dragon boat next to us. "Come to!" he ordered, and their course converged with ours. Thorfinn and I boarded it.

"Back to Vígríðr," I ordered.

We looped around our small fleet and headed back to the shore. I looked out past our stern and saw Hothbrodd's fleet. They were closing. His ships outnumbered ours.

Suddenly a yelling horn blasted from the open water. I cocked my ear to the sea, hoping to hear it again. It blasted again. *It's one of ours!* I looked across the water and saw another fleet heading toward Hothbrodd. It had to be Atli and Hrafn with Hunding's recruits.

"Hothbrodd will be hemmed in, forcing him to split his fleet to fight on two fronts, reducing its strength and effectiveness," I said to Thorfinn, feeling victorious as I spoke.

We walked to the masthead. *Nagalfar* had reached the shore and the Jötunn were pouring out of it and climbing single file to Vígríðr.

Behind them, Thør threw Mjölnir. It twirled in the air and struck *Nagalfar*, punching another hole in its hull. The ship tipped backward and the waves overwhelmed it, along with the undead still aboard. It disappeared under the waves and was swept out to sea.

We caught up to Thør. "Ahoy, Thør!" I yelled, hugging the bobbing masthead with my arm.

He turned, looking flustered, then brightened when he saw that it was Thorfinn and me. His chest was stained with Jörmungandr's venom.

"Get up alongside of him," I ordered.

I leapt into his boat, followed by Thorfinn.

"Get back to the sea battle," I ordered the master of this boat. Our fleet was closing, but Atli and Hrafn had already engaged Hothbrodd.

Thorfinn and I sailed with Thør back toward Vígríðr.

Partway, a small knarr drifted alongside our boat. Figures cowered in its belly, refugees from the fight. "Oh Your Grace, Prince Helgi!" a woman called as they drifted past us, drawing my attention to them. I recognized Lynza, Griet, and Lyana. They stretched out their hands.

"Oh great prince, will you rescue and protect us?" Griet pleaded. "We have no weapons."

"Here," I said, unstrapping Tyrfing and removing the twine holding it in the scabbard. I threw it into their knarr as they drifted by. "It's a sword you can use to protect yourselves."

Lynza gingerly touched the hilt with her fingertips, then wrapped her hand around it and drew the weapon.

"It is a charmed sword made by Dvallin. Its name is Tyrfing," I yelled as the distance between us lengthened.

Lynza dropped the sword and scuttled away from it in horror. "You have given me a cursed sword!" she screamed.

"I have?"

"It must be used, once drawn!" she screamed as they drifted farther away.

Terror continued to contort Lynza's face as some unseen and force overpowered her. Though she screamed and struggled, her body moved jerkily to pick up the sword and raise it above Griet's and Lyana's heads. "No!" she shrieked as the sword swept down, striking Lyana in the neck. Blood geysered and she collapsed, quite obviously dead.

Griet tried to defend herself, but the sword possessing Lynza sliced into her stomach, splitting it open. She slumped to the bottom of the boat, her life slowly pouring out.

"You betrayed our clan and my family," I yelled. "Those who looked to you for guidance and trusted you; those who kept you safe and gave you a purpose in the community."

The torture of resisting Tyrfing still twisted her face. "It still hasn't finished killing," she moaned. Tyrfing quivered and shook in her grasp. Slowly, though her arms shook with the effort to resist, its blade turned. She struggled, fighting to keep her arms outstretched and the weapon away from her. Then her arms seemed to collapse as the curse overcame her, and she thrust the sword through her own chest. She fell on top of Lyana and Griet.

"Ragnarök is just," I said, watching their coffin drift away.

We hit the shore on a wave. The keel dug into the pebbles and came to a stop and we leapt ashore before another wave yanked the boat out to sea.

Thør paused to put on his iron gloves, then nodded to me. We ascended the beaten trail to Vígríðr, following in the wake of the Jötunn. I heard a horse's neigh and looked up. Sleipnir flew by, circling Vígríðr and Hoddmímis Holt.

As the ocean rose higher and higher, we kept climbing to escape being swept away by the rising water. Longships filled with the remnants of Högne's fighters landed on the mountainside, abandoning their boats and scaling the mountain.

As we ascended, a black scar was becoming more prominent. It split through the mountain and disappeared into the ocean in a billowing cloud of steam and grey ash. Within it was as black as pitch, but as light moved across it, the contents of the gash churned and bubbled with fearful ferocity. The molten lava pushed through cracks and fissures, disappearing over the grey sloping rock to be cloaked in the mist created by its explosive contact with the ice. Its glassy black walls pulled in the light; black dust sparkled in eddies of rising heat and wisps of escaping vapour.

"It's Ginnungagap," Thør said. "It's where the world began."

"It's widening," I said. My thoughts felt sluggish, like they were crawling through my skull and being pulled into the crevasse.

"It looks like it's consuming the mountain," Thorfinn observed.

"Ginnungagap isn't threatening; it's divine," Thør said. "Its life force is taken from Ymir's saliva; it churns with endless possibility."

"It looks like it's spreading," Thorfinn insisted.

"It is. Whatever it touches will transform. Ymir is the power of creation. Whatever the outcome of the final battle on Vígríðr, the Æsir and the Vanir are powerless to stop Ginnungagap."

"Transformed into what?" Thorfinn asked.

"It doesn't matter," Thør replied. "Eventually it will transform all of us."

"Thør, you don't look well," I said, studying him.

"The wind on my face feels colder; it's a strange sensation," he said, staring into the abyss.

I looked up. The branches of the Great Tree seemed etched black in the misty clouds of smoke and steam. Its trunk towered into the sky.

"Ragnarök has progressed beyond me," Thør said.

"Thør, is Ragnarök the vengeance of the gods?" I asked

"No, they are victims of it, *by their own hand.* Miðgarð has been caught up in the very same war— only you kill each other. Helgi, despite knowing about Ragnarök, the Æsir and Vanir believed that our truce had ushered in an everlasting peace. And that creating humans would bind both sides *together*, eternally."

"You were wrong." I said.

Thør nodded.

Thør, Thorfinn, and I stepped onto Vígríðr, a vast glacial plateau that disappeared into the clouds. It stretched for as far as my eyes could see. Wind gusts blasted across the field in every direction. In front of us the undead Jötunn from *Nagalfar* rippled in and out of existence. Human fighters fell, spilling their lifeblood onto the ice and staining it red.

"Thrymr," Thør yelled.

A Jötunn turned around.

"It will be a pleasure killing you a second time," Thør yelled. He stomped across the ice and swung Mjölnir at Thrymr's moon-white head. His hammer hit the Jötunn square in the jaw, throwing Thrymr off Vígríðr and into the raging ocean.

I pulled out my sword, ready to take on one of the others in the party, but they scattered. Thør advanced and swung at another one. He missed. As the rest of *Nagalfar's* party dispersed, they blended into the other clusters of fighters. We advanced farther onto the field. The screams and cries, the clash of metal, and the moan of the incessant wind were overwhelming.

The Jötunn Hyrm stepped onto Vígríðr, towering over the humans and ready to eliminate those on the fighting field. His tail swayed and slapped the ice, sending frozen shards slicing into flesh. He roared, exposing shark-like teeth, and his tail struck Thør, sending him sliding across the ice. He regained his feet, unhurt. The Jötunn's tail waggled in the air as if daring us to try to attack it.

Thør threw Mjölnir. It twirled through the air and hit Hyrm's blubbery belly, easily tearing into the soft flesh. Thør caught his hammer and Hyrm wiggled his tail in the air like that of a rattlesnake. It swished and snapped, then slapped down on the ice with a boom as Hyrm tried to strike Thør. Thør lifted his hammer high and hit the Jötunn's tailfin, cracking the glacier in the process. Hyrm howled into the wind. With his shattered tail, he retreated farther into the field.

The roaring heavens, falling onto the mountain island, choked the sky with sulphur and filled the air with shrieks. Smoke trails converged on Fólkvangr, blowing holes through its ice core. The barrage slowly broke up sections of the floe. Large chunks of it tipped, to be swallowed by the ocean.

Freyja's undead marched and battled their way onto Vígríðr, killing everything in their path. Bodies dissipated into directionless wisps and afterimages.

"It's the beginning of the end," Thorfinn said. "Miðgarð is falling into the ocean right before our eyes."

Shapeless swirling objects burned across the grey sky. Fiery boulders pounded the ground with deafening ferocity, hitting the wave-beaten side of the mountain and exploding in clouds of rock and debris. A section of the escarpment dropped into the ocean.

Fiery rocks hit the icefield. Vígriðr shuddered and an edge of the glacier buckled, exploding into the gusting wind and sending razor-sharp shards ripping through flesh. Those boulders that hit the ocean sent jets of water and boats into the air, the geysers shaped like giant mushroom clouds. The air burned my skin and I ducked, trying to avoid the heat.

Thorfinn swung his sword, desperately fighting off an indigenous man. "Elsu, it's Thorfinn!" he shouted.

"I know, Thorfinn—I can't stop!" the man cried. "It feels like someone else is controlling my arms." Elsu bashed Thorfinn with his shield, then tackled him to the ice. Thorfinn's sword skidded out of reach. Elsu raised his spear, aiming for Thorfinn's head.

I bolted across the ice to his rescue. Another figure beat me there—I recognized Freydis. She swung her sword and decapitated Elsu. His body turned to dust and blew across the ice.

"Freydis!" Thorfinn shouted.

"I do that for my sister, Gudrid," she said, turning and disappearing back into the battling mob.

A storm kicked up, blowing ice pellets and freezing rain across Vígríðr. The sounds of battle were momentarily silenced by ice crackling all around us.

I grabbed Thorfinn's sword and helped him to his

feet. When I turned, Hothbrodd stood in front of me with his brothers, Gudmond, Starkad, and Dag, behind him. Apparently they were giving their older brother the first chance to kill. He stood ready with his shield and sword poised. We began circling one another, waiting for the other to make the first move.

He charged, slipping across the ice, and swung his sword. I blocked his swing and swung my axe into his shield, then yanked it aside. I kicked him in the groin and bashed my helm into his. He staggered back, shaking his head.

Recovering, he charged at me again, swinging. I dropped my axe and gripped my sword with both hands, preparing for the force of his blow. As he neared, I sidestepped and dropped to one knee to slice at his exposed underarm, He stumbled to the ground, screaming in pain.

"Hothbrodd, I expected more from you, as the heir to your father's throne," I taunted.

He turned and tossed aside his shield, then transferred his sword to his shield hand, favouring his injured arm. His face twisted with rage and fear, and he staggered slightly, struggling to breathe in the icy wind— he was tiring, feeling the effects of the blood loss. But like all of us, he wouldn't give up—couldn't give up. In the madness of Ragnarök, no one could afford to think and remain alive. It was act, or die.

He charged again and I swung, the edge of my blade catching the hilt of his sword and wrenching his hand backward as his sword flew out of his hand. He fell to his knees and his helm rolled off his head, exposing his mail hood. I sliced my sword down onto the back of his neck. His head dropped to the ice and blood gushed through the links in the chain mail on the back of his neck. I backed away as a pool of blood under him spread across the ice.

The sky lit up and a luminous figure appeared next to me. It was Sigrún. Smiling, she turned to the three brothers and shot through the air like an arrow, hitting Dag in the chest. His body turned to dust. She attacked Gudmond and Starkad next. Their bodies turned to dust too. Finally she stood in front of me, the ice pellets blowing around and through her body as she appeared to fade in and out of existence. She smiled at me, and my blood rushed through my pounding heart.

I reached through the storm-driven ice, grabbed the torc, and pulled it off. The centre stone was cracked down its centre. I threw it into the wind, across the ice.

She held out a golden belt to me. It was Thør's Megingjörð. I took it from her, and she disappeared into a million shards of glistening ice.

I looked for Thorfinn in the ice storm. He lay on the ground, dazed, but unharmed. "What in Hel's name was that?" he blurted.

"It was a beautiful Valkyrie princess, coming to save us," I said, helping him to his feet.

"Helgi!"

I turned as Sinfjötli and his guards approached through the storm. He had Mother walking before him, prodding her with the point of his sword. The left side of her face was severely bruised and swollen; I burned with anger. One of his guards prodded Gudrid forward with his sword; she carried Snorri, bouncing him on her arm to keep him calm. I heard Thorfinn gasp.

"Sinfjötli," I said, "let them go. What can you possibly gain? There is nothing left. We stand on the final battlefield."

He stared at me, then lifted off his helm. He couldn't see the end like I saw it. He tried hanging on, fighting for the victory. The edge of his mouth slowly curled, as I'd seen it do a thousand times before. His expression turned sinister as a thought seemed to possess him. "Helgi, choose who dies; the other one will go free: Gudrid and the baby, or your mother."

"Helgi—" Thorfinn said; I heard the panic in his voice. I raised my hand, trying to calm him.

The ice pellets changed to rain. Water started pooling on the glacier.

"Sinfjötli, these people are not involved in our family fight. They are not from any warring clan."

"You've chosen to save the woman and the baby," he said, putting his helm on.

"No—wait!"

He pushed the sword into Mother's back. As the tip protruded through her stomach, Mother opened her mouth in a silent scream and her eyes rolled back. She was dead before she hit the ice.

The guard pushed Gudrid over to Thorfinn.

I charged, my rage pulling me to Sinfjötli. My heart thumped in my chest and my breath pumped through my nostrils with the power of a mad bull.

Our blades met in the air and the sky lit up with arcing bolts that seemed to fracture the heavens. I felt Sinfjötli's madness on top of mine, giving him strength and taking it from me. He kicked me in the stomach. I stumbled backward, the weight of my chain mail trying to drag me to my knees. I heard swords clashing on my left and on my right. I straightened up as Sinfjötli charged me. He struck me on the shoulder with his sword.

The ground shook and the ice cracked, booming across the icefield. Along the crack, bodies shook and dropped to the ice, writhing in agony, as if the sound had shattered their bones.

Sinfjötli's blow knocked me to the ice, though his blade hadn't drawn blood. I swung my sword and struck him across his back, knocking him down. Slowly, I stood. Sinfjötli was on his hands and knees, struggling to stand on the slippery ice, his mail hood draped over his face. He regained his feet and we faced one another again.

"After I kill you," Sinfjötli yelled, "I'm taking *Hringhorni*. Gudrid said its Baldur's ship. It will protect me."

I slipped my axe out of my belt.

"We are evenly matched, thanks to the rain and the ice," he said.

I charged, my feet slipping beneath me, but I managed to remain upright and in control. Our swords clashed again and we fell to the ice. I hit him in the face with my elbow as we slid apart in a puddle of water. I lifted my head from the shallow puddle, tasting blood and salt water. My head, still on my shoulders, pounded.

We stood again. Blood dripped from Sinfjötli's nose, staining his mail hood. I licked my swelled lip, tasting blood.

I charged and swung. Sinfjötli blocked it and Vígríðr shook again. We slipped and fell to the ice. My axe spiralled out of my hand. I punched him in the side of the head, aiming for his face and hitting his hood. My fist felt like it had been crushed, but I heard a crack as his head hit the ice. Sinfjötli's sword skidded across the ice and he wrestled me for mine. I tried kneeing him in the groin, but his knee was blocking mine. I jumped on top of him.

He was still a little stunned, but his arms began flailing in my face. I managed to reach his throat and I wrapped my hands around it, squeezing his mail hood into his neck. As I squeezed, I watched his face as he struggled to inhale. His face turned red and his eyelids fluttered. I knew he was running out of air as I squeezed his life through my fingers. My arms trembled as I gripped his neck tighter and tighter. His head bobbed forward and I saw him dying before my eyes. He exhaled his last breath and I still squeezed until my hands went numb and I rolled off of him, crying.

The ice rumbled as I stood, composing myself. Then it shifted and flames shot into the air. Vígríðr was burning. The mountain began spewing flames and smoke. Blood and fire glowed through the ice. The glacier was turning to flames that consumed the ice in a jet of steam that shot into the sky. I looked around for Mother's body as the flames closed in around us.

"We don't have time!" Thorfinn yelled, pulling me off the glacier. I tried to fight him off, but eventually hope faded and I abandoned finding my mother.

We scrambled to the edge and ran up the trail to Hoddmímis Holt. There, I stood on a crag and watched as everything vanished, dissolving into flames and steam, leaving only the churning pitch from Ginnungagap where Vígríðr once was. All that remained was the churning volcano on one side and the ocean on the other. Thorfinn, Gudrid, and Þór stood next to me. I pulled off my chain mail, feeling the weight of killing leaving me.

Hringhorni spun, captured in the currents around Drogeo. The water was empty except for the rolling crests of the waves and the snaking tail of Jörmungandr. The storms and fighting had taken out the fleet and the rising water erased all life.

"Here," I said, handing Thør the golden belt.

"Megingjörð! Where did you get—never mind. Thanks," he said, strapping it around his waist.

"Helgi."

I turned as Dag approached me with a spear in his hand. He raised his hand over his head and thrust the spear through me.

I collapsed to my knees. "Why?" I asked, looking at him.

"Óðinn gave me the spear," he said. "I'm finished." Dag backed away until he fell off the crag. He fell into the volcano, disappearing into the molten pitch.

A flash of light warmed my face and someone caught me as I fell over. I looked up into Sigrún's eyes. "I don't want to leave you," I said, feeling scared. "You are *so* beautiful."

She lay me on the ground and I felt the heat that radiated from the mouth of the volcano. Thør sat next to me and carefully pulled the spear out of my side. I looked up at him and he smiled.

Sigrún gently picked me up. I drifted off as we flew away.

≈   ≈

Sigrún carried me to the base of Yggdrasil and lay me down next to the well. Two maidens stared into it, waiting. Their spindles lay on the ground, vines slowly crawling over them. They looked up at us with vacant eyes, then returned to staring into the pool. They were the Norns and the well they stared into was Mímisbrunnr, the well of Fate, home to the Mímir. I shivered, feeling the cold.

We sat in a garden on an island, the only dry land

as far as I could see. Yggdrasil towered overhead, its branches spread out over the woodland like veins running through the body. The only light touching the ground was a distant beam bobbing on the surface of the ocean.

Thør walked over to the well and scooped his hand through the pool. He held his arm over it, and the water dripped and trickled off his arm. "It looks like slobber," he said, awkwardly sniffing it.

"Thør, it must be the saliva of Ymir," Gudrid said, for they were all there now too. "The power of life that the Great Ash, Yggdrasil, feeds on."

"Then these are the fates, the Norns," Thør said, pointing at the maidens. "But, there's only two of them. Where's the third?"

"They must be Urðr and Verðandi," Gudrid said. "The Norn of what has happened and the Norn of what is. The Ragnarök must have taken Skuld, the Norn of what ought to be."

"Yes, I remember seeing her killed at Hunding's fortress," I said.

"The future is gone," the Norns said. "Skuld killed on one of her foolhardy missions."

The well gurgled. Bubbles rose to the surface and popped, slinging goo over the side. The water rose, pushing the slobber out onto the garden. Thør stepped away from it.

"Thør, what's happening?" Thorfinn asked.

"I don't know. I guess we wait with the Norns."

We sat with the maidens. There was an almost reverential stillness about it. Staring into the well was like staring into a single point and not seeing everything else floating around it.

"Look," Gudrid gasped.

A hand had emerged from the well. It slapped the ground, digging its fingers into the soil. Its arm emerged. No one moved; we were mesmerized.

"Oh, for Óðinn's sake," Gudrid said. "Thorfinn, hold Snorri." She handed the baby to him and walked over to the well. Thør followed. They reached into the well and lifted a figure from the goo and gently lay him on the grass.

He coughed and sputtered; his naked body beginning to shiver. He slowly sat up. He was an old man, his long grey hair plastered over his face. Gudrid parted it, pulling it away from his mouth and nose.

"Alfather," Thorfinn yelled, dropping to his knees.

"Hello, Thør," the old man said, slowly looking up. "Your father has returned to you."

"But, I saw you die," Thorfinn protested. "You were eaten by a wolf, Freyja in disguise."

"Nothing is ever as it seems." He laughed. "I see that all of my children are here." Óðinn stood up. His naked body dripped slobber.

"Except for Baldur," Thør said.

"*Yes there is that matter,*" Óðinn replied.

"Thorfinn," Óðinn said, turning to him, "In order for Freyja's plan to succeed, she had to eliminate her only rival in seiðr magic—me. I allowed her to consume me. But the best part of my plan was that I allowed Freyja to believe that she had succeeded. I hid inside of her in a bubble of seiðr enchantments. I was *right there*, under her nose all the time."

"Alfather?" Gudrid asked.

"Yes, my daughter," Óðinn said, walking over to Gudrid and taking her hand in his. "By the way, thank you for nourishing me."

"From my point of view, Helgi is a hero from *my* past," Gudrid said. "Have we—on *Hringhorni*—been sent into the past, or has Helgi been sent to my present?"

"Neither. The convergence of the past and the present was unexpected. Without a future, the present simply has nowhere to go. Think of it as a flowing river ending in a dam that allows it to go nowhere. The past keeps the present moving to the future. Without a future, the past will eventually catch up with it. I think that's what allowed you to exist in both times."

"You do not know, Alfather?" Gudrid said

"No. Ragnarök is new for me, too." He laughed. "Remember, I was foretold of Ragnarök by a völva prophetess."

"What will happen when the past catches up to the present?"

"It will be now; the end to *all* of our sagas," Óðinn said. "Now, I must finish what I came back to do."

I heard a neighing and Sleipnir trotted out of the woods.

"Sleipnir, my old friend," Óðinn said, meeting him and petting his neck. "It is good to see you; I missed you. But it's time for you to go, my boy," Óðinn added, rubbing his flank. "I want to remember you flying away." Óðinn slapped Sleipnir's rump and the horse took off, galloping to the precipice. His wings opened and Sleipnir flew away. Óðinn watched him with a wan smile. He giggled and lifted his arms in amused mimicry, enjoying his horse's freedom.

Óðinn turned and hobbled over to Yggdrasil. He looked up its colossal trunk that disappeared into the sky. Yggdrasil's incomprehensible size gave it divinity and power. Óðinn looked small and insignificant next to it.

The maidens dipped buckets into the well and dumped them over Yggdrasil's roots, feeding it. Vines crawled up its trunk.

Óðinn pressed his naked body against the Great Tree and moved his hand across its rough bark as if searching for the life pulsating within. "I can feel your agony," Óðinn yelled, closing teary eyes. "You are dying. The well no longer feeds you. Without Yggdrasil, we all die."

Óðinn's face contorted in agony and he wept for the tree, but I glimpsed fear there, too. His gnarled hand wiped his tears away, then touched Yggdrasil's weathered bark. He stroked it.

Suddenly Óðinn looked embarrassed. Why? I wondered. Had he believed that his power gave him immortality? He shivered. "I have nothing left," he whispered. "I am just a weak and foolish old man, standing here naked."

His saga was fading to nothing, I realized. There would be no one to tell it soon. "Alfather," I yelled. "What is happening?"

"It is the end, my son . . . for all of us."

Óðinn looked up; the sky had changed to fire, fed by the volcanoes erupting along the mountain chain. Dark, tumultuous clouds blew across it, carrying the flames. Yggdrasil swayed in the gusts. Limbs and branches cracked and snapped, shuddering, filling the air with the sound of a forest being ripped apart in the wind.

The alfather's naked body pressed against the tree. His bare toes groped for a foothold on the bark. He lifted his trembling, sinewy hand and grabbed a vine wound around the trunk. He slowly pulled himself up. The wind blew his long, wiry hair across his face and parted his beard at his chin, pushing and tugging at Óðinn as he crawled laboriously up the tree, hugging Yggdrasil.

The earth shuddered and the flames swirled above Yggdrasil's highest branches. I couldn't tell if the Great Ash was on fire, but I suspected the flames would settle down onto it as Óðinn scaled higher and higher.

The great ocean extended into eternity. The air screamed and juddered as flaming boulders plummeted through the fiery clouds, trailing black smoke, to hit the water in a mountain of bubbles and plumes of steam as they exploded beneath the water.

"Look," I said, pointing to a writhing swell of water.

"Jörmungandr," Thør said.

Sigrún carried me down to *Hringhorni*, followed by the others. We boarded. Thør moved the sail and we headed to the open water.

The world serpent slapped the ocean, sending waves toward us; its head coiled out of the water, then plunged underwater.

Hringhorni cut through the waves.

Jörmungandr writhed just beyond the rocky beach, carrying the skies along with its flailing tail; the rushing ocean churned wildly as its tail slapped into the ocean, pushing a wave so high that it covered the sky before crashing against us.

Thør slipped Mjölnir out of his belt and carefully stepped onto the gunwale. The ocean dipped and peaked. He peered into the water, appearing to have seen something. He jumped in. Suddenly the ocean rolled and *Hringhorni* tipped and yawed. Water shot up into the air off our bow and Jörmungandr's head and neck exploded from the water. Thør, with water dripping from his beard and hair, hung onto the world serpent's neck. It writhed and swayed, trying to knock him off. Its stinger tail slapped against the side of *Hringhorni* as it disappeared underneath the water.

I gripped the side and looked back to Hoddmímis Holt. Óðinn kept climbing, appearing oblivious to the destruction around him.

Thør had his legs around Jörmungandr's neck and was trying to shimmy up to the serpent's most vulnerable spot: its head. Every time he tried to hit Jörmungandr, the movements of the serpent diverted his blows. Thør raised his hammer again, and again Jörmungandr writhed and thwarted his attempt. Hugging its neck with his free hand, Thør took off the golden belt.

"What's he doing?" I said. "He needs the strength the belt provides."

He wrapped Megingjörð around the serpent's neck and twisted it around his hand. Repeatedly slipping his belt up the serpent's neck and tightening it, he shimmied higher and higher.

Jörmungandr's tongue lashed out into the air, whirling and whipping from side to side, trying to catch Thør. But Thør swung Mjölnir, swatting at the serpent's tongue. Jörmungandr screamed again and dived under the waves, trying to shake off Thør.

The flaming sky lit the ocean in a blood-red glow. Jörmungandr leapt out of the water and twisted, raising its hooked stinger and aiming it down at *Hringhorni*, intending to split the vessel in half. Still tightly gripping its neck, Thør threw Mjölnir at the tail. Mjölnir ripped through it, the wound spurting blood into the wind. Jörmungandr screamed in pain, shaking its head. Mjölnir returned to Thør just as the world serpent hit the water. The wave pushed *Hringhorni* out of Jörmungandr's reach, but the ship drifted sideways, caught in a swirling current.

The ocean boiled; Jörmungandr and Thør leapt from its centre, Thør swinging his hammer, gouging at the serpent's neck. Jörmungandr's neck burst open, releasing sebum. It oozed down Thør's arms and body. Thør tugged on the belt, jerking Jörmungandr's neck toward him as he tried to twist its head off. Jörmungandr's mouth opened and spit black poison, staining Thør's face and chest. Thør screamed in pain and dropped Mjölnir into the water. Jörmungandr rolled over and disappeared into the waves, taking Thør with him.

Thør was gone. We were alone, with no one left to protect us. My mind went numb.

Our gods were leaving us one by one, but despite that I fought to believe that Óðinn had sent us a saviour. Out of all the gods, it was Baldur's boat that gave us the means to save ourselves.

Glowing embers fell from the sky. Yggdrasil's celestial crown was on fire, the storm fanning its flames. Óðinn had shrunk to nothing.

I heard a faint wail, drifting through the storm.

Helgi.

Pain pierced my head and my ears felt like they were being pressed into my skull.

Helgi.

"Did you hear, that?" I said, turning to Sigrún. "It's the alfather; he spoke to me."

Sigrún put her arms around me and looked toward Yggdrasil. "I hear nothing," she said.

Helgi.

"He's calling me; you have to take me back."

Sigrún cradled me in her arms and Thorfinn held Gudrid and Snorri closer. I knew they'd be protected on

Baldur's ship as it sailed to the distant horizon. The light of Óðinn's son would light the way.

We launched into the air, and *Hringhorni* quickly diminished into a single point of light below us.

As we approached Hoddmímis Holt, I saw that Óðinn wasn't moving; his body was pressed spread-eagled against the tree, his bare feet wedged into the contours of the bark, his hands around vines above his head.

The Norns had not moved. The ocean was rising and waves were lapping against their knees. They stared at *Hringhorni*, bobbing on the water.

Óðinn was nowhere near Yggdrasil's crown. The vines were slowly crawling up the trunk, following him up the tree. They intertwined and coiled around each other.

"My children!" Óðinn cried out as we approached him. "You heard my call."

I realized that Óðinn hung upside down. The vines coiled around his arms, wrists, and legs, holding him against Yggdrasil. Vines moved around him. Next to him, an elongated knot on Yggdrasil was splitting down its length, like a sebaceous sore oozing and sputtering sap. It frothed and stained the bark and vines a milky white as it dripped down its side.

"I have seen the power of the runes," he rasped, and laughed. "I have seen the *ultimate* sacrifice."

The wind calmed.

"Óðinn," a voice whispered. "You must do what ought to be done; what needs to be done and what shall be done."

"I hear the dead," Óðinn said to us. "It is Skuld."

"I hear it too, Alfather," I said.

"That which is happening—" said Verðandi.

234

"—and that which happened," Urðr interrupted.

"Mustn't be undone," Skuld said.

"Sigrún," Óðinn whispered, his strength waning, "come closer."

As we flew closer, the vines lashed out and entangled us, holding us near him.

"Alfather," Sigrún screamed, "let us go! I must take Helgi to *Hringhorni*. I must save us."

"My daughter; it isn't me. I no longer have the strength to do it," he said as a vine pierced his stomach. Another vine pushed through his wrists and ankles. His mouth remained agape and his eyes stared into nothingness. Another vine pierced his neck. The vines slowly tore through him, ripping him apart. His blood dripped down Yggdrasil and burst into flames.

"I know what I must do," Óðinn said. "*Sacrifice myself unto myself.* If I don't . . . nothing will change."

Wheezing, he arched his back. He inhaled, filling his chest. "*Gungnir!*" he yelled, calling his spear.

The wind blew stronger and the sky moved again. The flames grew and the Great Ash burned. I felt the updraft of the growing flames, threatening to rise and consume us.

Sigrún's back arched and I felt something stab my side. I looked down. A spear had pierced through Sigrún and into me. I felt Sigrún go limp, her weight dragging on the vines.

I felt Óðinn's blood on me and the sanctity and the purity of the rising fire. I drew breath and it burned in my chest, the slow burning feeling like it was ripping through my head.

"Sigrún," I cried out, hoping she would answer. But Sigrún's arm was turning blue, the vessels running through her arms swelling. I felt her touch turning to cold stone and filling me with remorse.

Óðinn's eyes changed to black pearls and his head slumped to one side. His flesh began to burn; his blistered legs bubbled and suddenly the flames were tearing his flesh from his body.

Vines wrapped around Sigrún and me, dragging us toward the knot in Yggdrasil's trunk, now a gash swimming with sap. I stretched out my hand and feebly grasped Sigrún's arm. The tentacle-like vines were pulling us together. Reaching down, I pulled out Gungnir and threw it into the wind. I watched it twist and turn into nothing. Vines coiled around my and Sigrún's necks, dragging us into the gash in Yggdrasil's trunk.

Hringhorni was so far away that it was indistinguishable from a distant star in the night sky.

The lifeblood, the sugary sap oozing out of Yggdrasil covered us. My eyes were forced shut and I had to feel my way. I reached up and my arm penetrated the opening. The vines dragged my head into the hole; my hand gripped Sigrún's.

Inside Yggdrasil, the Great Ash pressed against my body, pushing me downward head first into its trunk. Sigrún followed behind as we descended.

The darkness in me was suddenly transformed into the light.

ᛥ   ᛣ

Who I knew myself as slowly diminished into a dream that lingered in the back of my mind. My feet felt planted and life moved all around me, beating in a softly nourishing, protective liquid state that surrounded me.

I felt legs, a torso, and a breast brushing against my chest in an embrace.

The destructive horror of separation, isolation, and death was a hollow resonance. My cold and lonely mind retreated from Miðgarð.

My eyes were opened and I became Yggdrasil and Miðgarð burning, my cries silenced by its sanctifying flames.

ഔ   ഽ

The ocean rose around my burned trunk, extinguishing the remnants of the flames and cooling my scorched bark.

The sky went dark and the ocean calmed. The water stilled and hardened; sheets collided and the air pounded, cracked, and shuddered.

Ragnarök had commingled the voices, the thoughts, and the sagas into a singular moment where nothing and everything existed. It compressed itself into the brief interlude between the end of one thought and the beginning of the next; a convergence into divinity.

It was *there* all the time. As simple as noticing the interlude between the end of the inhalation and the beginning of the exhalation.

Baldur rose and set, riding the horizon through the endless night. The heavens opened and bathed Miðgarð in a green aurora, moving across the night in endless rippling bands.

The moon circled in endless loops and the only movement on the surface was the night sky, spinning across the icy planet.

I felt the resonance of the gods' judgement at Iðavöllr. The Jötunn, including Loki and Freyja, were confined under Miðgarð forever, unable to interfere ever again. The gods that survived Ragnarök will build a new city and name it Gimli.

Baldur ignored the dark world, or didn't have the power to change it. And without light, change wasn't possible. But the son didn't abandon Miðgarð; he rode along the horizon to let us know that he was still there.

Óðinn had given his life and sacrificed the war-ridden world he had helped to create to rid Miðgarð of the fighting and the killing.

The Jötunn were now chained to Miðgarð, inseparable and transformative. Controlling their destructiveness became an internal process of introspection and reflection, to see the process of creation in its destruction.

It was the son's time to bring light and understanding to Miðgarð. The one and only light, illuminating the dark isolation of the human condition. It shone overhead, giving life to the surface and bestowing its nourishing love.

But when the dark overcame the son, humans huddled together in the gloom and shared their light till the son rose again. And thanked him for the good that he gave them when he returned.

As Óðinn said, whispering in Baldur's ear as he lay on *Hringhorni*, his funeral pyre, "You, my son, will rise again and give the light of your purity, beauty, and love to Miðgarð."

ဆာ   ရ

The first dawn broke the never-ending dark; the son returned, as had been foretold. The saga begins.

The son moved across the marble sky and it changed from blue to pink to yellow.

Below, the icy surface shifted and cracked, pushing into crags. The son rose higher; ice turned the colour of blood, shot into the air in shafts of vapour, and the oceans formed. Yggdrasil rose, its exterior still blackened, but its trunk hardening in the heat of the son, protecting the life inside. It stood like a monolithic fist, erect in Baldur's light.

The ocean boiled and steam rose. The fire Jötunn pushed up geysers of nutrient-rich water and vapour from the depths of Miðgarð, showering Hoddmímis Holt.

The sky let go its rain and washed Yggdrasil's stump, rinsing away the fiery scar. The sun heated the skies and the land. And Yggdrasil pumped life all around it.

I felt the stretching of its top to the skies. The vines emerged from the new earth where they were planted, their leaves nourished by the light of the son. They crawled up Yggdrasil, transferring its nourishment to the Great Ash's roots.

In time, a leaf-bearing branch stretched out of Yggdrasil's top, followed by more and more; eventually it took in more than enough light to feed itself. It grew and the garden at its base grew along with it. Its crown expanded, eventually covering the island.

A well, the only hole into the past, rose out of the receding water. Buds swelled on Yggdrasil, bloomed, and then bore fruit. Mímir's well nourished the soil with its life force; plants, shrubs, and eventually a woodland grew. The land was shaped into a valley filled with wild fruit and grains. Underneath it, edible roots grew in the cold earth.

The son's love nurtured it, feeding it light and showering it with rain without acknowledgement. The son did it for his father. The son loved his father so much that he wanted to take the fighting and the destruction and turn it into love. And to show that love, he would shine his light so Miðgarð would never see the darkness of war again.

Under the sea, life continued to flourish, unaffected by the events of Ragnarök. The life swam independent of the land.

ᔕ໐ ໐ᔕ

I begin to shrink; the universe grows. I open my eyes.

The walls surrounding me are pressing against me, like a breathing chest. I feel like I'm suffocating; my breathing no longer feels in sync with the life around me.

I see a slit of light and push myself to it. It gets brighter and brighter. Suddenly it surrounds me and I slip out onto the ground in a cold, gelatinous pool.

... *Eye—I feel out of time.*

I ... feel—I sh-shake—shiver. I ... I'm shiver ring— shivering.

I—my head—my body is pushing out, trying to break ... to breathe.

I open my mouth; the cold air enters me and chokes my insides. I exhale then breathe deeply, then pant, and my insides pound. I take a breath and the pounding diminishes.

The light stings my eyes. I squint, hear the howling wind, feel hard specks bite my face. I blink. My head moves and tips, then plunges into the soft ground. My nose and mouth run into each other, covering my chin. I lie still, trying to breathe, and cough my dizziness away.

A hand grabs me and drags me through the sap. I slither into movement.

I hurt. My body rumbles inside; my mouth gapes as my belly erupts, something rotted burning up my throat and chest and cutting over my tongue, throwing my body into spasms. I taste my breath; sweat drips down my face. I soil the ground's purity with a foul pool. My stomach erupts again and I heave onto the grass; the wind carries away my foul breath, leaving the taste behind.

I hear a burbling brook. The light doesn't hurt so much and I can remove my hand from my face, though I keep my eyes closed. I reach out and feel the ground. The trickling gets louder and louder. My hand plunges down into it. I lean over it and water splashes over my face and head. I feel the water flowing across my mouth and chin, soothing my cracked lips. I swallow and it soothes my dry mouth and throat. The cold water stings my eyes.

I slip into the moving brook and the water washes over me, washing away the sap.

I sit up and cover my face. Slowly I open my eyes and squint through the light penetrating my fingers, watching the white line change into the whitish-pink of my fingers. I open my eyes a little more. I can breathe a little easier. The wind blows into my hands and stabs my eyes. I feel a pressure in my head and I blink. I slowly remove my hands from my face and squint into the world around me.

White-barked trees tower over me and the ground is carpeted with grass. The son pierces through the overhead canopy and shadows criss-cross all around me.

I crawl out of the water and sit in front of the other, Lif. Lif's body is the power to create life and to nurture it.

I push myself up and slowly slide a leg underneath me, waiting for the ground to shift and tilt, but the cold wind settles my insides.

I slide my other leg under me, and push up to my hands and feet. I lean against a tree and wobble to my feet, hugging the tree to steady myself.

I reach out to Lif, take her hand and help her to her feet. We stagger, using each other for support, to the Great Tree towering into the sky.

The tree shakes above our heads and the ocean waves slap against the shore. The son gives the world his light and asks for nothing in return.

I see movement in the pool of sap. A snake twitches and slithers from the pool and suddenly disappears into the grass.

I stumble to the Great Tree, attracted by the brightly coloured fruit hanging from it, taking Lif with me. We reach up and pluck a handful.

The plump fruits burst, and their sweet-smelling juice flows down my hand. I hold out my hand to Lif's mouth; she extends hers and we bite into the fruit. Its sweet smell moistens my mouth and I taste the sweet juice on my lips and in my mouth.

In the distance, white clouds rise from the water and disappear into a rainbow. The son's love shines and we sit under the cool shade of the tree, brushed by the ocean breeze.

The saga begins . . .

Glossary

Ægishjálmr (The Helm of Awe, or Helm of Terror) is a protective symbol, giving its bearer the power to deceive its enemies. Possibly originated, as the power of illusion, forgetfulness and deceiving of sight in seiðr magic.

Æsir is one tribe of Norse gods.

Alfather is literally: "all father," or "father of all;" another name for Óðinn, the leader of the Norse pantheon.

Althings in the Viking age, were rudimentary assemblies where grievances were heard, decisions were rendered and laws were passed.

Álfrs are elves.

Asgard means "enclosure of the Æsir." It's one of the nine worlds and is home to the Norse gods and Valhalla, Óðinn's enormous hall.

Austr is east.

Baldur is the Norse god of light and Óðinn's second son. It's said that he's so handsome, wise, and bright that light shines from him.

Dökkálfar are dark elves.

Dægur is half a day

Fólkvangr means army field. Freyja receives half of the slain, to fight at Ragnarök. The other half go to Óðinn's hall, Valhalla.

A **hóf** is a covered place of worship

A **hörgr** is a type of outdoor altar; usually an arrangement of rocks.

iViking means that you are going to raid a specific place, most commonly on land or on ships.

Jötunn (pl. **Jötnar**) is a class that includes giants, elves (both light and dark), dwarves; a race of nature spirits with superhuman strength. They sometimes intermingle and intermarry with the tribes of the Æsir and the Vanir.

Megingjörð is a belt worn by Thør: "Megin" means power or strength, and "gjörð" means belt.

Miðgarð literally means the "middle world" inhabited by men.

Norðr means north.

Ragnarök or ragna-rokkr literally means "the twilight of the gods."

Seiðr is the most powerful of all magic. It is the power of delusion. The goddess Freyja had seiðr magic. Óðinn asked her to teach him.

Suðr is south.

Vestr is west.

Vanir are another group of gods once separate from the Æsir, now a subgroup of them. They loosely represent the emotional side of human nature.

Völva (pl. **völvur**) literally means "wand carrier;" they practised shamanism, sorcery, and prophecy.

About the Author

R.G. Johnston grew up in central Newfoundland. The province's cultural and natural beauty inspired him at an early age to write.

He won a bronze medal for Best Regional Fiction – Canada East for his first book, Vinland: The Beginning.

Other Books by R.G. Johnston

Vinland: The Beginning
Vinland Ragnarok: Twi-light of the Gods

Undead at Groom Lake